Noah gently lifted her chin with his forefinger to meet his eyes. Those same captivating blue eyes she'd fallen in love with three years ago. "You've had little time with Daniel compared to the three years we were together. Those years must mean something."

He was right. Their time together had created precious memories of laughter, fun, and serious plans for their future before they encountered their differences and he left Berlin. Those years loving him did mean something, whether she wanted to admit it or not. She and Daniel hadn't needed much time to fall in love. They were compatible and comfortable with each other. They shared the desire for the same lifestyle. He hadn't attempted to change her or the way she did things. She owed it to herself, Noah, and Daniel to sort out her feelings before she could commit to either one of them. . . .

Books by Molly Jebber

CHANGE OF HEART

GRACE'S FORGIVENESS

TWO SUITORS FOR ANNA

Published by Kensington Publishing Corporation

Two Suitors for Anna

MOLLY JEBBER

ZEBRA BOOKS
KENSINGTON PUBLISHING CORP.
http://www.kensingtonbooks.com

ZEBRA BOOKS are published by

Kensington Publishing Corp.
119 West 40th Street
New York, NY 10018

All Kensington titles, imprints and distributed lines are available at special quantity discounts for bulk purchases for sales promotion, premiums, fund-raising, educational or institutional use.

Special book excerpts or customized printings can also be created to fit specific needs. For details, write or phone the office of the Kensington Sales Manager. Attn.: Sales Department. Kensington Publishing Corp., 119 West 40th Street, New York, NY 10018. Phone: 1-800-221-2647.

Zebra and the Z logo Reg. U.S. Pat. & TM Off.

First Printing: February 2017
ISBN-13: 978-1-4201-3765-1
ISBN-10: 1-4201-3765-4

eISBN-13: 978-1-4201-3766-8
eISBN-10: 1-4201-3766-2

10 9 8 7 6 5 4 3 2 1

Printed in the United States of America

To Ed, my soul mate, loving husband, and partner.
My best encourager and supporter!
To Mitch, the best brother a sister could ask for.
I'm so thankful for you and love you so much.

ACKNOWLEDGMENTS

Thank you to:

Dawn Dowdle, agent, and John Scognamiglio, editor in chief, for their support, kindness, and guidance.

Misty, my beautiful, talented, and smart daughter, who lights up my life and helps me in so many ways.

Sue Morris, my mother. Beautiful, elegant, and amazing woman. Love you, Mom.

Lee Granza, Debbie Bugezia, Sigrid Davies, Mary Byrnes, Ginny Gilmore, Elaine Saltsgaver, Donna Snyder, Melanie Fogel, Linda Schultz, Connie Melaik, Darla Landren, Ann Wright, Lynn Smith, and Marsha Kaiser.

I love my Southbridge friends. You know who you are and how much you mean to me. Your support, love, and encouragement have touched my life in such a special way. Words can't express how much I value each and every one of you.

My precious Sunday School and church friends in Ohio and Naples. Thank you so much for your prayers.

Patricia Campbell, DJ Welker, and Southwest Florida Romance Writers' group for your advice, love, and friendship.

Marilyn Ridgway—You've lifted me up more times than I can count! You're such a blessing!

Sandra Barela, Celebratelit.com—Thank you for your friendship, advice, and encouragement!

My readers—Thank you so much for your support and encouragement.

I apologize if I've forgotten anyone—but you know my heart and how much you all mean to me.

Chapter One

Berlin, Ohio, 1903

Anna flipped the sign on Grace and Sarah's Dry Goods to open to show she was ready for business on Monday morning and glanced out the open window. She chuckled. A young newspaper boy waved a paper high above his head with his back to her. He was perfect for the job with his loud voice.

"Exciting news! On July fourth, we reported The Commercial Cable Company, Great Northern Cable Company, and the Eastern Telegraph Company have made it possible for President Roosevelt to deliver the first telegraph message around the globe! Read another article on telegraph messaging today!"

An Englischer smiled and approached the red-haired boy. "I'll take one. Thank you." He pressed coins in the eager boy's hand, tucked his purchase under his arm, and whistled as he headed across the street.

A mamm ran after her little maedel heading for the bakery. "Nancy Lynn, get back here!"

The blacksmith had a line of customers outside his

door. Berlin bustled with activity. Men and women entered and left the shops, restaurants, post office, and livery. The sun glinted off the window. Anna squinted.

A man beeped his horn and raised his fist. "Watch where you're going!"

She gasped. *Noah!* He'd almost been struck!

"Sorry, sir." Noah crouched, hurried across the street, and waved to her.

She pressed a hand to the nervous flutter in her stomach and waved back with the other. She loved his sandy-blond hair, sky-blue eyes, and tall, thin frame. Restless and carefree, Noah loved change. During their three-year friendship, he had rearranged his chore schedule often, experimented with growing different kinds of herbs, and built numerous household products out of pine, maple, cherry, and oak. While Noah was interesting and a delight most of the time, she didn't share his enthusiasm for change. She found comfort in going about her tasks the same way. He'd pushed her to do things more like him for the last several months. They'd argued more often and his latest obsession to relocate to Lancaster for no good reason had added to her confusion as to whether they were meant for each other. To imagine life without him would be painful.

All he talked about was leaving Berlin, Ohio, to live in Lancaster, Pennsylvania, to make new friends and enjoy a different community. She had no desire to return to Lancaster. Living in Berlin the last three years, she'd enjoyed managing the dry goods shop and making good friends. She looked forward to raising a family here.

Would Noah ever be satisfied living in the same place for long? His need for adventure worried her.

She'd kept quiet on the matter, hoping he'd forget the silly notion. He'd hinted at marrying her, but he hadn't proposed. She, her family, and her friends assumed they'd wed someday.

What if he asked her to marry him? She had no idea what to say. He'd been quieter than usual before and after the church service yesterday. Something was apparently heavy on his mind. Was he getting closer to asking her? She had always thought they'd marry, have kinner, and build a future together. Giddy with excitement at the idea until now. Why did he have to shatter the day she'd waited for since she'd fallen in love with him by choosing to move away from family and friends? Things had changed for them. He picked at everything she did. Would Noah ever be satisfied with her or living in one location planning for kinner and their future? She couldn't stand to think about this anymore today.

Noah walked into the shop and interrupted her thoughts. "Good morning. It's only the sixth of July, and already, the sun is blazing hot. I'm ready for winter. I abhor this heat, but I enjoy all the colors in the fields and gardens. All the plants and flowers are in full bloom. They are pretty, like you." He grinned and touched her nose. He glanced at the walls and waggled his finger. "You need to change your quilt display, like I told you. Change is good."

She stiffened and fought to keep from rolling her eyes. "Noah, I don't need to move things around every other day. Let's not argue." She pointed to the box under his arm. *The man can be exasperating.* "What are you carrying?"

Noah set the box on the counter and patted the lid. "I finished handcrafting a sewing box out of cedar, and I wanted to show the piece to you before I delivered it to Mark's shop next door."

She peeked inside. "You varied the sections in the lift-out part. What a wonderful idea. The cedar is beautiful." She gave him a grateful smile. "This sewing box is almost as pretty as the one you gave me last year. Mark will be pleased. The sections kumme in handy for needles, pins, and spools of thread." She admired Grace and Mark's relationship. Both were good friends to her and Noah. Mark had graciously given his time to Noah teaching him how to handcraft household products before he'd married Grace and they'd had a child. Grace had hired her and later entrusted the management of the shop to her. She could talk to Grace about anything and trusted her friend would not repeat what she told her. She wished their lives weren't so busy and they could sit and chat more often.

"I can't take all the credit. Mark's been a good teacher and friend. Taking care of his livestock and farm is a pleasure rather than work. He's an excellent craftsman, but he makes the same things. I modify them to offer a little something different. I'm excited he's offered to sell my products in his store. I'll need the money for *our* future." He winked.

She wasn't surprised he wasn't satisfied to construct his creations the way Mark showed him. His creative mind was always kumming up with new ways to alter his projects. Anna opened her mouth to ask about his plans for the money but decided against it. An attractive Amish man strolled into the shop. He looked familiar, but she couldn't place him. He was several inches shorter than Noah. He had broad shoulders and powerful muscles bulged tight in his sleeves. She guessed him a couple of years older than Noah. "May I help you?"

He removed his hat, revealing a full head of thick, brown hair, and gave her a sheepish grin. "Jah, I'm here to purchase much needed kitchen towels."

"I'm Anna Plank, and meet Noah Schwartz. I'll be glad to show you what we have for choices."

"I'm Daniel Bontrager, and I'm new in town. I relocated here from Lancaster, Pennsylvania." He shook Noah's hand.

Daniel Bontrager. Where would she have met him? Anna snapped her fingers and smiled. "I recognize you from the church I attended in Lancaster. We moved to Berlin three years ago."

Daniel nodded his head. "Jah, I remember you. We'd moved to Lancaster from Middlebury, Indiana, after my mamm's parents passed. Daed had to get away from all the memories. Our families were acquainted, but I didn't have much time for attending social gatherings, and I missed Sunday services quite a bit. Mamm got sick, and I stayed home to watch over her. She had good and bad days. The neighbor took care of her during the workweek."

"I'm sorry about your mamm."

"Me too." Noah cocked his head. "I'm considering relocating to Lancaster. Anna has no desire to return there. Did you enjoy living there?"

"I did."

Noah crossed his arms. "Are you any relation to Jonathan and Adele Bontrager?"

Daniel cast his eyes downward. "Jah, he was my bruder."

Anna swallowed the lump in her throat. Daniel's bruder's fraa, Adele, had been a sweet woman and news of her and her boppli's passing during childbirth had spread like wildfire in the community. She gave him a sympathetic smile. "Adele was pretty with her soft voice, dainty features, and kind personality. I was shocked when Jonathan died from a tragic heart attack a few months after the loss of his fraa and infant. You have my deepest sympathy."

"Danki. I miss them."

Noah cleared his throat and put a hand on Daniel's shoulder. "I'm sorry about their passing, too. They were a wonderful couple. What made you choose to move here?"

He acknowledged Noah's concern with a nod. "I needed a fresh start. My parents were murdered in a robbery while shopping in the General Store in Lancaster almost two years ago. Mamm was having a good day, and Daed offered to take her with him. The robber shot them, along with the owner. The sheriff was next door and heard the gunfire. He rushed in, but they were already dead. The robber turned his gun on the sheriff, and he shot and killed the criminal. Violence is rare in our town. The way they died was a shock to us and the community."

Anna blinked and blinked again. She pressed her fingers to her parted lips. He must've been devastated to find out his parents had been brutally murdered. Amish did everything to avoid trouble. "Where were you when your parents were in the store?"

"My bruder and I were working at home when the sheriff and the bishop came and told us the dreadful news. I'll never forget the date. It was February second, nineteen one. Two months later, Jonathan and Adele married and moved to Berlin." He shuffled his feet. "Jonathan wrote how much he loved living in this town. I'd planned to move closer to him, but I kept putting the move off. I decided to sell everything and take over Jonathan's haus and property. I regret waiting."

He was young to have been the last one left in his immediate family. He must feel so alone. The violent event would most likely stay fresh in the Amish community's minds for a while. "I would probably want to do the same if I were in your position."

Noah stretched out his hand. "I'm sorry you suffered the loss of your parents in such a horrific way, and Jonathan and his family, too."

"I didn't mean to share my whole life story." Daniel diverted his eyes to the window.

Noah slapped Daniel's upper arm. "Don't apologize. We're a close community, and we want to get better acquainted with you." He lifted his box. "My mamm and I live on the last farm on the left on South Road. Stop in and visit anytime." He headed for the door. "I'm happy to help with whatever you need, and please don't hesitate to ask. You may want to move or purchase a few new pieces of furniture to make Jonathan's haus more like yours."

"You're kind to offer, but I'm comfortable with the furniture at present. I may buy new pieces later."

Anna held her breath a moment. Noah couldn't resist imposing his ideas onto someone else. He was too pushy. Being content with leaving things the same wasn't a disease! Maybe Daniel found comfort having his bruder's things around him.

Anna lifted a towel. "Daniel, there's a stack of these on the shelf next to the wall to the side of the counter. You'll find they differ in fabric and color. Would you like to browse through them, while I walk Noah to the door? I'll be quick."

"I'd be glad to. Take your time." He headed toward the shelf.

She followed Noah and smiled, as he walked with a lilt in his step and hummed as he went to the door. He'd been empathetic and extended a warm wilkom to Daniel. The Amish helped each other, but Noah had gone above and beyond to befriend Daniel. She had her concerns with Noah, but she admired his cheerful attitude, his solid work ethic, and ability to make friends easily. "Would you like to kumme to supper this evening?" She'd ask him later why he was so quiet yesterday.

"Of course. I'd never turn down your mamm's cooking." Noah winked. "After supper, we will discuss our future." He turned and switched the stack of aprons she had displayed on a shelf to a small table against the side wall under the hanging quilts. "Much better." He waved to Daniel and left through the connecting door to Mark's shop.

She paused. Her heart sank each time he moved her dry goods. Why wasn't the shelf where she had set the aprons good enough? She had them where she wanted them. What would he say about their future? She wanted to ignore her doubts and get excited about his possibly proposing, but her conscience wouldn't let her. She glanced at Daniel. She didn't have time to dwell on her problems with Noah. She should help Daniel. Walking to him, she held up the top towel. "We also have a variety of sizes." She gestured to another table.

Leah rushed in minutes later and threw her bag under the counter. "Good morning."

Anna gestured her over. "Please meet Daniel Bontrager. He's moved into his bruder Jonathan Bontrager's home. You probably don't remember him, but he attended our church in Lancaster."

Smiling, Leah stood next to Anna. "I'm Anna's schweschder Leah. I apologize. I don't remember you."

"Don't worry, I'm not offended." He tipped his hat. "I'm pleased to make your acquaintance."

"Daniel came in to buy some dry goods." She gestured to the towel rack. "Did you find what you wanted?"

He selected three of them. "I'll take these, please." He passed the towels to her. He paid for his purchase and waited while she wrapped them. "Danki." He scanned the coverlets. "You have an interesting arrangement of patterned quilts on the walls. Do you and your schweschder stitch them?"

"We and other Amish women in the community."

"Anna, you should show him our keepsake pocket quilts."

He fingered a brown-and-white one with a star pattern. He patted the pocket. "What do you put in here?"

Anna removed a quilt from the hooks, draped the coverlet over her arm, and untied the ribbon holding the pocket closed. "You write a letter to the person receiving the quilt and tuck the note inside. The quilt and letter become keepsakes. The person receiving the letter will have the giver's words to read again and again for comfort and joy for years."

"What a creative idea. I'll purchase it along with my towels."

Anna opened her mouth in surprise. She hadn't had many men purchase the quilts. His enthusiasm and interest in the idea of the pocket warmed her heart.

Leah joined them. "I'll wrap your purchase for you while Anna accepts payment."

Anna removed the dented gray metal cashbox from under the counter and recorded the sale.

He passed her the correct change and accepted his package from Leah. "Danki for your help. Pleasure meeting you both. The sun is shining in spite of the pouring rain." He pointed to the window. "There's a rainbow."

She strained her neck to look out the window. "The rainbow's arch stretches far."

Leah pressed her nose up to the glass. "The pink, green, and blue in the rainbow paint the prettiest picture across the sky. I wish they would appear more often."

Anna stepped around the counter and walked Daniel to the door. On the way, a drop of water wet her sleeve. She paused and touched the damp spot. Pointing to the ceiling, she grimaced. "We must have a leak in the roof."

He peered at the moisture on the ceiling. "I'd be glad to fix the damage for you for a minimal cost."

She clasped her hands to her chest. "Danki for offering. I'll ask Grace King, my employer, for permission. She has to approve maintenance costs."

"I'll stop in on Friday to take a look at the damage and give you an estimate. Please assure Mrs. King I'll give her a fair price. If she agrees to me doing the work, I'll schedule a time with you for next week."

Leah grinned. "Kumme back anytime. These are my favorite towels because they're homespun cotton and keep their shape and absorb the water much better than the rest of the ones we sell."

He smiled but kept his eyes on Anna.

Her cheeks heated. "Have a pleasant day, Mr. Bontrager. Wilkom to Berlin."

"I'll talk to you Friday, Miss Plank."

"Call me Anna."

"Only if you call me Daniel."

"Agreed."

Daniel paused and put his hand on the doorknob. "It truly was a pleasure meeting you, Anna." He grinned and shut the door behind him.

Leah closed the sales journal and stowed the book under the counter. She chuckled and nudged Anna's shoulder. "Noah better hurry and ask you to marry him. He's got competition. Daniel Bontrager couldn't pry his striking dark brown eyes away from you."

Anna sucked in her bottom lip. Daniel had matured and was more attractive than she remembered. His brown hair and eyes complemented his high cheekbones and structured jawline. Now she understood why she'd only seen him a few times in the church services. He'd experienced a boatload of sadness in his life. No wonder their families hadn't gotten better acquainted.

She had noticed Daniel staring at her earlier, but she wouldn't admit this to Leah. Noah was her first love, and she hoped they could reach a mutual understanding about their differences and the confusion in her mind would vanish. "You missed Noah. He came in earlier."

"Did he meet Daniel?"

"Jah, they got along well." She hung another quilt in place of the one Daniel bought. "Noah's kumming to supper tonight. He wants to talk about *our* future."

Leah's brown eyes rounded, and she put a hand to her mouth. "Tonight could be when Noah proposes to you! A night you'll never forget."

* * *

In the evening, Noah joined them for their evening meal. She pushed the corn on her plate from side to side. Her stomach was in knots. Mamm prattled on about new, heavier scissors they were selling at the General Store. Leah told them about meeting Daniel, and Noah chimed in about his good impression of him. Beth asked questions about him. Anna fidgeted with the blue cloth napkin in her lap. All this small talk was getting on her nerves.

Noah wiped his mouth. "Mrs. Plank, your chicken and dumplings were excellent." He squared his shoulders. "Anna, I was going to ask your mamm to step outside to ask her an important question, but what I have to say concerns your entire family." He darted his eyes to each one of them. "If Anna agrees to marry me, do any of you object?"

Anna gasped and froze.

Mrs. Plank smiled. "You've got my blessing, sweet Noah, but you and Anna need to discuss your proposal in private."

Noah stood. "Your mamm has a point. We should step outside. I'm sorry I caught you off guard. I shouldn't have put you on the spot."

Leah and Beth squealed. "Say jah, Anna!"

Mamm put a finger to her lips. "Don't push Anna for an answer. Let her and Noah have time alone to discuss this."

Her mind whirled with enthusiasm and confusion. Eyes pooling with tears, she exchanged an endearing look with Mamm and her schweschders before going outside with Noah.

He clasped her hand, and they walked toward the pond. With puppy dog eyes, he cocked his head. "I'm afraid I've handled this all wrong. Forgive me?"

"Of course I do." She had wished he'd asked her

first. They had important issues to discuss before they could agree to marry. On the other hand, he hadn't mentioned a word about leaving Berlin in his proposal. Had he reconsidered moving to Lancaster? Her other problem with him had gotten worse. Why had he nagged her the last several months to change her displays, recipes, routines, and other things to suit his way of thinking? She went to the same spot they sat last time. She'd wanted to claim the area under the big oak tree near the edge of the pond as *their* spot. She'd told him this numerous times, but her request fell on deaf ears.

Noah pointed to another thick, green, grassy area a couple yards farther away from the soothing calm of the water. "Sit here with me."

She bit her tongue and squelched telling him again why his ignoring her request hurt her feelings. She glanced at the purple and yellow wildflowers lining the perimeter, and a cluster of fully leafed green oak trees stood off to the right side. Summer was her favorite season. Darkness came much later, and the temperature couldn't get hot enough for her. These favorites usually calmed her, but not here with Noah at this moment. Her heart thudded against her chest like a heavy hammer. She'd let him speak first.

Noah reached for her hand and turned her chin toward him. "Anna, I love you. I want you with me for the rest of my life, but I want to travel to other Amish communities and consider moving to the one we are the most comfortable in. If we wait to have a boppli, we could move to Lancaster, live with my aunt and uncle, and work for them on their property. After a year or so, we could move again and settle down for good in whichever place we choose. You've avoided my questions concerning living in Lancaster. Are your feet firmly planted here?"

She shouldn't have dared to hope he'd abandoned his idea. He was tenacious once he had a plan. Her deep sigh came from the bottom of her heart. "I want to raise a family with my loved ones near me, Noah. I treasure my job and friends here. Berlin suits me. I have no desire to leave. Lancaster was a pleasant place to live, but I like Berlin much better."

"You are older and you might find Lancaster more interesting now. You can work in an Amish-owned store and meet new friends, as well as get reacquainted with past ones. My aunt and uncle will wilkom you with open arms." He gently squeezed her hand. "My mamm and your family will be fine. We'll visit them. You can exchange letters and keep up on the gossip."

Why couldn't he leave things the same and be content in Berlin? His restlessness set her teeth on edge. "Your wanting to relocate isn't our sole problem. I question whether we are compatible anymore. You've asked me to alter many of my tasks to suit your way of thinking the last several months. We've argued a lot over your obsession to change the way I do things. Why have you done this recently and not before?"

Noah frowned and stared at the pond. "We got better acquainted and more serious as time passed. I got more comfortable with telling you how I felt. I wish you would be more spontaneous and share my enthusiasm for adventure, but I still want to marry you." He gave her a sheepish grin. "Don't get upset over my showing you how to do things better or when I make suggestions. I can't help myself. I don't mean to ruffle your feathers. I'm confident we can overcome any obstacle we face together." He kissed her hand. "Marry me and kumme with me to start a new adventure."

Their times together had changed from joyful to worrisome. She'd kept her mouth shut each time he mentioned joining his relatives and making new friends away from Berlin. He'd pushed her to change her life, tasks, and way of thinking for several months. All of which made her uncomfortable.

Had he really thought through this major change in his life and maybe hers? "You have Mark and your mamm to consider. Mark has been a good teacher, employer, and friend to you. Won't you be letting him down by taking off to live somewhere on a whim and not for a good reason?"

"I haven't told Mark why and when he'll need a replacement for me yet, but I'm confident he'll understand. There are plenty of young Amish men waiting to take my place."

She was disappointed in him for abandoning his mamm and asking Anna to abandon hers. They were widows and needed help. "What about our mamms? They need us." Jane Schwartz worked in the bakery in town, and she had Amish farmers helping her with her hay and garden, but Noah cut her wood and did repairs. They had a close relationship. Anna's income at the shop and help at home would be missed by her family.

"Mr. Zook and Mr. Beiler insist on tending to the hay field, garden, and livestock for mamm. She's comfortable managing the rest of her property. She earns enough money to live comfortably working at the bakery and has enough produce for food. Mr. Zook and Mr. Beiler will continue to supply her with meat. Your family is doing fine as well, and Mr. Zook and Mr. Beiler look out for your family, too. I'm confident our families will support our decision to move to Lancaster."

Staring at crows getting ready to pounce on a dead squirrel on the edge of the pond, she shivered and hugged herself. She didn't like crows or this conversation. They were at a crossroads. As she searched her heart for an answer, her head began to ache. "Noah, I love you, but I'm uneasy leaving Berlin and need more time to find out if you can accept me for who I am and not try to change me."

His serious brown eyes stared into hers. "I was quiet yesterday because I was afraid you wouldn't want to leave here. Today I couldn't wait any longer to ask you to marry me and find out. Anytime I brought up the subject, you avoided commenting. The one problem we have, in my opinion, is your unwillingness to relocate. The rest we can resolve. I'll show you new ways to do things to help you. Remember, Anna, I love you, and you can trust me to provide a good living for you."

His dismissal of her worries filled her with dread. "Will you leave anyway if I refuse to go with you?"

He cut his glance to a squirrel clambering up the tree. "I'm counting on you being by my side for the rest of my life. I refuse to consider the alternative." He hopped up. "The sun is lowering. We'll discuss your problem with me suggesting you change certain things again after you've had time to consider a date for the wedding and what you'll need to take to Lancaster."

Hadn't he heard a word she'd said? He assumed she'd leave with him. She blamed herself a little. Her throat constricted. Her life was about to change, and either direction she chose didn't thrill her. She walked with him to his wagon.

He lowered his head and pressed his gentle lips onto hers. "Good night, my sweet Anna."

Her heart skipped with joy. She touched her lips and gazed into his eyes. "Good night. I love you." She watched him leave, and her joy vanished. Her concerns returned. She took slow steps to the haus as tears dripped onto her cheeks. She dabbed them away with her sleeve and went inside.

Leah and Beth sat together on the settee knitting.

Beth raised her head. "When are you getting married?"

"Where's Mamm?"

Beth pointed. "She's in her room putting away laundry. Tell us your plans."

Leah grinned and stopped knitting. "Jah, tell us."

"Brace yourselves. Noah's proposal has a hitch. His plan is for us to marry and move to Lancaster and live with his aunt and uncle, Mr. and Mrs. Schwartz."

Beth pursed her lips. "What! You can't leave us! Why can't he stay here?"

Leah stood and crossed her arms. "Jah, why?"

Anna's head jerked. The anger in Beth's and Leah's tones rang out like a strike of lightning amid dark storm clouds. She expected no less from them. They'd formed a close bond, especially after their daed passed.

Hands on hips, Mamm stood in the doorway. "What are his reasons?"

Anna's eyes swept around the cozy room she loved. She slumped in the chestnut cedar chair in the corner. "He wants to experience living in other Amish locations and meet new folk. He's always craved change."

Beth's face reddened. "He's being ridiculous."

"I agree with Beth. He's being selfish satisfying his

desires and giving no thought to his mamm and us."
Leah narrowed her eyes.

Mamm sat in the other cedar chair across from
Anna. "What do you want to do?"

"I love Noah, but I have no desire to leave my
family, job, and friends. We have other problems to
resolve too."

"Then don't leave. And what other hitches do you
have with Noah?" Beth pouted.

Mamm moved next to her youngest child. "Leave
your schweschder alone. She has a right to her privacy. She'll tell us what information she deems appropriate. We must support Anna in whatever path she
chooses to take."

"Not me!" Beth stormed to her room.

Leah went to Anna and knelt at her side. "Will
Noah settle in Lancaster, or will he want to move somewhere else in a few years? Relocating several times
wouldn't be an easy life for you or your kinner."

Anna touched her dear, sweet schweschder's hand.
"He mentioned moving at least one more time after
relocating to Lancaster, and you've made a good point.
He may want to lead a vagabond life. I have no guarantee he won't want to pick up and move again and
again. I would be miserable moving from place to
place. Noah's sense of curiosity and adventure were
interesting to me when he shared learning woodworking from Mark, finding a new way to use a tool,
or changing the furniture arrangement in his
mamm's haus, but his constant criticism of the way I
do things is unsettling."

Mamm kissed Anna's forehead. "Pray to God for
guidance. I trust you to do what's best for you and
Noah. I'll not stand in your way if you choose to leave
Berlin with him." She hugged Leah. "I'm going to bed

after I say good night to Beth. I suggest the two of you do the same."

"I'll speak with Beth in a few minutes." Anna gently squeezed her mamm's arm.

Mamm dipped her chin to her chest and left the room.

Leah gripped Anna's hand. "Please, don't go. If Noah loves you, he'll stay here."

Her family's reaction to her news added more heaviness to her chest. They mimicked the thump of hurt in her heart, picturing herself leaving them behind. "I surmise Noah is set on going to Lancaster with or without me. To be honest, I've struggled the past few months, wondering if he is the husband for me. His restlessness has put a wedge between us. I'm worried we're drifting apart."

"I'm sorry, Anna. We love Noah, but I'm angry he's being immature and thoughtless. I've noticed he badgers you to change our displays, your recipes, and other things. I find it irritating, so you must too. Have you told him how you feel?"

"Jah, but he's been dismissive of my worries when I've brought them to his attention."

"He has to accept you for who you are or, in my opinion, you'll live a life of frustration."

She understood all too well what her schweschder meant. Anna hugged herself. "Believe me, I agree with what you're saying. I'm afraid to admit it and to let him go, though." She yawned. "I better go to Beth before she falls asleep. I may already be too late."

Leah nodded.

Peeking around the half-closed door, Anna smiled at her youngest sibling. "Do you mind if I kumme in?"

Sliding back and giving Anna room to sit on the edge of the bed, Beth pouted. "Please don't leave me."

Beth's sad eyes and worried look pained her. She'd done her best to answer questions and relieve any fears her little schweschder had over the years. "I have no plans to go anywhere as of yet. Let's not waste time arguing over whether I stay or go. We want to enjoy each day we have together. Besides, if I go, we can write letters and you can tell me everything that's happening in your life, and I'll do the same."

Beth's chin trembled. "You understand me better than Leah or Mamm. When you have kinner, I want to spend time with them. We won't be able to bake, laugh, play games, and have family meals together. There's so much we'll miss out on."

Her schweschder simplified the jumbled thoughts in her head in minutes. These things were important to her, too. "I understand, and I'll tell you when I've decided what to do. Get some rest. Did you say your prayers?"

"Jah, and I prayed Noah would kumme to his senses and build a haus for you here."

She wanted the same. Anna chuckled and tousled her schweschder's hair. "Good night. I love you."

Leah slowly opened the door and sat next to Anna on Beth's bed. "Tell me why you're both laughing."

Beth told Leah, and Leah grinned at Anna. "I'm praying the same prayer before I go to sleep."

Anna had a tight-knit bond with her schweschders. A future without them near wasn't something she could fathom. Anna wished them each a good night and went to her room with its plain pine bed, small table, and stool in the corner. She knelt by her bed. "Dear Heavenly Father, what is Your will for my life? Please give me the clarity I need. Is Noah the husband for me? Am I wrong to not follow him to Lancaster? Can he go back to accepting me for who I am and the way I do things? I love You, Heavenly Father. Danki for Your grace and mercy. Amen."

She flipped through her King James Bible and scanned the Book of John. Shutting her Bible, she breathed in the gentle breeze coming through the window. Noah filled her mind, and she couldn't concentrate on anything else. How long would he give her before he pressed her for an answer?

Daniel peeked in the windows of the Berlin Restaurant. They stayed open the latest, besides the saloon. The scent of mouthwatering fresh bread and fried chicken wafted out their open window. He strolled inside and nodded to two Amish couples dining at two small tables in the corner. He eyed their full plates of chicken and dumplings. The waitress carried a slice of flaky-crusted cherry pie past him and set the dessert in front of a gray-haired, short and stout Englischer in a linen suit and fancy leather shoes.

The waitress, a young blond woman, wore her hair in ringlets pulled back and tied with a pink ribbon. Her printed ankle-length dress was tight-fitting with a white ruffled apron covering the front and tied in a bow in the back of her neck and waist. "You walked in two minutes before we close, but you have enough time to order and enjoy your meal. We won't rush you." She tapped her pencil on her pad of paper. "I'm Bridget. I haven't seen you in here before. Are you new in town?"

He removed his hat and set the straw topper in the empty chair beside him. "I'm Daniel. Jah, I moved to Berlin from Lancaster." He breathed deep. "The chicken aroma drew me in."

"We've got good food, except for today's apple pie. The cook burnt the crust."

"I'll have chicken and dumplings, please." He studied the covered glass shelves lined with desserts. "Would you mind saving me a piece of cherry pie?"

"I'll put one aside for you. Smart selection. You won't be sorry." She winked and headed for the kitchen.

Daniel nodded. The restaurant had red-and-white checked curtains and white tables and chairs. The tablecloths and napkins matched the curtains. The two couples paid for their meals and left. He and the Englischer were the restaurant's remaining customers.

The waitress delivered his food. "Enjoy, and if you need anything, wave me over."

"Danki." He dipped his big spoon in the mixture and savored each bite until his plate was empty.

The waitress approached him. "Are you ready for your cherry pie?"

He nodded. "I'm full, but I can't pass up dessert."

"I'll be back." The waitress scampered away, returned a few minutes later, and set the pie full of cherries on a small plate in front of him. "I found two pieces and hid the other one back for you if you want another slice."

"Danki." He slid it close and devoured the sweet-and-sour-tasting pie in minutes.

The waitress handed him his bill and collected his payment. "I hope you come back. You're a cute one." She flashed a big grin.

Daniel's cheeks warmed. He blushed and rushed out the door to the livery. Leaving the livery, he drove home. He'd never be comfortable around Englisch women. They wore their clothes too tight and were too forward. He much preferred Anna. She was plain but pretty with her thin frame, soft voice, and kind eyes. He couldn't get her off his mind since meeting her. She and Noah had exchanged endearing looks. They were most likely more than friends. He envied Noah. He wished he could've gotten better acquainted with her to find out if it would grow into something more.

He went home and stowed his horse and wagon in the barn. He pumped water in a bucket and lifted the salt he kept in the far corner. He sprinkled salt in the water and sprinkled the hay with the mixture. He offered the combination and fresh water to the horse. He petted the animal. "You're doing a good job for me. Danki."

He crossed the yard and opened the door, and Otis ran and jumped on him.

He caught the medium-sized brown dog in his arms. "Good to see you, my friend."

Otis licked his master's face and wagged his tail.

Daniel chuckled and set him on his feet.

Otis took care of business and returned to Daniel.

They went inside, and Daniel filled Otis's bowls with food and water. "Here you go. Enjoy your grub."

The dog dug his muzzle in the mixture until the bowl was licked clean. He drank his water until there was no more.

Daniel laughed. "You do enjoy mealtime."

Otis moved his paw to clang the two dishes together. He tilted his head and barked.

"No more for you. You've had enough."

Daniel pushed the door open and waited for Otis to join him. He sat in the white swing on the porch and stared at the orange sun peeking through the tall green trees. "What a beautiful evening."

Otis raced through the yard and chased a butterfly

then a squirrel. A few minutes later, he jumped onto
the swing and rested his head on Daniel's lap.

"I'm enjoying Berlin, Otis. I met a lovely Amish
woman named Anna. Noah is a fine Amish man and
very wilkoming, but I wish he didn't have his eyes on
Anna. She's the first woman I would consider for a
potential fraa. She's a beauty and quite delightful."

Meeting Anna had taken him by surprise. His
breath caught in his throat at the sight of her. A wisp
of her pretty brown hair had escaped and her hazel
eyes sparked. She was radiant.

Women in Lancaster had shown their interest by
bringing him meals and desserts, but he'd been too
busy to invest the time he would need to get acquainted
with a potential fraa. With the sale of his parents' property and his things in place at Jonathan's, he could
concentrate on finding a woman to share his life.

He scanned his wide pond, with its water rippling
in the breeze, and chuckled at the ducklings strug-
gling to paddle behind their mamm. To the left of the
pond, the garden had vegetables lined in perfect rows.
Hay covered the field in golden waves farther back
from the garden. His haus had enough room for him,
a fraa, and several kinner someday. The covered porch
was a pleasant place to rest at the end of a long day.

He went inside and removed his bruder's and
schweschder-in-law's clothes from the dresser drawers
and clothespress. He found infant blankets he assumed Adele had knitted and clothes she'd stitched
for the boppli who had died along with Adele during
childbirth. The soft coverlets brought back sad
memories of cleaning out his parents' home after
they died.

He pressed Adele's white prayer kapp to his cheek.
The fabric was soft like her voice. She'd been like a

delicate flower. Quiet and soft-spoken and always smiling and sweet. Jonathan had told him how much he cherished his fraa. Glad his bruder had found love and married Adele, he hoped to experience the same happiness with a fraa of his own someday. He put the worn, thin cotton bonnet in the crate, along with the other garments. He grasped the boppli blanket and closed his eyes. An ache of loss ripped through his chest. At least they were in Heaven together.

Jonathan had written letters to him about what a smart and supportive partner Adele was. He said they could discuss any problem and resolve their issues without raising their voices. He claimed, although she was shy, she offered advice when she had a strong opinion about something. He wished his bruder and sister-in-law would've remained in Lancaster where they could've spent more time together. He felt guilty for not moving to Berlin sooner.

He hoped to marry a fraa he could depend on for advice. He clutched the hairbrush and comb from the top of the dresser and tossed them on top of the clothes. He went to the kitchen and smiled as Otis's tail swiped his leg as they walked. After picking up his new kitchen towels, he folded them and set them on top of the counter. He'd ask Anna Friday if she knew of a family who would want the garments he'd tossed in the crates.

He reached in the drawer to check for anything he'd missed, then grabbed and pulled out a wooden-handled pocketknife, the one his daed had given Jonathan on his wedding day. Turning the cherrywood handle from side to side, he admired the craftsmanship, then put his newfound treasure back in the drawer. The knife would be a memorable keepsake of the times he'd practiced target shooting, fishing, and working alongside the two most important men in his life.

He stood and rubbed the ache in his back. Pulling the door open, he stepped out onto the porch and inhaled the humid, dark night air. He wished to enjoy summer all year long. He wilkomed hot weather. He yawned and stretched his arms, stepped back inside, closed the door, and headed for his bedroom. After shrugging into his nightclothes, he turned down his kerosene lamp, whispered a prayer, and went to bed. Anna's grin and heart-shaped face came to mind. A pang of guilt washed over him. He shouldn't dwell on his attraction and wanting to know Anna better. But his mind wouldn't listen.

Chapter Two

Anna approached two customers on Tuesday afternoon. A smiling Englisch woman in a calico printed ankle dress with reddish hair pinned in a tight bun came in accompanied by a young man with fierce, dark eyes. He strutted inside like he owned the place and flexed his muscular arms. He was of average build, but his thrown-back shoulders and raised chin irked Anna. The man oozed rudeness. She guessed his age would be close to Leah's at sixteen.

She forced a professional smile. "May I help you?"

"I'm Mrs. Donna Winter and this is my son, Butch. Would you please show me your pinwheel quilts?"

The obnoxious man didn't acknowledge her but waggled his eyebrows and smiled at Leah. "Hi, little lady."

Leah dipped her head and gave him a shy grin.

Anna shivered at the young man's boldness. Leah eyed him like she'd met him before. Her schweschder had a giddy air about her, and the way she swayed and gazed at him set Anna's teeth on edge. She forced a smile at Mrs. Winter and gestured to the quilts on the wall. "We have an assortment in various patterns and colors. We also have keepsake pocket quilts."

"What is the purpose of the pocket?"

"You tuck a letter to a loved one inside."

Mrs. Winter's cheeks dimpled. "What a clever idea."

The woman had a pleasant tone and kind demeanor. She certainly didn't match her son's arrogant tone and stance.

"Take your time to browse. I'll be here if you need me."

Anna noticed Butch and Leah were grinning and conversing as if they'd been friends for quite some time. Her schweschder's brazen behavior wasn't appropriate.

Anna frowned as Leah batted her eyelashes and Butch whispered in her schweschder's ear.

Their familiarity sent waves of trepidation through her. She was more than ready for the obnoxious young man to leave. "Mrs. Winter, do you have any questions?"

"I would like to purchase the yellow, blue, and white pinwheel quilt."

Anna moved the wooden stepladder to it and unhooked the quilt from the pegs. She stepped down and carried the woman's selection to the counter. She couldn't stand to watch her schweschder's delight in the Englischer's interest in her one more minute. "Leah, would you mind wrapping Mrs. Winter's purchase while I record the sale?"

Leah rushed to Anna's side and pulled out paper and twine.

Butch stood back and rocked on his heels. His intimate gaze swept over Leah. His mouth curled in an inappropriate and sly grin while he eyed her schweschder from head to toe.

Stifling her urge to ask him to leave immediately, Anna hurried to accept payment from Mrs. Winter and stowed the journal under the counter. "Danki for coming in."

"Thank you for your help." She hooked her arm through Butch's. "Come along, Son."

Butch ogled Leah again with a cunning smile, stepped to her, and leaned close to her ear. "See ya soon, little lady."

Blushing, Leah smiled wide and waved to him.

Anna stiffened and pursed her lips. Her obedient and faithful Leah had shocked her.

The door banged shut, and she whirled around. "I'm ashamed of you. You shouldn't act so familiar with Butch Winter. Batting your eyelashes and hanging on his every word. The way he stared at you was not honorable or respectable. You encouraged him with the sway of your skirt and shy smiles. You acted like you've met him before."

Eyes swimming with threatening tears, Leah pressed a hand to her chest. "I ran into him in town a few times and we chatted. I didn't mean any harm." Leah darted her eyes away from Anna and wrung her hands.

Her schweschder's embarrassment and anxiousness worried her. Leah had wilkomed Butch's attraction to her. She was young and innocent. She didn't understand Butch's intentions might not be honorable. The man scared Anna. Leah would be considering marriage in the next couple of years, and she'd assumed to an Amish man. She swallowed and stared at her. "Leah, would you consider an Englischer for a potential husband?"

Her schweschder bit her trembling upper lip. "I'm not sure."

Anna's breath caught in her throat. She'd been contemplating leaving with Noah and living in another Amish community. The thought never entered her mind Leah or Beth might become interested in an Englischer and leave the Amish community. The reality of either of them leaving Amish life would tear her and their mamm's hearts in two. "Leah, answer me. Could you leave us and handle being shunned?"

Leah shivered and thrust her chin stubbornly. "I don't want to discuss this anymore."

"Keep away from him. He's not a gentleman and certainly didn't treat you with respect. And until you choose whether to remain Amish, you shouldn't complicate your life considering an Englischer. And not a man such as Butch Winter."

Leah had been responsible, smart, and loyal. Her schweschder hadn't inquired about the world outside their community, and she possessed a deep-rooted faith in God. Butch had put this temptation in Leah's head. Leah was too inexperienced to realize the danger she put herself in. Anna hoped she never encountered the arrogant Englischer again. Her schweschder hadn't responded to her warning. She wanted to protect her from harm. Would Leah listen to her?

She and Leah waited on customers the rest of the afternoon. The small talk between them had been strained after Butch and his mamm left. Anna closed the shop at five and hooked her arm through her schweschder's. "I don't like this dissension between us. You've got me worried over you and Butch Winter."

Leah patted her hand but looked away. "Don't be silly. We're fine."

Anna wasn't convinced, but Mamm would be joining them on the way home. She had to trust Leah for now. Leah had been trustworthy and sweet and had never exhibited flirtatious behavior like she had with Butch Winter. She didn't want to make more out of it than necessary. She had enough on her mind with Noah's proposal and stipulation they move to Lancaster.

She and Leah retrieved the buggy and picked up Mamm. They headed home.

Mamm talked about her day. "My feet are hurting. We worked hard today. We had a constant flow of customers in our shop. Tuesdays aren't usually so busy."

Anna drove the buggy and nodded now and then. Arriving home, she halted the horse and put the animal in the barn.

Beth ran from Mrs. Hochstetler's next door to greet them. "I gathered and mixed the ingredients to make butter cookies. Mrs. Hochstetler helped me a little bit." She held up a basket of cookies. "She sent some home with me for us."

The sun shone bright on her schweschder's full cheeks and freckles across her small nose. A red curl escaped her kapp and hung above her eyes. She pushed her hair back in the kapp.

Anna grinned. "Good work, Beth. They'll make an excellent dessert."

Patting Beth's shoulder, Mamm beamed. "I can't wait to bite into one after supper!"

Leah grinned. "Me too!"

Mamm yawned and stretched. "Anna, I'll cook."

"I'll cook for us if you'll feed the animals. I know

how much you enjoy them. There's enough mixed feed for the horses at present, but I'll need to make more for tomorrow. I'll prepare the ingredients to soak overnight after we finish our supper. Leah can help me prepare supper."

"I'm going to the cellar to get canned peaches, salted ham, and green beans." Leah headed to the cellar doors.

Beth handed her basket to Mamm. "I'm going to talk to Thomas." She ran to him not too far away.

Mamm sighed. "Danki. I do need to keep your little schweschder from pestering Thomas all evening. She doesn't understand why he won't commit to marrying her when they grow up." She shook her head. "He's at a disadvantage living next to Mrs. Hochstetler. He probably wishes she wasn't taking care of Beth. I'm certain she watches for him to go outside and play each day."

Anna chuckled. "Poor Thomas. He doesn't have a chance. She's determined to win him over."

Leah grinned and approached them, carrying her pickings for supper. "I overheard what Anna said, and I agree. You can't sway Beth's opinion on anything. Believe me, I've tried more than once." She gestured to her arms. "I'll take these in and open them."

An hour later, Anna glanced at her family sitting around the table. Mealtime was her favorite time of the day. The food was good, but the conversation was better. She and her family discussed customers, supply orders, and the latest gossip in town. They had to talk out troublesome issues at times, but they solved their problems together. Having time, with her family erased from her life if they left Berlin, would be like losing one of her limbs. She blinked back tears and forced a smile on her face.

Leah extended her hand. "Hold hands, and I'll give thanks to God for our food." She raised her head after completing her prayer and passed dishes of steaming boiled potatoes and ham. "Mamm, Anna and I met Daniel Bontrager yesterday. He's new in town, but he lived in Lancaster. Anna remembered him from church a couple of times, but I didn't."

Anna shared with Mamm Daniel's story about his parents' passing. "Do you remember them?"

"How tragic! And jah, I had met and saw them in church, but I didn't know them well. I had heard his mamm was in bad health. They weren't in Lancaster long before we moved here. So Daniel is Jonathan's bruder then?"

"Jah, Daniel took over Jonathan and Adele's place."

Anna mashed her boiled potato and added butter and a dash of salt. "He's a roofer, and I'm asking Grace if he can repair our leak at the shop. He promised to quote us a fair estimate."

Raising her eyebrows, Beth tilted her head. "Is he handsome, Leah?"

"Jah, he has dark brown eyes and hair. His arms bulge with muscles threatening to tear through his shirtsleeves. He likes Anna. You should've seen the way he smiled at the sight of her. No one else existed for him but her. I was invisible."

"Leah, stop your silliness. He was kind and a gentleman. Nothing more." She scooped out another helping of green beans. "Noah and Daniel met at the shop. Daniel overheard me inviting Noah to supper. I'm sure any interest he might've had in me diminished, so you can put your silly notion out of your head." Anna's cheeks warmed with embarrassment.

"If Noah leaves, maybe you'll give Daniel a chance. Anything can happen." Beth grinned and forked a piece of ham.

"I wish life was as simple as you make it sound, my dear little schweschder."

"Life can be simple, Anna. Let Noah go and get better acquainted with Daniel. Thomas is stubborn and won't admit he loves me, but he does and we will get married someday."

Leah and Mamm chuckled at Beth's innocence.

Anna raised her hands in dismay. "You all are maddening at times, but I love you." She smiled.

They chatted about the day, finished their food, and enjoyed fresh peaches topped with fresh cream for dessert. After they were finished, Anna carried her plate to the dry sink, and Leah pulled out containers for the leftovers. "We love you too, Anna. I shouldn't have teased you about Daniel. You're not upset with me, are you?"

"No, but the last thing I need is you trying to match me with another man. Noah is all I can handle."

Mamm lifted a large kettle with a wooden handle off a peg. "I'm not getting involved in this conversation. I'm going outside to pump water."

Leah and Beth put their plates on the counter.

"Anna and I will wash the dishes." Mamm set her pan of water on the counter. She poured half of it in the dishpan and the other half in a drinking pitcher. She lifted the teakettle off the stove and added hot water to the dishpan.

Anna stuck her finger in the water and grinned. "The temperature is just right." She put the dirty plates, glasses, and utensils in the water.

Mamm smiled. "I'll wash and you dry the dishes, Anna."

"I'll wipe the table." Anna slid a damp cloth across the smooth wooden surface.

Leah waved to Beth. "Let's play checkers."

Her schweschders skipped to the sitting room.

Anna rinsed the lightly soiled rag in the dishwater and then hung it to dry on a peg next to the sink. She stepped to Mamm, grabbed a clean dishtowel, and accepted a clean wet plate from her. "Did Daed ever go through a phase where he suggested you change the way you do things?"

"No, he and I were content and the thought never occurred to me to change him, and he didn't try to alter me or anything I did."

"Noah's strongly suggested I alter the way I do things."

"Give me an example."

"He asks me to rearrange the furniture, quilts, and other dry goods more often than I prefer. I don't hold a fishing pole to his satisfaction. I don't alter my routine enough to suit him. I could go on and on."

"I don't believe you can change someone. They have to want to change. If you don't wilkom his suggestions, you need to contemplate if Noah is the man you want to commit your life to. Search the Scriptures and pray to God for answers."

"But I love him so much."

"Love may not be enough. What sacrifices are you willing to make to marry Noah? You may not be compatible at this point. You've had time to learn more about each other. Maybe you and Noah are too different." She dried her hands on her apron and circled her arm around Anna's shoulders. "Like I told you yesterday, whatever your decision may be, I trust you, and I'll support you. Your happiness is what's important to me."

"Danki, Mamm." She dried the rest of the white porcelain dishes she'd eaten from all her life and stowed them in the cabinet. Anna grabbed a large pail with a thick wire handle, went outside and pumped water, returned to the kitchen, and placed it on the stove to boil. Using hot pads, she tackled the handle of the hot pot of water. She carried the big pail to the barn and made it without spilling any. She returned to the kitchen to gather two quarts of oats, one of bran, and a half pint of flaxseed. There was just enough of each. Tomorrow Mamm would have to buy more at the General Store and replenish the supply. She returned to the barn, snatched a stable bucket, poured the oats in it, and added the flaxseed. She drenched the dry mixture with the boiling water, dropped in the bran, and covered the blend with an old rug.

Standing back, she studied the bucket. The contents should be fine in the corner behind the hay. The combination needed at least five hours to rest. The time would allow it to absorb the water and the flaxseed to bind the oats and bran together. The horses hadn't experienced any digestive problems since she'd started them on the combination. She was careful with their portions and made certain they were given enough hay to maintain their good health. She wished she could fix her and Noah's problems this easily.

She drew in a deep breath. *I need private quiet time.* She went to her favorite hidden spot by the pond not far from the haus. She threw a stone in the water and watched it disappear, leaving an ever-widening ring of ripples. She wasn't sure if she could watch Noah walk out of her life any more than she could envision leaving her family and friends. Were their problems temporary? Would he accept her as she was like he had when they first met, given time?

Leah's joyful personality had been more so this evening. She hoped her schweschder had put any notions of taking up with Butch Winter out of her head. Her schweschders needed her counsel, and she wanted to share life with them. Another reason to stay in Berlin. Hopefully, reading her Bible before bed, saying her prayers, and getting a good night's rest would give her clarity.

The sun streamed through the window Wednesday morning. Anna had enjoyed doing chores in the warm air on this beautiful day. She returned to her room and poured water from her white porcelain pitcher into a large bowl sitting on the washstand. After splashing her face, she blinked her tired eyes. She'd tossed and turned most of the night. *I'm exhausted. Noah and I have to kumme to an understanding soon, so I can enjoy life again.* She grabbed a thin white cotton towel off a peg a few feet above the washstand and dabbed her face and wiped her hands. Returning the towel to the oak peg, she peeked out the window and listened to the birds sing. A warm breeze brushed her cheeks.

Clothes changed and ready for work, she joined her schweschders and Mamm in the kitchen.

They hurried to finish their biscuits and beef gravy.

"Make sure you have your bag before leaving!" Anna grabbed hers. "Enjoy your day."

Beth scampered to the neighbor's haus.

Anna, Leah, and Mamm climbed in the buggy and headed to town. She listened to Leah and Mamm discuss the yellow chicks that had hatched early in the morning. After pulling in front of the General Store, her Mamm climbed out. "I'll meet you at the livery at five, like usual."

Nodding, Anna drove to the livery and left her buggy. She and Leah strolled to the shop.

"Anna, you were quiet on the way here. Have you kumme to any conclusions regarding Noah?"

She had kumme to a conclusion, but she wasn't ready to discuss her decision with anyone yet. She wanted to give herself time to mull over the conversation she would have with Noah. "I'm getting closer to making a decision."

"I won't press you. Tell me when you're ready." Leah touched her arm and smiled.

Anna nodded and unlocked the store, and they entered the shop.

Several minutes later, Grace came in bouncing Joy, her beautiful little maedel, on her hip. "Anna, Leah, how are you?"

"Grace, what a nice surprise." Tucking her fingers into Joy's tiny fist, Anna smiled. "You have such cute rosy cheeks and beautiful hazel eyes. You are a pretty little maedel."

Joy grinned and wriggled in her mamm's arms.

"Grace, how are you?" Leah reached for Joy. "Let me hold you, little one." She carried her to the colorful quilts displayed on the wall. "Do you like these colors?"

"I'm fine, Leah. Joy takes to you easier than she does most people."

"Her name fits her. You and Anna talk. I'll entertain her."

"Your dochder is mesmerized by the quilts. Maybe she'll like stitching them and carry on the tradition of the keepsake pocket quilts." Anna stole a glance again at Leah and Joy then shifted her attention to Grace. "Have you talked to Hester lately? Does she have any news about Becca?"

Grace lowered her tone. "I miss Becca each day. I could tell her anything, and she never passed judgment on me. I'm blessed to have Hester to keep me informed about her. Even though she's not Amish, I'm relieved our laws allow me to birth bopplin with her. She visits Becca a couple of times a year. Becca's got two kinner, she's involved in her church, and happily married to Matt."

"Does she still work as a nurse in his office?"

"Hester said she stays at home with the kinner. Mrs. Carrington, Matt's mamm, keeps her busy with fund-raising events and parties." Grace's lips quivered. She lowered her chin to her chest. "Danki for asking about Becca. You're the only one who understands. You and Mark are the only Amish I can talk to about my dear friend without being reprimanded, or worse, shunned for mentioning her name since she became an Englischer."

"You can always share what's on your mind with me. I'm sorry you both can't spend time together. Shunning is a difficult law for me to follow, so I understand. I'm glad she's happy. I'm blessed she and Ruth suggested you and Sarah sell the keepsake pocket quilts in your dry goods shop. I love working here."

She gave Anna an endearing smile. "I'm so blessed you came into my life when you did. Your timing was perfect, and you're doing a great job." She beamed. "I'm excited Mark bought the shop from Levi, Sarah's husband, and my father. He's finished the new sign, 'Grace's Dry Goods Shop,' and I'm anxious to have the marker hung." She winced. "Mark's more interested in building products for his store than he is in hanging my sign."

"I have a solution for you. Daniel Bontrager, Jonathan's bruder, has moved to Berlin. He's living in Jonathan and Adele's haus. He has offered to repair the shop roof. He'll give me an estimate Friday, and I'll run his price by you first before giving him the go-ahead. If you choose to accept his offer, he could repair the roof, and I could ask him to hang the sign. He said the cost for the repair would be minimal."

"If you consider his price fair to hang the sign and repair the roof, tell him to go ahead. I trust you. He can pick up the sign at Mark's store. He's got it in the back." Her facial features turned sad. "Poor Daniel. He must be sad with the loss of his family. I miss Adele and Jonathan. They were such a sweet couple."

"He's lost his entire family. His parents were killed in a robbery at the Lancaster General Store. In spite of suffering such tragedy in his life, he has a positive attitude. I admire him for not allowing the tragedy in his life to weigh him down."

"I hope he's successful and content in Berlin." She cocked her head to the side. "Do you have anything else you'd like to discuss about the shop?"

"Everything is good. I enjoy the customers, keeping the records, and ordering supplies. Of course, having Leah work with me is wonderful." Grace allowed her to display the dry goods however she chose, and she had given her the freedom to raise the prices or put things on sale. Grace's leniency made managing the shop easier and more fun.

"I'm so pleased Leah accepted your offer and enjoys working in the shop. She's such a sweetheart, and my neighbors have told me how helpful she's been with them when looking for dry goods." Grace touched Anna's shoulder. "You aren't your usual cheery self today. Your eyes are ringed with dark circles. Is something weighing heavy on your mind?"

They'd formed a close bond since the day Grace had hired her on the spot when she inquired about a job. Anna blew a sigh of relief. Grace was here. She could talk to her about Noah. Grace wouldn't mince words or sugarcoat her answer to anything Anna asked her. "Noah asked me to marry him."

Eyes big, Grace hugged her. "When?"

"Before we set a date to wed in Berlin, he wants me to agree to move to Lancaster shortly after our wedding. His aunt and uncle have offered to have us stay with them. He would work for his uncle managing his farm and livestock."

"He wants to leave here? Why? He and I don't get a chance to chat much when he's working on our property. We're both so busy. Mark hasn't mentioned Noah's leaving Berlin. Noah must not have shared his plans with Mark yet. I assumed you two would get married eventually and maintain a life here. I'm shocked."

"Noah craves change. He wants to experience living in a new location."

"Do you want me to ask Mark to talk to him? Your families should kumme first. He's being immature."

"No, please don't ask Mark to speak to Noah. They have a special friendship, and I don't want to cause trouble between them." Anna leaned on the counter. "My heart rips in two when I consider packing up my belongings and waving good-bye to those I love. He and I haven't seen eye to eye on a lot of things for the past several months. He suggests I change one thing after another, and his constant interference and dissatisfaction with my ways irritate me."

Grace's tone became serious and she held her gaze.

"I'm fond of Noah. He's a good man, but he is different from most Amish men. Mark has told me about Noah's need for adventure, and his desire would be unsettling for most women, I'd suspect. He can't stand to leave things the same in his life. You are the opposite. In my opinion, you have to accept each other for who you are to find happiness together." She put a hand to her chin and shook her head. "I never thought he'd want to leave Berlin, since you and he have become serious. When did he first mention his idea to you?"

"He brought up moving to Lancaster more than once this past year. I'd hoped he'd abandon the notion."

Grace put a hand to her stomach. "I hurt for you. These are major decisions."

"What should I do, Grace?"

"You have to consider what type of life you want. Would you enjoy moving from community to community, or do you want to grow roots here and maintain long-lasting relationships with your friends and family? Would you resent him as time goes on if he asks you to continually change things you're content to have remain the same? You must ask God if Noah is the man for you. Marriage is forever. You want to choose a husband who shares your values." Grace patted her arm. "I'll always be close with you no matter where you live. We can write letters and, hopefully, you'll return to Berlin for occasional visits."

Anna beheld her dearest friend. Grace had an apple-sized birthmark on her cheek, but it did nothing to diminish her loveliness. Her wisdom, kindness, and close friendship meant more to her than she could put into words. The woman was a midwife, shop owner, fraa, and mamm. Grace was determined, strong, caring, and dependable. She admired her deep faith in God. "I'm glad we had a chance to talk about Noah. Danki for listening."

Grace brushed Anna's cheek. "I love you, dear friend. Your happiness means a great deal to me. Face your fears and don't give in to them. You are questioning marrying him for good reasons. Don't ignore them. Settle these problems with him before you commit to marriage."

Anna dipped her chin to her chest. "Danki for your advice. I'm not sure what I'll do yet."

"I don't envy you."

Leah bounced Joy on her hip and approached them. "Your little maedel is a sweetheart. She's easy to please and delightful." Leah came alongside Anna, cuddled Joy, and nuzzled her face in the boppli's neck.

Wiggling and laughing, Joy reached for her mamm.

Taking her boppli from Leah, Grace chuckled. "She is good most of the time."

Joy fisted her hands and rubbed her eyes.

"Time to get my dochder home for a nap."

"Take care, Grace." Anna waved.

"Enjoy the rest of your day." Her dear friend grinned over her shoulder.

"Bye, bye." Joy flapped her hand, then stuck her thumb in her mouth.

Anna and Leah waved.

Shutting the door, Leah paused. "Did you enjoy your time with Grace?"

"I really did. She's not afraid to speak her mind, but she's kind and gentle when giving me advice. I admire her for not letting her birthmark destroy her confidence. I don't know if I'd be as strong had I been born with it. I've noticed the strange looks she gets from Englischers. It can't be easy for her."

Leah nodded. "I admire her too." She wrinkled her

nose. "Anna, did you tell Grace about Noah pressing you to relocate? I'm curious as to her reaction."

"Jah. She was surprised and concerned. She told me to consider if I wanted change or consistency in my future."

"You are a homebody and comfortable in your routine. Noah's innovations in constructing wood products and rearranging how he does his chores are harmless, but constantly suggesting you change the way you do tasks to suit him is troubling. Moving to Lancaster would disrupt your orderly life in a big way, and resenting him for trying to alter you would cause problems for your marriage."

"I love Noah, but love may not be enough to overcome our differences." The words hit her like a thunderclap. Her head began to throb. Losing Noah would be like losing a loved one to Heaven.

Customers strolled into the store, and Anna went to greet them. She bit her tongue to not rush the short, indecisive Englisch woman dithering over whether to purchase the wedding ring or the pinwheel quilt. Glancing at the clock, Anna hoped the woman would choose her selections before the clock struck five.

At closing time, the woman chose the pinwheel quilt and passed Anna the correct change with a smile. "Thank you for being patient with me."

"I'm glad you're pleased with your purchase." Anna wrapped the package. "You're wilkom in our shop anytime. Good day."

Anna listened for the door to close behind the customer. "Ready to go, Leah?"

She missed their usual closeness and comfort before Butch destroyed it yesterday. Leah had been quiet and avoided her all day. Her heart ached at the tension between them.

Leah nodded, stepped outside, and waited for Anna to lock the door.

Pointing, Leah squinted. "Mamm's waiting at the livery."

They met Mamm, climbed into the buggy, and headed home. They discussed their workdays at the General Store and dry goods store and what to have for supper.

Anna couldn't shake the guilt of holding back Leah's transgression from Mamm.

After pulling up to the barn, Anna waited for them to climb out and open the big, rustic, white barn doors. She drove the buggy in.

Beth walked over from Mrs. Hochstetler's and greeted her family. "Mrs. Hochstetler taught me a different knitting stitch today." She held up her needles and a small patch of knitted yarn. "She let me bring it home to show you."

Mamm smiled. "I'm glad you like knitting. Your stitches are perfect. I'm proud of you."

Beth blushed. "Danki. I worked on it all morning."

Leah touched Beth's sample. "I like the dark blue yarn you chose."

"Me too." Beth grinned.

Patting Beth's shoulder, Anna beamed. The sun shone bright on her schweschder's full cheeks and freckles across her small nose. A red curl escaped her kapp and hung above her eye.

She pushed the hair back in her schweschder's kapp. "You've got the most beautiful hair."

"Danki, Anna." Finished securing the horse in a stall, Anna fetched water for drinking, while Mamm and her schweschders went inside the haus to prepare

their evening meal. Anna strolled inside and she set
her pan on the counter. She wiped her forehead with
the back of her sleeve and listened to her family discuss Beth's fascination with the new fuzzy chicks in the
chicken coop while she washed and cut the vegetables. The discussion of everyday events took the edge
off her troubles. If she left Berlin, she'd miss these
special times with her family. The joy in their voices
and the way they used their hands to aid them in
telling their stories were just some of the things she
loved about being around them.

Time had gotten away from her. Beth was ten already. Leah was sixteen, and she'd be considering a
man for a potential husband soon. A twinge of appre-
hension whipped through her at the thought Leah
might choose an outsider. She shuddered. Butch
Winter came to mind. She couldn't stomach the
thought of Leah's considering him. She loved her
schweschders so much, and she wanted them to
choose husbands who would respect and love them. If
she left Berlin, she'd miss out on what was to kumme
in her schweschders' lives. The thought sent chills up
her spine.

The table set, she helped carry full dishes of
ham, vegetables, and potatoes to the table. Quiet,
she finished half her food and pushed her plate
aside, distracted from the conversation around her,
thinking of Noah. She loved him, but their wants and
desires seemed too different to ignore. She hugged
herself and a gloom of sadness enveloped her.

Leah carried the dishes to the dry sink. "I'll wash
the dishes tonight."

Beth popped up. "I'll dry them."

Mamm hugged her dochder. "Danki, I could use
a rest."

"Go lie down, Mamm. I'm going to take a stroll before turning in for bed." Anna held the door open and breathed in the heavy scent of honeysuckle.

Going toward her room, Mamm grinned. "Danki, my thoughtful girls."

Anna stepped on the porch. The warm air and slight breeze fluttered her sleeves and skirt. Serene, the picturesque crystal-clear pond lined with trees and the worn white barn against the bright orange sun calmed her.

Bowing her head, she prayed. "Dear Heavenly Father, please guide me in the path You would have me go concerning Noah. Is he the one You would have me to marry? My heart is torn. Danki for Your loving mercy and grace. Amen."

Later, she went to her room. She turned her head to a noise that startled her. "Beth, you scared me."

"I'm sorry. I didn't mean to." She frowned and sat. "I need to talk to you."

Something was definitely wrong. Beth's sad eyes and worried face sent her heart racing. "Beth, you can tell me anything. What's bothering you?" Beth was pensive and tense. Way out of the ordinary for her schweschder's usual disposition. Beth was positive and cheerful most of the time.

"Leah thought I was asleep when she climbed out our bedroom window last night. After she was outside, I peeked out. In the light from the lantern she carried, I saw a young man dressed in a red shirt and wearing a fancy hat waiting for her. They disappeared into the woods."

Gripping her apron and fighting to control the volume of her voice, Anna sat quiet. Butch Winter was most likely the man her schweschder had met. The boorish Englischer had lured Leah to the woods.

Her stomach churned with angst. He could have forced himself upon her. She was innocent and would've trusted him. How many times had Leah and Butch met?

She had to put a stop to Leah's meeting with him, but how? "Do you have any idea how long Leah was gone?"

"I fought to stay awake until she came back, but I fell asleep. I was frightened she wouldn't return. When I woke up, she was in her bed." She crossed her arms. "I'm afraid she'll sneak out and meet him again."

Leah's behavior was out of the ordinary. In the past she'd obeyed and was eager to please God and their mamm. Anna couldn't imagine what attracted her schweschder to Butch. "I'll talk to her, but don't mention this to anyone."

Shaking her head, Beth raised an eyebrow. "Shouldn't we tell Mamm?"

"Let's not tell Mamm yet." She rested her hand on Beth's shoulder. "Let me talk to Leah first."

Beth put a finger to her lips. "I won't say a word."

Anna gently squeezed Beth's shoulder. "Danki for telling me. Go to your bedroom. I'll go speak with Leah."

Drawing her mouth in a grim line, Beth walked through the open doorway.

Anna couldn't believe Leah had put Beth in such a predicament. She was foolish to think her little schweschder wouldn't wake and find her missing. Leah's actions were thoughtless and reckless. She went to the kitchen. Leah was there, wiping off a dish. "Would you please kumme to my room?"

Wiping her hands on a towel, Leah didn't meet her gaze. "What do you need?"

Deceitfulness hung in Anna's mind. "Kumme to my room, and we'll need to shut the door. We need to talk." She couldn't tell what was going on with Leah. A fire ignited inside her and fueled her anger. She glared at Leah. "Beth told me you climbed out the window last night. She peeked out and noticed you meeting a young man. Were you with Butch Winter?"

Face red, Leah's chin trembled. She nodded. "Jah, but don't worry. I'll not have anything to do with him again. He scared me. Oh, Anna, I'm full of guilt. I wouldn't want to leave our Amish community. I was foolish to let myself get carried away with an Englischer in the first place. I'll marry an Amish man when the time kummes. Please forgive me."

"Why did you agree to meet him? How reckless of you! I can't believe you went with him to the woods at night alone!"

Sitting next to Anna, Leah stared at her lap. "The day he came to the shop, he asked me to meet him in the woods after dark so we could get better acquainted. I didn't think of being in danger. His broad shoulders and confident way about him sent my heart in a spin. He was so handsome and pleasant. I trusted him." She bit her trembling lip. "You were right, Anna. He's not a gentleman."

Something had happened to change her schweschder's mind about Butch. What had he done? She shivered and crossed her arms against her chest. "How many times and where did you meet him?"

"Twice behind the apothecary before he and his mamm came into the store to shop. Last night was the only time I left the haus at night to join him." She dabbed the tear escaping her eye with the corner of her apron. "I'm sorry I deceived you. I've prayed and asked God to forgive me. Please, Anna, please forgive me."

"I have trusted you when you left the shop to run errands. I'm livid you've been meeting Butch, knowing it was wrong. What you've done was thoughtless and risky." The fire inside her dwindled. Leah's plea for forgiveness tugged at her heart. Her pledge never to have anything to do with Butch again eased her mind. Keeping a constant watch on her would've been difficult for her or Mamm if she hadn't agreed to not have anything to do with him again. "Why your sudden change of heart toward him?"

"He held my hand and walked me to an area where we could spread the blanket he carried. We put our lanterns down and talked. He grabbed my arms so tight they hurt and kissed me. I pushed him, and he fell back. I ran home as fast as I could. He didn't follow me." She held her deeply flushed face. "I've never been so frightened."

Anna closed her eyes tight and shook her head. Unspeakable things could have happened to Leah. Emotional and physical scars could've damaged her schweschder forever. She was certain God had his hand of protection on her schweschder. Especially after meeting Butch and observing his disrespectful behavior. "He could've harmed you. You have more sense than to meet a man in the woods at night." She placed her hands on Leah's shoulders. "You have defied God and our family and gone against Amish law. I'm ashamed of you. You hid your transgression by acting like you hadn't met Butch before he came to the shop with his mamm. I'm hurt and angry you deceived me."

"I'm sorry, Anna. I feel terrible for what I've done. Please, please, don't tell Mamm. Discussing my foolish behavior with you and facing your wrath is hard enough, but Mamm will insist on informing the bishop. She wouldn't want to chance that someone may have seen Butch and me together and told him. We were careful. I'm confident no one paid attention to us. I don't want the bishop to find out and think less of me. He may suggest I be shunned for a period of time for my indiscretion."

Anna stared at her hands in deep thought. Leah was right. Bishop Weaver wouldn't be happy her schweschder had invited trouble from an Englischer. Amish did their best to avoid any unpleasantness from Englischers. If he insisted she be shunned for her transgression, they'd have to ignore her, and she'd have to sit at a separate table for meals. No conversations, no advice, no interaction. She scanned Leah's face. Her quivering lips and trembling hands showed her sincere remorse. They could keep this secret among the three of them. There would be no need to upset Mamm. The risk of the bishop telling the members in church and asking Leah to stand before them and ask forgiveness sent shivers through her. Her schweschder should be held accountable for her actions in this way, but she just couldn't do it to her. She'd protect her.

"Anna, please say something."

"Do you agree to never meet him, or any man, in secret again?"

"Jah, I promise."

"If you consider an Amish man for a friend or potential husband, you are to tell me about him first. Understood?"

"I promise. Does this mean you won't tell Mamm?"

"I'm not going to tell her for my own selfish reasons. I'm afraid she'll tell the bishop, and I couldn't stand to ignore you for whatever length of time he'd impose. I'm hoping Butch will stay away, but I'm fearful he'll show up at the shop again. He doesn't seem like the type of man to accept rejection well. If he does, we'll have to tell Mamm." Her mamm would expect her to share Leah's transgression with her. A wave of guilt passed through her. She'd given Mamm a reason to distrust her for the first time.

Leah hugged her. "Danki, Anna. I'll not dishonor you or our family again. Are you confident Beth will keep our secret?"

"I'll speak with her again. If she expresses any opposition, we'll have to tell Mamm."

"May I go with you?"

Anna nodded.

They went to the bedroom Leah and Beth shared. Anna folded her hands and squeezed them tight.

Beth stood and crossed her arms. "I had to tell Anna you snuck out the window to meet a strange man. I was afraid he would hurt you." She narrowed her eyes. "Besides, you were wrong to sneak out like you did."

Leah held Beth's gaze. "I was wrong. I should never have done such a thing. I regret my actions. Forgive me?"

Beth nodded and relaxed. "I do forgive you, but don't ever sneak out of our window for any reason again."

"I won't."

Anna's chest swelled with relief. The three of them shared a special bond. Leah's foolishness had threatened to rip them apart. Nothing was worth severing their close relationship.

"Beth, we'd prefer to not tell Mamm what Leah's done. Will you agree to keep this from her?"

"I don't want to tell her, but if she finds out we've kept this from her, she'll be angry." She pushed her pencil above her ear. "Leah, please don't ever put yourself in danger again. I'd be heartbroken if anything happened to you."

Leah slumped on the bed next to her little schweschder. "I'm sorry I put you in this position. Rest assured I've learned my lesson."

Anna stepped closer to them. "We are fortunate to have one another. Let's not take our relationship for granted. We must always trust one another. If any of us has a concern, we are to discuss what is on our mind among the three of us. No matter how embarrassing or difficult the subject matter, we mustn't keep secrets. Agreed?"

Beth and Leah nodded and reached for Anna's hands. The three of them stood in a circle and bowed their heads.

Leah prayed, "Dear Heavenly Father, please forgive me for being disobedient and disappointing You and my family. Danki for Your mercy and Your grace. Amen."

Unclasping her schweschders' hands, Anna hugged and wished Beth and Leah good night and went to her room. Again, shame took over her mind. Not sure if she'd made the correct decision by not informing Mamm about Leah's behavior, she plopped on the bed and pictured herself shunning her schweschder. No, she couldn't risk being told to ignore Leah. She'd stick to her plan.

* * *

Daniel gazed out over his newly painted white fence Friday morning and grinned. Thursday he'd mucked the stalls, mended his own fence, and repaired his neighbor's roof. Standing back, he scrutinized his work. Sturdy and strong, the stakes should withstand the weather for years.

He shrugged on clean clothes, secured his wagon, and whistled on his way to visit Anna at the shop. She had lingered in his mind since the day he met her. He chastised himself over and over for entertaining thoughts of her, but his mind wouldn't cooperate.

The newspaper boy had a stack of papers sitting at his feet. "Read President Theodore Roosevelt's speech on preserving our natural forests!"

He smiled at the boy. Pushing the dry goods shop door open, he beheld the woman who had captivated his thoughts the last few days. "Good morning. Did you have a chance to ask Mrs. King if I may repair the roof leak?"

"Daniel, danki for coming in. Grace visited me the other day. She would be obliged if you would give us an estimate. You're wilkom to use the ladder we have in back."

"Jah, I'd like to inspect the damage if you don't mind."

Leah came in from the back room. "Good morning, Daniel. Would you like a cup of coffee? I threw in fresh firewood and lit our stove a short while ago. The coffee should be ready."

He'd take any chance to linger with Anna. "Danki. I'll take a cup. I cleaned out Jonathan's and Adele's drawers and clothespress. I'd like to donate them. Where should I take them?"

"After church services, we have tables for the meal

and one table for things people are giving away. You can put the donations there after the next service."

"Good suggestion. Most of the clothes are in good condition. I'm hoping they can be of benefit to people in need." Accepting the mug from Leah, he glanced at the front door clanging open.

A young man, head cocked back with a sly smile, strode in. The Englischer had a demanding attitude. Anna and Leah paled and stepped back. The man's bold stature and shrewd dark eyes alarmed him. The women apparently didn't feel safe.

He moved next to Anna. "Sir, may we help you?"

"I'm Butch Winter. Leah's my woman. Tell 'em, Leah."

Daniel gaped at him. Was Butch out of his mind? He couldn't imagine gentle Leah having anything to do with such an impolite man, and he was an Englischer.

Red-faced, Leah gasped. "No! I'm not your woman. Go and leave me alone."

Butch scoffed at her. "You gonna be angry over a little kiss? I don't understand why you rushed off from me after our special time together in the woods." He moved closer to her. "Don't be coy. You want me to kiss you again. Don't you? Come on over here. I won't bite."

Temper at its highest peak, Daniel stepped between Leah and Butch. "Leave and don't ever bother Leah or kumme here again."

"Leah doesn't want me to leave. She's being a typical woman. She'll be angry for a while, but she'll be mushy for me later." He chuckled, pulled a toothpick from his pocket, and held the skinny stick between his teeth.

Disgusted and having a hard time keeping his fisted hands at his sides, Daniel wasn't prone to violence and had never used them to solve a dispute, but Butch was testing every fiber of his self-control. "Get out!"

"Leah, honey. Tell the man he's wrong."

"He's not wrong. I want you to honor our wishes."

Daniel pointed to the door. "Go!"

Butch drew his eyes in a cold stare, huffed, and slammed his fist in the side wall, winced, rubbed his knuckles, and stomped out.

Staring at her feet, Anna sighed. "I'm sorry you had to stand up to Butch on our account."

Leah bowed her head. "I made bad choices, and I've brought trouble to us. I've been a foolish woman." She cast a forlorn look at Daniel. "I met him a couple of times. He was kind at first, and then he turned forceful and scared me. I'm ashamed of myself for flirting with an Englischer. I've upset my schweschders, and I'm sick about what I've done."

Lifting his hat, Daniel ran a hand through his thick, dark hair. "Leah, we all make mistakes, but the lessons we learn from them are what counts. Have you asked God to forgive you?"

Blushing, she bobbed her head up and down, tears pooling in her eyes.

"Good. I recommend you put the ordeal behind you." Glancing at the women, he saw the color had returned to their cheeks and their trembling had eased. He'd hidden his astonishment about Leah's surprising revelation. Young and innocent, Leah could've been attacked physically and scarred in her perception of men for the rest of her life. Thankfully, she'd escaped unharmed. Uncertain whether Butch would return, he was glad he'd be working on their shop roof for a few days.

"Danki for your understanding, Daniel." Leah startled when the door opened. She ran to greet the two young Amish women entering the shop.

Sheepishly Anna held his gaze. "I'm embarrassed you were drawn into our family problems with that unscrupulous man, but I'm relieved you were here to defend us. His stance and temper are unsettling. I'm grateful you stepped forward and helped us. Please don't tell anyone what happened."

"I won't." Anna was sweet. She was protecting her schweschder from worry. If only she were free to consider him for a suitor. He longed to pursue her. "You can ask me for anything. I'm happy to help you or your family in any way." He swallowed. Maybe he'd been too forward. It wasn't his intent. He hoped he hadn't created an awkwardness between them. Hiding his attraction to her proved more difficult than he had anticipated.

"I trust you to keep our secret, Daniel. I suspect most Amish men would've been appalled at Leah's conduct and lectured her. You spoke your mind and pointed out her actions weren't acceptable, but you showed her compassion. Danki."

He breathed an inward sigh of relief. He hadn't offended her by offering his help. "There's no need to admonish her any further. Her slumped shoulders and trembling lips were enough to tell me she understood the magnitude of her actions. Besides, I'm not in a position to reprimand her."

Anna waggled her finger. "I don't agree. When you

defended her, you earned the right to speak your mind."

Smiling, he stood at attention. "I stand corrected." Her approval of his response to Leah delighted him. "I hope never to lay eyes on Butch again."

Chapter Three

Noah pushed the door open. "Daniel, I'm surprised to find you here." He flashed Anna a big smile, then shook his head. "You still haven't moved those quilts." He dragged a small table of linens to the far wall. "A little change can make all the difference. Don't you agree, Anna?"

Anna swallowed and gave him a curt nod. Daniel was here, and she had customers. No, she didn't agree, but she'd bite her tongue. Why did Noah find it necessary to rearrange her displays? There was nothing wrong with them.

Leah waved. "Good morning, Noah." She returned her attention to a customer.

"Good to see you, Leah." Noah waved back to her.

Daniel turned to Noah. "I'm here to give Anna a price to repair the roof."

Noah glanced at the blemished spot on the ceiling. "It's good to fix the damaged roof before a big storm kummes and makes the leak worse."

Anna nodded. "I'm grateful to you, Daniel. I wouldn't want to lose our dry goods due to water damage." Why wasn't Noah working at Mark's? What

an odd time of day for him to kumme to the shop.
"You're usually working for Mark this time of day."

He removed his straw hat and held it tight at his
side. "I should wait until after work to speak to you,
but I didn't want to wait. Can we talk in private?"

Daniel cleared his throat. "I'll get the ladder and
check out the roof damage."

Anna smiled at him. "I won't be long, Daniel." She
sighed as the door closed. She was relieved Daniel had
excused himself and separated from them. What she
had to say to Noah should be said in private. Leah was
helping another customer. "Leah, would you mind if
I left with Noah for a short while? We'll be in back of
the apothecary if you need me."

"No, take your time. I'll fetch you if I need you."
Leah nodded to Noah and returned her attention to
the patron.

Anna walked with Noah outside into the sunshine.
The heat warmed her cheeks. She led him to their
quiet and private destination. She waited for him to
speak.

Noah pressed his hat to his chest. "I was anxious to
hear your answer. I don't have much time to wait. Are
you going to marry me and relocate to Lancaster,
Anna?"

She'd contemplated her answer and had kumme to
the right conclusion for her. She hoped she wouldn't
regret her decision. She loved him, but they both
sought different lifestyles. She gazed into his sea-blue
eyes and tears welled in hers. "I'm sorry, Noah. I'm
staying in Berlin. For the past few months, our conversations have been strained and we've grown apart. I
love you, but we also need to have shared values and
accept each other for who we are if we're going to
commit to each other for a lifetime."

Noah reached for her. "Please, Anna, reconsider. You're making too much of my little suggestions to you. I love you. Please leave Berlin for me."

His last words frustrated her. Why couldn't he remain in Berlin *for her*? "If I leave for you, I'll be making a mistake. To go with you shouldn't be such a heart-wrenching decision for me or for you to make a life in Berlin. You're set on moving to Lancaster, and I'm set on remaining here. I disagree your 'little suggestions' to me are insignificant. Your constant need to show me how to improve my ways makes me feel inadequate. There's nothing wrong with my choices. I need to be sure you can accept me the way you did when we first met. Stay and give us this time."

Noah hung his head. "I understand you're having a difficult time leaving your family and job, but I assumed you would choose me when making your final decision. I don't agree we need more time before we marry. I'll stop imposing my suggestions onto you, since they bother you so much. But we're bound to have problems. No marriage is perfect."

Since his suggestions bother me so much? She couldn't get through to him how troubling his trying to change her every move was to her. His disregard of her concerns validated her decision. "I have other reasons why I need to reside in Berlin." She recounted her story about Leah and Butch. "My family needs me. Leah is going through an impressionable time. I have a good job, friends, and family in Berlin. You and I haven't gotten along lately. You're not willing to stay and work through our differences. Remaining here is best. I feel it in my heart."

Noah jerked his head back wide-eyed. "I'll find and have a serious talk with this Butch Winter."

Waving a dismissive hand, Anna shook her head

"No. Daniel was here when Butch came in earlier. He told Butch to leave us alone. I doubt he'll grace us with his awful presence again."

Shoulders relaxing, Noah's face softened. "I'm relieved Daniel faced off with him. No telling what could have happened." His nostrils flared and he crossed his arms. "I'm surprised Leah would agree to meet him in the woods. What she did is a disgrace to your family."

His judgment pained her. She wished she hadn't confided in Noah. The least number of people aware of Butch causing havoc in their lives, the better. "Please don't say a word to anyone about her and Butch. She's regretful, and I'm confident she has learned her lesson."

He relaxed and softened his voice. "Berlin is a tight-knit community. Your family and my mamm have lots of friends willing to help them with whatever they need. They'll be in good hands if you kumme with me. Don't do something you might regret."

"My heart hurts. I'll need time to heal, but I'm confident I've made the right choice."

Noah held her gaze. "Don't shut the door on us yet. I'm leaving for my aunt and uncle's tomorrow. If you change your mind, meet me in the morning at my haus by five o'clock. Tell Leah good-bye for me. I'll go around front where I hitched my wagon." He lingered with pleading eyes, squeezed her hand, and, moments later, left.

Tomorrow. He'd shattered her heart. Their problems couldn't be fixed in a day. Anna hugged herself and swallowed the bile rising in her throat. She blinked back tears and went back inside the shop.

Holding an armload of aprons, Leah rushed to her. "Why are you frowning? What happened?"

"I told Noah I wouldn't marry him and move to Lancaster." She pressed a hand to her throat. "He's leaving in the morning." She fell against Leah and cried.

Leah held her and stroked her back. "I'm sorry you're in pain. I can't imagine how awful you must feel. Noah's been a part of your life most of the time we've lived in Berlin. Your love was evident in the adorable way you looked at each other, but maybe your parting is best, considering what you've told me."

She wanted the angst to end. She'd miss his lop-sided grin, his enthusiasm for their simple and big victories. He'd brought a smile to her lips more times than she could count with his thoughtful words and acts of kindness. He'd delivered cut wood to her family in the winter, carved Amish dolls for her, and brought her favorite desserts to the shop. She would run out of room on a sheet of paper if she wrote down all the wonderful things he'd done for her. They had outweighed their differences, until the last few months when things had turned troublesome. "Mourning his loss will be the hardest thing I've ever done."

"You're strong, courageous, and determined, Anna. Pray and ask God for grace to accept Noah's decision to leave. Do you believe not leaving with Noah is God's will for your life?"

"I do and after reading the Bible and praying about my decision, a peace came over me and the answer was clear. I should remain here."

"Selfishly, I'm relieved. I hope you, Beth, and I will marry good Amish men and live close. I want our kinner to grow up together. I'm fond of Noah. I'll miss him too. I wish him the best."

Anna enjoyed the natural rhythm of rural life in

her Amish community. The rolling land and the daily and seasonal routine of working in the soil beside family and friends represented security and provided all of life's needs. She couldn't think of anything Lancaster could provide for her to entice her to leave Berlin. She stared at her feet. "Let's discuss something else. Daniel may kumme back in any minute."

Daniel returned with a cheerful grin, turning sympathetic in seconds.

She suspected he noticed her tearstained cheeks. He was too much of a gentleman to ask why.

He took off his hat and traced the brim with his fingertips. "I've got good news. The leak isn't as bad as I'd anticipated." He handed her a note. "Here's my estimate." He scanned the shop. "Did Noah leave?"

Leah knelt to pick up a loose thread off the floor. "He left the shop a few minutes ago." She tossed the thread in the trash box. "You won't see him in Berlin after tomorrow. He told us he's moving to Lancaster."

Anna bit her lip. Daniel's eyes had widened. She hoped Daniel didn't ask any questions about Noah. She knew Leah's remark was innocent, but she wished Leah had let him find out the news from someone else.

She quickly glanced at the note. "Daniel, your price is a generous one. I hope you aren't underpaying yourself." She waited, hoping Leah or Daniel wouldn't mention Noah again.

He waved a dismissive hand. "If you're satisfied with my work, you'll tell others in the community. Your recommendation will help grow my business. Working for you would be my pleasure."

She relaxed her tense shoulders. Changing the topic of Noah to Daniel's price for repair had worked. She wouldn't argue with him, but she doubted he was collecting enough money to pay for the supplies. He was a kind man. "Grace granted me permission to accept or reject your price. I'm ready for you to do the work once your schedule permits. She and her husband, Mark King, are the sole owners of this shop now. Mark constructed a new sign, but he hasn't had time to hang it. Would you mind hanging the sign and how much would you charge?"

"I'll hang the new marker the same day I repair the roof for no additional charge."

"We must pay you something to cover your cost for the extra work and time."

"I wouldn't turn down a batch of oatmeal cookies." He wore a friendly grin.

Leah chuckled.

Anna managed a half grin in spite of her sadness. "Oatmeal cookies aren't a fair trade for hanging the sign, but I'll accept and provide you with a basketful." The single man was probably starved for homemade meals and desserts. Feeding him was the least she and Leah could do for his trouble.

"Is tomorrow soon enough?"

Leah nodded. "We'll bake your cookies tonight and have them ready for you in the morning!"

New in town, he hadn't a chance to meet many people yet. Anna would've chatted with him further and not rushed him off, but she couldn't concentrate. Her heart was heavy from her discussion with Noah. "Tomorrow would be perfect. Danki."

He gazed at her. "I'll meet you here around eight." He patted his stomach. "I'll have some cookies for breakfast."

She grinned in spite of her dark mood. "We'll have coffee to go with them."

She and Leah bid him good-bye. She waited until

the door closed to speak. "Smiling when my heart aches is difficult."

"Your bloodshot eyes and tearstained cheeks are hard to ignore. Daniel must have noticed and sensed the time wasn't right to engage in casual conversation." Leah glimpsed at the note in Anna's hand. She gasped. "He's almost working for free at this price."

"We haven't represented our Amish community in the best light. Most of the women in our community wouldn't have let him leave until they'd offered him food and three cups of coffee. He must wonder if we have any manners."

"We should bring him some of Mamm's leftover chicken stew along with the cookies. He can enjoy the food for his supper."

"I agree. Doing something nice for someone else might cheer me up."

An Englisch couple came in. Leah greeted them and showed them blankets.

Anna walked to the back room, grabbed a towel, and buried her face in it. Tears wet the cloth. She mourned the loss of the happy life she'd envisioned with Noah as his fraa before he'd suggested they start life anew in Lancaster. What did God have in store for her? Would she ever get over Noah and find love again? She couldn't dwell on her hurt. She had to work. Wiping her tears, she breathed deep and forced a smile on her face. She pushed Noah out of her mind and focused on the customers. "What did the couple purchase?"

"A green blanket and the pretty embroidered apron Mrs. Beiler brought in last week. They traveled here from Canton by motorcar to visit a sick aunt, and they are going home in the morning." She peeked out the window. "The couple argued about what to buy. I couldn't wait for them to leave."

"Traveling can be draining and tiresome. I have sympathy for them driving such a long distance. No wonder they might be grumpy." Her mood wouldn't be the best if she had traveled with Noah to Lancaster. She and her family had a rough time coming to Berlin from Lancaster three years ago. A wheel broke, they ran out of water, and Leah had an upset stomach. She could've endured the ride to Lancaster with Noah, but not the uncertainty of whether she would have a happy life with him.

"I don't share your sympathy for them. The husband bragged about his motorcar he bought in May in Toledo." Leah gave Anna an impish grin. "Traveling by motorcar would be easier and faster than by buggy."

"We don't need such worldly experiences or material things. The simpler our lives are, the better. Our attention should be on our Heavenly Father. I should heed my own advice. I'm guilty of concentrating too much on myself lately."

"God understands you're sad. Don't worry. My curiosity about a motorcar won't steer me away from my present life." She tapped Anna's hand with her finger. "I'm afraid you're stuck with me."

"I wouldn't have it any other way." A wave of relief washed over Anna. Leah had scared her mentioning her interest in motorcars. She didn't want any sign her schweschder would entertain further thoughts of worldly desires after her encounter with Butch.

Customers strolled in the rest of the day, purchasing quilts and towels. Heavyhearted, Anna forced a smile and glanced at the clock. Five o'clock couldn't kumme soon enough for her to lock up and go home.

Two Englischers walked into the shop. The older woman had her hair wound in a gray, braided bun. She supported her hunched back and thin frame with a smooth oak cane. Her beautiful green silk dress had a smart white collar and gold buttons from top to bottom. She had a sparkle in her eyes and cheerful tone. "Juanita, my cousin, wrote me a letter. She bragged President Roosevelt visited Wyoming where she lives. She stood in front of the crowd and he shook her hand before he spoke." She beamed. "He's the youngest man we've had as president in the United States, and he's doing a fine job. I wish I could've been there to listen to his speech to preserve our natural forests and other news."

"Sharon, I wish we'd both been there."

Anna admired the woman's attitude. Her struggle to take each step had been evident, and she hadn't uttered one word of complaint. Instead, she focused on her cousin's story and had a positive outlook. The woman had lifted her mood.

She and Leah showed one quilt after another to women asking questions about the patterns and purpose of the keepsake pocket quilts. The customers were kind and speaking with them passed the time quickly.

The last Englischer left, and Anna glimpsed at the clock. "We sold eight quilts in seven hours. A first for us."

Leah grabbed their bags and dragged her feet to the door. "My back aches from straining to take them off the wooden pegs. Let's go home."

Anna, with Leah beside her, stepped outside and locked the door. "Mamm's waiting in front of the livery. She must've left work a few minutes early."

Placing a trembling hand on Anna's sleeve, Leah

stopped her. "Are you going to tell Mamm about Butch?"

"We no longer have a choice. He may show up again. We were wrong to keep your involvement with him from her. She'll be upset with us for not telling her about him and question our loyalty to her. I feel terrible about it."

Leah stared at their mamm in the distance. She lowered her voice to a whisper. "I can't convince you to keep quiet about him, can I?"

Anna didn't want Leah to pay dearly for her mistake. Her schweschder had agonized over her bad behavior long enough, but the repercussions of her actions would be far worse if their mamm or the bishop found out from someone else. Shunning her schweschder was a painful prospect. She hoped the bishop and her mamm wouldn't suggest this. Standing by Leah's side, she'd continue to support her. "No, but we'll tell her together. First, we'll have to inform Beth of our plan. She should be there with us, but I'll take the blame where she's concerned. Beth is innocent. We never should've asked her to keep quiet about what happened."

"Mamm will be furious. I'm scared she'll tell the bishop."

The bishop was a stern but compassionate man, but if Mamm told him about Leah and the rude Englischer, she had no idea how he would react. "I'm certain she will insist on telling him."

Leah took her hand. "I'm sorry to add my troubles on top of your burden of Noah's leaving."

Anna squeezed her hand. "We'll get through this together." They joined Mamm. "Did you have a good day, Mamm?"

"Jah, but I was ready to leave. A steady stream of

customers came in and out of the store. I did learn
something new from Mrs. Zook, who bought a new
broom this morning. She dips her broom in boiling
suds once a week to toughen it. She claims the broom
is like new and lasts much longer. Might be worth
trying sometime."

"Sounds like good information, Mamm." Anna
smiled at the liveryman and accepted the reins.

They got into the buggy, and she guided the horses
toward home.

"Noah is leaving for Lancaster tomorrow. I chose not
to go with him." Saying the words out loud brought
another tightening to her chest.

"I'm sorry. You must be hurting. Noah's moving to
Lancaster saddens me. I assumed he'd stay and marry
you and limit his adventures to Berlin. Selfishly, I'm
happy you're remaining with us."

Leah clasped Anna's hand. "Noah brought a lot of
joy into our lives with his jokes and cheerful personality. I wish him well in his new life in Lancaster. I'm
confident God will bring the man He wants Anna to
marry to Berlin when He's ready."

"I agree, Leah."

Anna took a calming breath. "You're both right.
Noah's a good man. I wish him well too. We just have
conflicting goals in mind."

"Do you think Noah will eventually abandon his
Amish upbringing?"

"No, Mamm. I'm certain Noah will follow God and
the Amish laws wherever he goes."

Mamm reached across Leah and patted Anna's leg.
"If there's anything I can do to help you through your
heartbreak, please tell me."

"Having Noah gone from my life is heart-wrenching,
but I'll be fine. The healing will take time." She had

hopes and dreams, all involving Noah. They'd vanished when he left her. She blinked back tears. She'd never regret loving him. She hoped she'd never regret letting him go.

Anna halted the horse and waved as Beth came running toward them. She stepped out of the buggy last.

Beth hugged each of them. "I learned a new knitting stitch today! Mrs. Hochstetler is going to help me make a small blanket."

"I'm pleased you enjoy knitting." Mamm pressed a hand to her chest.

Anna and Leah nodded in agreement.

"Mamm, Leah and I will water and feed the horse."

"Good. I'm hoping we have plenty for our meal tonight." She waved Beth over. "Do you want to help me cook or stay with Leah and Anna?"

"I'll stay with them for a few minutes, and then I'll kumme and help you."

Mamm nodded and took a brisk walk inside.

Anna led Beth and Leah inside the barn. "Beth, I need to tell you something important."

Beth hurried to her. "What's wrong? You're not sick, are you?"

"I'm fine. Noah stopped by the shop, and we had a difficult but good conversation. Noah and I won't be getting married. I told him I couldn't marry him if he insisted we had to move. He's chosen to go to Lancaster anyway. I wanted you to hear the news from me." She sighed. "Leah and I are going to tell Mamm about Butch, but let's wait until after supper."

Beth stepped back and her face paled. "All right. I don't like keeping secrets from her. I'm scared she'll never forgive us." She bit her bottom lip. "I want to be there when you tell her. I just want to get it over with."

"I'm sorry we put you in this position."

Beth said, "I forgive you." She held Anna's hand. "I'm sad Noah is leaving, but I'm overjoyed you're going to live here. Noah's selfish trying to take you away from us."

Anna kissed her younger schweschder's head. Beth's enthusiasm warmed her heart. "You're a sweetheart. Go help Mamm. Leah and I will be in shortly."

Beth nodded and walked toward the haus.

Anna and Leah led the animal into the barn. Mamm worked hard at home and the store. She stopped whatever she was doing to listen to their latest news, good or bad. Her hugs were the best. Nonetheless, she expected them to behave in a manner pleasing to God. Anytime Anna had misbehaved, Mamm's steely stare of disappointment hurt worse than the actual punishment she had received. "I feel better we are going to tell Mamm. It isn't fair to Beth to have her worrying about keeping a secret from Mamm. It isn't right for us to do so either."

"I'm afraid to face her wrath. She may never trust me or you again. I'm so sorry, Anna."

Mamm would be shocked and worried when they told her about Leah and Butch. Would Mamm question Leah's integrity in making decisions once they told her about Leah's transgression? Anna believed her schweschder was remorseful, and she wanted Mamm to forgive Leah and still trust her. They'd betrayed her. She hoped Mamm would learn to trust her again too. "She'll be disappointed in us. You'll have to convince her you won't deceive her again. I'll have to do the same."

Leah nodded.

Anna hooked her arm through Leah's, and they walked to the haus.

Beth ushered them to the table. "We're having pancakes and eggs for supper. Sit and relax. I've got the table set."

Anna rubbed her younger schweschder's back. "You're a good helper."

Serving each of them, Mamm emptied the pan of eggs. She passed Leah a plate of pancakes. "Let's hold hands and bow our heads." She prayed a prayer of thanks for the food.

Anna noticed Leah hadn't eaten more than a few bites of her food. She was relieved Mamm was pre-occupied with Beth's story.

Beth held her glass. "Mrs. Hochstetler and I had a picnic for lunch, and she forgot to put cookies in the basket for dessert. While she was inside fetching them, a raccoon climbed on the table and snatched her ham sandwich and scampered away. He was bold and my being there didn't bother him a bit. Mrs. Hochstetler came back and screamed, and I laughed. He was adorable. I wanted to hug him." She shrugged her shoulder.

Mamm squinted. "Don't ever pet a raccoon. They may look cuddly, but they can be a mean animal."

Beth finished sipping her water. "Mrs. Hochstetler warned me about wild animals and not to get close or bother them. Don't worry. I won't."

Beth told the best stories. Her arms waved and her eyes widened with excitement. She was a delightful child. Kindhearted and full of energy, she did more than her fair share of chores. She was thankful Beth had entertained them. She hadn't been in the mood to participate much in the conversation. Noah's leav-ing and Leah's ordeal had worn her out and the night wasn't over yet.

Leah scooted her chair back and took her plate to the dry sink. "I'll fetch water for washing the dishes."

Anna stood. "Mamm, I'll clear the table. Leah and Beth will help me wash and dry the dishes."

Mamm yawned and stretched her arms. "I'll check the cellar for canned peaches. I might make a pie sometime this week. I'm not sure if we have any left. Then I'll sit for a few minutes in the front room." Mamm pushed the door open and stepped outside.

Beth frowned. "Do I have to do dishes?"

Shaking her head, Anna grinned. "Leah and I will do them. You go play."

"Yippee!" Beth skipped out the door.

Anna nodded and carried over a stack of dirty plates to the dry sink. Guilt inched its way into her. She should never have agreed to involve Beth in keeping a secret from Mamm. What a terrible lesson to teach her sibling. She wouldn't want her family to keep anything from her. *Deceit* was an ugly word, and she cringed at succumbing to it.

Leah brought in the washbasin full of water. She poured it in the big pot on the hot stove. "I'm nervous about talking to Mamm."

"Me too. After we're finished in the kitchen, let's get some fresh air and our thoughts together before approaching her about Butch."

They washed and dried the dishes, then passed by Mamm in the front room. She had her head back and eyes closed. Her heavy breathing and mouth wide open showed she was asleep. Anna put a finger to her lips and gestured for Leah to go outside. She and Leah found Beth in the barn.

Beth ran to her. "Where's Mamm?"

"Sound asleep," said Leah.

Anna said, "Telling Mamm about Butch won't be

easy. We must express how sorry we are to have kept this from her."

Leah and Beth nodded.

Horses neighed, and Anna's heart thudded. She whirled around and froze. *Mamm.*

"Tell me what? I came to search for all of you. I found your quick disappearance after supper odd. What is going on?"

Quivering, Leah stepped to her. "I met a handsome Englischer, Butch Winter, in town and kept him a secret from all of you. I assumed Beth was asleep the night I crawled out the window to meet him, but she wasn't. She told Anna. When Anna confronted me, I'd already decided I wouldn't have anything to do with Butch Winter again or any other Englisch man. I promise. Please forgive me, Mamm, please." She buried her face in her hands and sobbed.

Anna and Beth came alongside her.

Her schweschder had rambled what happened out so fast, Anna wasn't sure Mamm understood everything she'd said, but her pinched lips and angry eyes said she'd caught the gist of Leah's story.

Hands on hips, Mamm stood red-faced. "I'm shocked and appalled at your behavior. You've dishonored God and your family. How long have you been meeting with him?"

Leah wiped her eyes with her apron and wrung her trembling hands. "The one time I met him in the woods, he grabbed my arms and pressed his lips with force on mine. I pushed him away and ran home as fast as I could. When Anna confronted me with what Beth told her, I begged her and Beth not to tell you. I was so ashamed of what I'd done."

Squaring her shoulders, Mamm waggled her finger. "Anna, I'm ashamed of you. You're the oldest. You shouldn't have hidden Leah's bad behavior from me and even worse, to ask Beth to do the same. Your deceit and bad behavior are out of the realm of your normal character. I'm sick about this."

Filled with remorse, Anna met Mamm's angry gaze. "There's more to tell you. Butch came to the shop today and confronted Leah. He had charmed her, but she soon found out what a rude and arrogant man he is. Daniel Bontrager was there and asked him to leave, and he did. His return to the shop is why we're telling you. We hoped he wouldn't kumme back, and we wouldn't have to tell you about him. I'm hoping we've seen the last of him, but I can't be sure."

Mamm pinched her eyes shut for a moment. "Leah, did you allow Butch Winter to kiss you or more? Is there anything else you're not telling me?"

"He held my hand a few times, but nothing more until he kissed me in the woods. I'm afraid of him, and I don't want anything to do with him." She held her red cheeks. "Please, forgive me."

"I'm hurt and angry all of you deceived me. I'm sick Butch may harm you, Leah. From what he's done so far, he doesn't sound like he gives up easily. You've been taught to avoid trouble. I don't understand why you would do such a thing."

Anna hadn't prepared herself for the harsh anger and painful disappointment in her mamm's face and voice. Never had she witnessed such a strong reaction from her mamm. "Frankly, we were afraid you'd tell the bishop. We aren't prepared to shun our schweschder if he demands we do so."

Mamm glared at them. "He may ask our community to shun her. If he does, we'll abide by his wishes. Leah and I will go to the bishop's haus. I don't want anyone to tell him about Leah's transgression before we do. Someone could've walked by the store window and seen or overheard him. I hope not." She climbed in the buggy. "Leah, let's go."

Anna hitched the horse to the buggy and joined them. "I'm going too."

"Me too." Beth's lips trembled, and she nodded in agreement.

Leah swiped her wet face and exchanged a grateful glance with her schweschders.

Mamm drove out of the barn.

Anna and her schweschders stayed silent on the way there.

Anna grimaced each time the wheels hit a rut on the bumpy dirt trail on the way to the bishop's haus. The silence was deafening, and the ride was miserable. Clouds shielded the sun and the gray sky matched her mood. This day would be a bad memory. Noah had walked out of her life, and she was sick about this dissension in her family. She bit her bottom lip. The answer was prayer for her family, for Noah, and for herself. Now she had to face Mamm's wrath and suffer the consequences. She and Mamm were close. She was rife with agony. She shouldn't have kept Butch Winter's interference in their lives from Mamm and asked Beth to do the same. She should've known better.

After halting the buggy in front of the bishop's haus, Mamm tied the horse to the hitching post and marched to the door.

Clasping Leah and Beth's hands, Anna walked with them to the porch.

The bishop opened the door before Mamm knocked. "Horses hooves clip-clopping down the lane alerted me. I peeked out the window and recognized you. Kumme in. Why the long faces? Has something happened?" He motioned to them. "Please sit."

They stood until Mamm sat. They chose to sit close together on the settee.

Mamm twisted her hands in her apron and breathed deep. "Leah met an Englischer, Butch Winter, several times in town and once at night in the woods. My family kept this from me. I found out this evening and wanted you to hear the story from my lips. Her punishment from me is to write Psalms, Chapter Twenty-three, fifty times and give her homework to me tomorrow night. At the same time, she is expected to recite the passage by memory."

Mamm must've kumme up with her punishment for Leah on the way there. The price Mamm was making Leah pay for her transgression wasn't as bad as she'd worried her penance might be. The bishop's punishment could still be to shun Leah.

The bishop peered over his spectacles. "What do you have to say for yourself, Leah?"

Tears sliding down her cheeks, Leah met his stern gaze. "I'm ashamed and horribly embarrassed. He kissed me forcibly and I ran away." Her lips quivered. "Nothing else happened between us. I assure you I will not make this mistake again. I've asked God to forgive me, and I hope you and my family will also." She closed her eyes and dropped her chin to her chest.

"Anna, do you have anything to say?" The bishop waited for her to answer.

She swallowed and grasped Leah's hand tight. "I believe she is sorry for her transgression, and I have forgiven her. She's filled with grief about her behavior. I would ask you take her blemish-free past into consideration. I'm guilty of keeping this a secret from Mamm and also of involving Beth."

Anna slid closer to Leah. She glanced at Mamm's pinched lips and taut jaw. Would their bad judgment sever the bond her family shared? She had gone against Amish law, and her decision had been wrong.

Beth put her hand on Anna's lap and rested her head on Anna's shoulder.

The bishop leaned back thoughtfully and steepled his hands. "Leah, you haven't joined the church yet."

"I'm not going to participate in rumspringa. I have no desire to experience the world. I want to marry an Amish man and remain in Berlin. I'll join the church when I'm eighteen."

A wave of relief settled in Anna's chest. Leah's declaration would help to erase the bishop's and Mamm's concerns that her schweschder would abandon her firm belief in God and Amish values. She was happy Leah had voiced her regret again. Her schweschder's remorse solidified in her mind that Leah had grown from this unfortunate incident.

"I'm happy you've chosen to make a commitment to Amish life and join the church when you're eighteen, but please don't commit to Amish life for your mamm's or my benefit. This decision must kumme from your heart."

"Englisch life isn't for me. I desire an Amish life with a man with my same upbringing and values."

The bishop leaned closer and put his elbows on his knees. "You've been an exceptional example of a kind and honest young woman from the time you moved to Berlin three years ago. No one has ever uttered a negative word about you to me. I can tell by the anguish in your face and tears flowing from your eyes, you have genuine repentance for your actions."

The bishop's face had softened and his tone was even. Anna closed her eyes and prayed a silent prayer for mercy for Leah.

"I won't ask you to relay to the congregation what you've done. Nothing would be gained but gossip from sharing this story with anyone else. But if you are caught again in the act of disobedience to God and against the church and your transgression is brought to my attention, you will be shunned for a period of time. We don't want to invite any trouble from the Englischers. If you had already joined the church, I would've asked the community to shun you. Do you understand?"

Leah bobbed her head.

"Stay on the path you know God and your family would have you take as you go through life."

Leah's tortured expression was mixed with relief at his kind judgment.

"I will, sir." She choked on a wrenching sob.

Mamm stood. "Danki, Bishop Weaver. I'm sorry to have troubled you. You've been generous and kind to us. I'm grateful for your leniency."

"Leah's past is why I've been easy on her. She's young and finding her way. I trust she'll not stray again. Most importantly, don't blame yourself. You're a good mamm."

Anna got up with Leah and noticed Mamm's shoulders had relaxed and color had returned to her cheeks. She'd respected the bishop before, but she admired him more now. He'd kept calm, listened, and advised Leah in a stern but loving manner. He was more compassionate than she'd anticipated.

The bishop raised his palm. "Let's pray before you leave. Dear Heavenly Father, forgive Leah for her bad decision. Guide and direct her path through

Scripture. Heal the hurt her transgression has caused for the Plank family. Mend their broken bond and bring them close. Danki and Amen."

They bid the bishop farewell and went to the buggy. Anna untied the horse and got in. Mamm clucked at the horse, and they headed for home. "Leah, you will write out Psalms, Chapter Twenty-three fifty times. I want you to complete your homework by tomorrow night, and I expect you to recite these verses by memory to me at the same time you hand me your written pages."

"I'll do as you ask. I promise. Again, I'm sorry."

Anna nodded. When would Mamm warm up to them again? She'd hoped the bishop's prayer would soften her temper toward them. Her relaxed shoulders and moist eyes were encouraging. She wished her tone would change. Leah's trembling had ceased, but her anguish remained.

Arriving home, Mamm handed the reins to Leah. "You stow the horse and buggy."

Waiting with Leah, Anna watched Mamm and Beth go inside the haus.

Leah wiped a tear from her cheek. "Danki for your support. The bishop was easier on me than I'd imagined or deserved. I'm glad our visit to him is over. I'm afraid Mamm will never forgive me."

"Give her time. You're fortunate the bishop was kind and forgiving to you. Let's bend over backward to help Mamm and show her we love her and want to regain her trust in us."

Anna and Leah took care of the horse and putting the buggy away and then went inside the haus.

Beth sat in the maple chair and practiced her knitting skills.

Anna glanced over her shoulder. "I'll be in my room if anyone needs anything."

Beth smiled.

Noah's last night in Berlin was tonight. She would no longer run into him in town, he'd not visit her at the shop, and there would be no more walks together. Their future together had been shattered. Pain crept into her throat. She stepped into her room and froze. *Mamm.*

Mamm pointed. "Shut the door."

Closing the door gently, Anna stared at the floor. "I'm sorry for not telling you in the first place."

"You must never hide anything from me again. You've been an excellent example of a fine Amish woman to your schweschders, and I've trusted you implicitly until now. Please tell me I can trust you, Anna. You're my rock. I need your honesty and support. What were you thinking? Beth's a child. You are teaching her to be deceitful!"

Anna touched her arm. "I am your rock, Mamm. I feel horrible I've let you down."

"You exercised bad judgment keeping this from me."

"My wanting to protect you from being angry and wanting to shield Leah from being scarred by her indiscretion clouded my judgment." She put her hand on Mamm's. "Please, please, forgive me, Mamm. Leah longs to have your forgiveness too. She's really sorry."

"She knew better than to go alone with a man to the woods, Amish or Englisch. Her doing such a thing infuriates and scares me. Butch could've forced himself on her, and she could be with child or worse, he could've killed her. We don't know him." She slumped on the bed and wept.

Stroking her cheek, Anna whispered, "She's safe,

and he didn't harm her. She's learned a hard lesson. Can we put this behind us and move forward?"

Mamm straightened and wiped her eyes. "Of course, with prayer and time. I'm afraid Butch might kumme to the shop again. Some men can't take no for an answer. I'm thankful Daniel was there to ask him to leave. I can't imagine what might have happened if he'd found the two of you alone."

"Daniel was so brave and didn't blink when he stood up to Butch. I'm glad he was there too. He'll not say a word to anyone about this. We can trust him. I'm baking oatmeal cookies for him in the morning and taking them to the shop to show our appreciation. He's been hired to repair the leak in the roof."

"I'm relieved he'll be there. We should invite him to supper to show our appreciation."

Mamm might be joining Leah in matching her and Daniel. *No, don't be silly.* The supper invitation was payment to a friend who'd stepped in to help and protect them. Nothing more. "I'll ask him when he's free."

Chapter Four

Anna lifted the oatmeal cookies off the much-used metal sheet and arranged them in a cotton-lined basket Saturday morning. Chewing the last bite of her cookie, she grinned. The extra teaspoon of sugar had worked to sweeten the flavor more than usual.

Beth padded into the kitchen dressed in her traditional blue dress and white kapp. Wide-eyed, she peeked in the basket. "May I have one?"

"You can have one. These are for Daniel." Anna handed her a cookie.

Mouth full, Beth put a hand to her lips. "I could eat the whole batch. They're scrumptious."

Leah joined them. "Is there enough for me to steal one?"

"Jah, but like I told Beth, only one."

She bit into the cookie and cupped a hand to her chin to catch the crumbs. "Daniel's going to enjoy his oatmeal cookies. They're mouth-watering good."

Mamm ignored Leah's comment and walked into the cozy kitchen. "The horse is hitched to the buggy. We'd better get going."

"Do you want a cookie, Mamm?" Anna presented

the basket. She hoped the tension would disappear today.

"None for me, danki." Waving a dismissive hand, Mamm turned to her. "Anna, don't forget to ask Daniel to supper. We don't want to wait long to show our gratitude."

Anna nodded. "Beth, have a good day."

Snatching her puzzle, Beth grinned. "You too. Have a good day!" She went out and skipped toward Mrs. Hochstetler's haus.

Her younger schweschder hadn't let the awkwardness looming over their family alter her usual happy mood. Anna wished she could push the tension hovering over them out of her mind. She passed the basket to Leah. "Hold this for me, please." She thanked her, clicked the reins, and drove to town. The sun warmed their cheeks and brilliant honeysuckle patches along the way scented the air with a heavy, soothing sweetness. She breathed deep and waited for Mamm or Leah to speak. *Nothing.* "Isn't the weather beautiful?" She pointed to a stretch of pasture. "Mr. Beiler's coal-black horse is grazing. He's got the shiniest coat I've ever seen." The rides to and from work would be awkward if these long silences kept up. They had to have more than one-word conversations sometime. Mamm and Leah had said little to each other. She and Beth had tiptoed around both of them this morning.

Arriving at the General Store, Mamm got out, gave a curt nod, and went inside.

Mamm's stern expression wasn't lost on Anna, or on Leah either, she suspected. She drove to the livery and left the horse. Her heart ached at the breach within their tight-knit family. Mamm or Leah had to give in. "Leah, you should've spoken to Mamm on the way here."

"She's not happy with me. I'm staying out of her way."

Pausing in front of the shop door, Anna squared her shoulders and squinted. "You are the one at fault. Open up conversations with her. Show you want to build the broken bridge between you."

Lips quivering, Leah blinked back tears. "I will."

The newspaper boy shouted, "Jack Morrissey talks about his time with the Cincinnati Reds and retirement. Read the full story here!"

Anna glanced at the boy and her lips parted in surprise. Daniel was behind him kumming toward her. She smiled.

He crossed the boardwalk and joined them. "Good morning."

"Coffee?" She lifted her bag. "We brought some from home. It should still be warm." She unlocked the door and noticed Leah relax. She was certain her schweschder was relieved Daniel showed up and halted her earlier lecture.

Handing him the basket, Leah grinned. "Anna baked oatmeal cookies for you."

Blushing, Anna cleared her throat. "*We* wanted to show our appreciation to you for speaking to Butch on our behalf, and for charging us such a fair price to fix the shop roof." She pulled out a container. "I brought a serving of Mamm's chicken stew for you. I'll put it in our icebox until you're ready to take it home. The cookies are under the counter. You can snack on them whenever you like and take the rest home."

He lifted up the covering, sniffed favorably, and removed a cookie. He took a bite of the cookie and closed his eyes for a moment. "These cookies are delicious. I'll savor them. The chicken stew will be perfect for my supper tonight. Danki."

The twinkle in his eye and the way he cocked his head a little each time he met her gaze had become pleasantly familiar. "Are you interested in kumming to our haus for supper? We told Mamm you stood up to Butch, and she'd like to have you over. You can save your chicken stew for another time."

"I was happy to help." He shuffled his feet. "Jah, danki. I'd love to kumme."

Leah reached for his empty cup. "Kumme around six. More coffee?"

He shook his head. "Danki, but I've had enough coffee."

Tonight. She was thinking later in the week or next. She had wanted to wait until she'd had a few more days to quit her heavy brooding over Noah and until Mamm was at ease talking to Leah. She couldn't recant the invitation. It would be rude. Leah had been too quick for her. She would have to be cordial and put her hurt aside. "I'd be pleased if you'd join us for supper."

He grinned and cocked his head a little. "What can I bring?"

Anna shifted her eyes from his gaze to the floor. "Please don't bring anything. Kumme and enjoy Mamm's excellent cooking."

"I'm looking forward to it." He shifted the tool belt around his waist. "I should let you get to work. I'll go next door and fetch and hang the sign. Next, I'll repair the roof."

She waited until the door closed behind him and whirled around to Leah. "Why did you invite him to join us tonight? Mamm is barely speaking to you, and I'm not in the frame of mind for company yet. Noah's leaving has been painful for me. Entertaining is the last thing I want to do. I could've used at least a few more days."

"All good reasons why Daniel should kumme to our haus after work. Mamm will be hospitable and not let on a thing is wrong between us. You'll be forced to engage in conversation with him and it will take your mind off Noah. First and foremost, Mamm and I don't want to let too much time pass to show our thanks for his goodwill gesture."

Anna clutched her apron. *How selfish of me.* Leah's words of wisdom pricked her heart. They should wilkom Daniel with open arms and learn more about their new friend. She had caught his big brown eyes gazing at her and his mouth drawn in a sweet smile. He wore his emotions on his sleeve. Leah had been observant. He showed interest in her, but she was far from ready to open her heart to someone new.

Daniel could be a man she would consider if her heart was free. He had a calm and strong demeanor. The tragedies in his life hadn't left him bitter or hard. She would put her troubles aside and be friendly to him tonight. He needed friends, and she hoped he would enjoy her family and a good home-cooked meal. "I stand corrected. I will put on a smile and be a good hostess."

"I don't mean to diminish your hurt over Noah, but Daniel has no family and Berlin is unfamiliar to him. I'll go to the General Store and tell Mamm he's kumming to supper tonight. I'm taking your advice and starting a conversation with her. I worked hard on my writing and memorization assignment, and I'm through with both. I'll have plenty of time today to work on my assignment between customers. I'll hand her my pages and recite the verses this evening. I'm hoping it will help mend her deep disappointment in me and bring us a step closer to restoring our once-close relationship."

"Telling her about Daniel accepting our invitation is a perfect way to begin bridging the gap between you and Mamm. Go. I'll mind the shop."

Daniel entered Mark King's furniture store. He approached the tall man behind the counter. "Good morning, I'm Daniel Bontrager."

"I'm Mark King. Grace told me she and Anna spoke about you the other day. I understand you offered to repair the roof. Danki. I was friends with your bruder and his fraa. I'm so sorry for your loss."

Daniel bowed his head and nodded. "Danki." He glanced at Mark's display of products. "You've hand-crafted beautiful pieces to sell. I admire your talent." He ran his hand over an oak headboard. "What a beautiful piece of furniture."

"You're kind. Woodworking relaxes me."

Daniel pointed to the sign leaning against the back wall. "I came to fetch the new sign for the dry goods shop. I'll hang it for you. The new name will stand out in town. You did a wonderful job carving out the letters."

"Danki."

"I've got the time, and I'm pleased to help out. It's been a pleasure to meet you, but I better get to work. Have a nice day."

Mark opened the door for him. "Good to see you. Stop by anytime."

Nodding, he left. Mark was wilkoming and humble.

He looked forward to meeting more people in the community. He was glad he'd moved to Berlin.

He propped the sign in front of the dry goods shop, fetched the ladder, and removed the existing sign and replaced it with the new one. How did the new marker measure up to the rest of the signs in town? He went across the street and studied it. GRACE'S DRY GOODS SHOP had oak letters big enough for everyone to notice. The marker was the best-constructed one in town.

He returned to the ladder, tightened his tool belt around his hips, moved the ladder to the back of the building, and set about repairing the roof. He couldn't stop thinking of Anna. Noah had left for Lancaster, and Anna and Leah had invited him to supper. Praying last night before bed, he'd asked God to have him meet the Amish woman meant for him. Every time he looked into Anna's eyes, his heart raced.

He wished Noah the best. The man had been wilkoming to him. He would've liked getting better acquainted, but he'd gladly forfeit Noah's acquaintance to have a chance to win Anna's heart. How could Noah leave her? Daniel didn't understand Noah's determination to relocate. Was God paving the way for Daniel? He shook his head. He shouldn't jump to conclusions.

Anna's eyes were swollen and puffy this morning. Was she grieving Noah and having trouble sleeping? He longed to tell her how beautiful she was and how she'd captured his interest. It was out of the question. He had to wait. She would need time to adjust to Noah's being gone. In the meantime, he would befriend her and her family. They could use a man to chop and stockpile wood and do repairs. Helping them would be a pleasure.

He went inside. Anna was helping two women. They were Englischers with their noses in the air and pinched lips. Her cheery voice and warm smile emphasized her natural charm and beauty. She treated them like they were her friends. Her heart-shaped face and dainty features painted a beautiful portrait. Leah was helping a patron peppering her with questions. He'd bide his time until they were finished. She was worth the wait.

He unhooked the pinwheel and patchwork quilts the patrons had chosen and carried them to Anna at the counter for her to fold and wrap.

She smiled at him. "I'll be with you in a minute."

Returning her attention to the customer, she accepted payment from the women and registered the sales in the shop journal, then wrapped and handed them their packages. "Enjoy your quilts and have a nice day."

She reopened the cashbox and paid him for his work. "Danki. What a relief to have the roof fixed. I can't wait to take a look at the new sign."

"It's the best sign in town." He opened the door for her.

They went outside. She stepped back and studied the sign. "Mark did a wonderful job, didn't he?"

"He's talented and a perfectionist. A good combination of traits to have for a carpenter."

"Danki for hanging it."

He opened the door for her. "I'll return in a few minutes and load my supplies. I put the ladder in the back."

"Is there anything I can do to help?"

"I can manage." He fetched his wagon and hitched

the reins to the post in front of the store and loaded his things. He returned to the shop and Anna handed him his cookies and container of stew. "I have everything."

"We'll look forward to seeing you at six. Our haus is on Brown Road. The second farm on the left."

"I look forward to it." He waved to Anna and Leah and held the door open for the Englischers, then followed the customers out. He drove home, and inside his haus, he fed Otis and let him outside. He checked the clock and crossed the yard to the barn. The hours would drag by until the time came to clean up, change clothes, and go to the Planks' for a good home-cooked meal.

Later in the day, he took off his dusty boots, went to the living room, and checked the maple mantel clock above the fireplace again. *Five o'clock.* Finally, the time had arrived to wash and get dressed to go spend time with beautiful Anna and her family. His razor sharp, he swirled the brush in the shaving-soap mug, scraped away the whiskers from his jaw and neck, and poured water from his mamm's white china pitcher into its matching bowl to rinse his face. Running his hand over his chin, he grinned. He hadn't cared about being perceived as attractive by a woman until he met Anna.

He changed the water, washed, toweled off, and dressed in his crisp, clean black pants and white shirt. After pulling his suspenders over his shoulders, he snapped them in place. He went to the kitchen and emptied the cookies in a clear jar and poured the chicken stew in a bowl from his cupboard. He poured water from a pitcher into the dishpan, rinsed, and dried the Planks' container to take back to them.

After throwing wood into the wagon bed, he paused to count how much was there. "This stack of firewood should last a while." He petted his dog and opened the back door. "Otis, time for you to go inside. Your water and food bowls are full. Help yourself."

He hummed familiar hymns on the way to the Planks' and enjoyed the orderly Amish farms along the way. Grand horses, fat cows, and herds of sheep grazed contentedly in pastures. The trip didn't take long. The Planks didn't live far from him. He liked living close to Anna. Arriving, he halted the wagon and tied the horse to the worn white hitching post. Their plain white haus had a wraparound porch with two rocking chairs out front. The pond lay off to the left side with oak trees providing shade throughout the property. The worn-planked barn stood off to the left side. The garden had perfect rows of vegetables and the hay field spread over about five acres.

A younger maedel with big emerald-green eyes and the sweetest dimples in her cheeks greeted him at the door. "You must be Mr. Bontrager. I'm Beth." She opened the door wider. "Kumme in, please." Her impish grin brought a smile to his face.

"It's a pleasure to meet you, Beth. Call me Daniel." She didn't resemble Leah or Anna with her green eyes and red hair in a tight bun under her thin cotton bonnet.

Beth put a hand to the side of her mouth and lowered her voice. "Mamm has prepared company beef roast for tonight. My favorite. She only cooks her special dish if we're having special guests."

He raised his eyebrows. "I like being a special guest."

Beth giggled and covered her mouth. "You can

take a seat in the sitting room until the food is ready. Would you like something to drink?"

"I'm fine. I'll wait until dinner to have a glass of water. Do you mind taking the basket to the kitchen? Anna let me borrow it and the bowl inside." He studied the mantel above the fireplace and admired the oak clock. The pine settee and chairs had feather-stuffed black cushions, and a green-and-white pinwheel quilt hanging on the maple quilt rack in the corner created a comfortable atmosphere.

Beth accepted the basket and container from him. "I'll put these away and kumme back and keep you company until the food's ready."

She returned and chattered about making her first apron under Mamm's instruction.

Mamm wiped her hands on a towel and approached him. "I'm pleased to meet you, Mr. Bontrager. Beth should have brought you to the kitchen right away for us to give you a proper greeting. I apologize."

"I wanted to talk to him by myself for a little bit." She gave Mamm an impish grin.

Mamm frowned and shook her head. "No doubt."

"I don't mind. Beth's been very good company." Beth beamed.

Mamm smiled. "I'm grateful for all you've done to help Anna and Leah. They've told me you defended them against Butch Winter and about the repairs you've made at the shop. I'm glad you could join us. Kumme to the kitchen."

He nodded.

Mrs. Plank had a stout, round body, but her heart-shaped face and button nose resembled Anna's. Her demeanor was serious but kind.

"Call me Daniel, and danki for the invitation. I'm

new in town, so I'm glad to meet new friends. Dining with your family is a treat for me." Daniel followed her and Beth.

He met Anna's gaze, and her mouth tipped at the corners to a smile. His heart flip-flopped. He yearned for a sign of encouragement she found him attractive and was delighted to see him. She confirmed it with her sweet smile. The Planks carried dishes of green beans, beef, beets, and boiled potatoes to the table. Warm, puffy, fragrant biscuits steamed in a round basket in the center. The meal was fit for a king. "Greetings, Anna and Leah. The food looks scrumptious."

"Daniel, good to see you." Anna grinned.

"Glad you're here, Daniel." Leah carried over salt-and-pepper shakers.

Beth pulled out a chair. "Daniel, you sit between Anna and me."

He hoped he didn't fumble over his words or spill anything. He wanted to leave Anna's family with a good impression. "My pleasure, Beth." He waited until the women were seated, then took his seat.

Mamm glanced at him. "Would you say grace, Daniel?"

"I'd be honored."

Mamm reached for Leah's and Anna's hands.

He held Anna's hand and Beth clasped his. Anna's dainty fingers and soft skin sent tingles coursing through him. Shutting his eyes, he bowed his head. "Dear Heavenly Father, forgive me for displeasing You in any way. Danki for providing this food and bless the women who have prepared the meal. Danki for bringing me to Berlin and introducing me to this kind family. Amen."

Beth passed him the steaming-hot parsley potatoes. "Leah told me you're Jonathan's bruder. I'm sorry he and Adele died. I liked them very much. She said your parents died too. You must get lonely." She paused and smiled at him. "You can kumme to our haus anytime to eat with us."

Anna's younger schweschder hadn't taken a breath between sentences.

He wouldn't have to worry about any lulls in the conversation. He liked her spunk. "Your offer is a generous one. My old friend, Otis, keeps me company at the farm, but I would much rather be here with your family sharing supper."

Beth tilted her head. "Who is Otis?"

"My dog. He's an average-sized mutt, and he has short brown hair and big brown eyes. He's friendly and behaves well."

Leah cupped her water glass, ready to take a sip. "Bring him over next time. I want to meet him."

"I'm not sure your mamm would approve of a dog in the haus."

Mamm moved her hand in a backward wave. "I don't mind. I'd like to meet him too."

Beth pushed the green beans to the far corner of her plate. "You must be sad your family died. Anna's sad too. Noah, our friend, asked Anna to marry him, but she told him no. He wanted to move away and she didn't. I heard her tell Mamm he wanted her to change the way she liked to do things, and she doesn't want to. If Thomas asked me to change my ways all the time, I'd tell him to mind his own business. I'm glad she stayed here. If he'd loved her enough, he would have married her and never left."

Anna's eyes widened and her mouth flew open.

"Beth, please don't discuss my private business with Daniel."

"Why? My friends played with me at Mrs. Hochstetler's today. They're gossiping about Noah leaving. Daniel may as well hear it from me." She whirled her head to Daniel. "Besides, if he didn't love Anna enough to stay, he doesn't deserve her."

Daniel was in agreement with everything Beth had said. He wouldn't have left her if he'd been in Noah's position, and they'd apparently had more problems than his leaving. He'd tried to change her, but why?

"Beth Plank, enough! We've told you not to discuss our personal business outside of our family." Anna's cheeks flamed bright pink.

Mamm splayed her hand on the table. "Beth, you listen to Anna. You've said too much. Stop it."

Daniel stifled his smile at Beth's innocence. "She means no harm. I won't repeat anything Beth has told me."

Anna stared at her lap, then raised her eyes to meet his. "I'm sorry you are again being privy to our personal problems."

Leah spread butter on her biscuit, then passed the small bowl to Mamm. "We could use a change of subject. Mamm, your biscuits are better than usual tonight. Would you like butter?"

"Jah, dear, danki. How was your day?"

"We had a pleasant day at the shop. The customers were enjoyable, and the time moved fast. How about you?"

"I stocked the shelves at the General Store today, and my back hurts a little, but the day was fine otherwise." She stood and smiled. "I made apple pie for dessert."

Anna turned to Daniel. "You're in for a treat. Mamm's apple pie is the best in town."

Daniel found Leah's attempt to change the conversation endearing. Evidence of their closeness was reflected in the easy way they related to one another. Tension must have built between Mrs. Plank and Leah over the incident concerning Butch. Raising her kinner alone must be hard for her. No man to help with the property, care for her, or lend advice. Anna's poignant reaction to the exchange of conversation between Leah and her mamm had hit a soft spot in his heart. He couldn't explain it. Anna had swooped in and stolen his heart the minute he'd walked into her shop. Each time he encountered her, a flutter of excitement filled him. The more he knew her, the more he liked her.

Her delightful family brought back wonderful memories of conversations with his parents and bruder. Beth had confirmed his suspicions. Noah had left to fulfill his need for adventure, and Anna had declined to follow him. He smiled at Mrs. Plank. "Apple pie is a favorite of mine."

Beth rose and grinned at Daniel. "I'll cut and serve the dessert." She set the first piece in front of him. "Don't be shy. We have plenty if you'd like a second piece."

Daniel chatted about selling his home in Lancaster after the untimely passing of his parents.

Mrs. Plank collected his empty plate and paused. "I'm sorry, Daniel. You must've been devastated to lose your family at such a young age. Like Beth said, you are wilkom here anytime. Don't be a stranger."

Beth forked a chunk of fragrant apple oozing with

cinnamon-flavored syrup. "Daniel, did you consider marrying an Amish woman in Lancaster?"

Anna gasped. "Beth Plank, where are your manners?" Dismay covered her sweet heart-shaped face.

Mamm glared at her. "Beth, if you can't behave, you'll go to your room."

Clearing his throat, Daniel said, "Her question is a fair one, and I don't mind answering it. I was busy working and hadn't made the effort to meet anyone. I would like a fraa and kinner someday."

Beth grinned and nodded. "I want to marry Thomas Mast and have kinner someday too, but he doesn't like to talk about marriage yet."

Daniel bit back a laugh. Beth was a cheerful and delightful maedel. She was determined to speak her opinion, in spite of her family's warnings. He liked her forthrightness.

Leah stretched and put a hand over her yawn. "Beth and I will do dishes. I'll be back." She returned a minute later with her written verses. "Mamm, here's my assignment. I'm prepared to recite Psalm Chapter Twenty-three."

"Go ahead."

Leah recited the Psalm, Chapter Twenty-three.

"Very good, Leah." Mamm didn't smile.

"I'm grateful God knows our hearts and forgives our transgressions. I've prayed and asked Him for forgiveness, and I hope you can find it in your heart to forgive me too. I'm so ashamed, and I'm sorry, Mamm." Leah stared at her trembling hands.

"I hope so, Leah. Your actions were serious and could have scarred you mentally and physically for the rest of your life. I ask you to obey Amish rules for your safety and to teach you good values to live by.

I love you, Leah. My heart would break if anything happened to you. I forgive you."

"I have learned my lesson, Mamm."

Daniel suspected Leah had passed her assignment to Mamm and recited the Bible verses in front of him to show her remorse since he had been privy to her trouble with Butch.

Mamm nodded and reached for the half-empty serving dishes. "I'll stow the leftovers and send some home with you, Daniel."

"I won't turn them down. Danki."

Leah threw Anna a mischievous grin. "Anna, why don't you show Daniel the pond and flowers we planted?"

Leah had a sparkle in her eyes. She was definitely matchmaking and finding a reason for him and Anna to spend time alone together. He was grateful for her efforts and waited for Anna to answer. She might excuse herself and ask one of her schweschders to show him around. He hoped not.

Anna gestured to the door. "Do you mind taking a walk?"

"I'd be pleased to." His heart pumped fast. There was no place he'd rather be than with her. He had a lot more to learn about her. Their walk would provide the opportunity.

"The evening sun shines on the water like a blanket of shimmering glass. I enjoy the boppli ducklings paddling behind their mamm and scrambling to keep pace with her." She pointed to the hyacinth not far from the pond. "We planted those. They're doing well." She gestured to the field of daisies. "Such a simple flower, but the white and yellow colors and its shape make it one of my favorites."

Daniel grinned. She delighted in the little things God created. His Amish friends in Lancaster were busy and let life pass them by. He'd mentioned how much he loved the beauty in flowers, the sun, and green pastures. They frowned and shook their heads as if he was out of his mind to waste time on such things. "I like them too. Early evening in the summer is pleasant. The balmy breeze, quiet water, and big orange sun lowering behind the trees are such a wonderful sight. God's creations are amazing."

He wished he could sit in the same spot often and have discussions with her. He wanted them to have a special spot. Anna had affected him like no other woman. He couldn't explain it. "My daed was too busy working from dawn to dusk to notice the beauty of nature. I'm glad you find joy in these things."

She picked up a small stone and threw it in the brush, avoiding his gaze. "Noah delighted in all God's wonders too."

Her comment about Noah put an unwilkom damper on his hopes. "I'm sorry I didn't have a chance to get better acquainted with Noah. Do you think he'll return?"

"I expect he will return to visit his mamm."

She hadn't mentioned hoping Noah would return for her. Her gaze went to her feet and her voice was a notch above a whisper.

Lifting her mood wouldn't be easy, but he'd try. "The first night I found Otis on the side of the road and brought him home, he dragged every pillow I had in the haus into a pile and pulled them over top of him. I searched all morning to find him."

She laughed and met his gaze. "Otis sounds like a joy to have around."

"He is a good companion." He ran his foot over a thick grassy patch. "Did you enjoy living in Lancaster?"

"Lancaster was fine, but Berlin is a more close-knit community. Maybe it's because I'm older, but I'm more comfortable in a smaller town and community. I have found getting acquainted with people here has been easier. I have no plans to ever leave. What about you?"

"I prefer a small community too. I'll miss my friends, but I was so busy. I hardly had any time to spend with them. I plan to settle in Berlin." It might not register with her at the present that he was planting roots here, but later, his revelation might matter to her if their friendship grew. He hoped so.

The sun had lowered. He walked Anna back to the haus and bid the Planks farewell. Anna strolled to his wagon with him.

"Danki for the delicious meal. I've enjoyed spending time with your family. I hope we'll run into each other again."

"Stop by the shop or kumme for supper anytime. We've always got plenty, and Mamm loves to feed guests. You've made quite an impression on our family. She'll be crushed if you don't visit again." She gave him a shy smile. "Mamm might think you didn't like her cooking, and you wouldn't want to hurt her feelings. Leah is thankful for what you did for her, and Beth took to you the minute she met you."

He was gratified by her small joke about her mamm's cooking. She was inviting him back. He couldn't help but think their friendship was growing. He unloaded the wood and stacked the pile in the woodshed. "I've got more wood. I'll drop another pile off next week.

Danki for your generous hospitality. I'll say a word to your mamm before I leave."

They went inside.

"Mrs. Plank, danki for supper."

"You're wilkom. Don't be a stranger."

Beth chuckled. "Jah, don't be a stranger, Daniel."

He smiled, bid them farewell, and left.

Anna walked him out. "Enjoy your ride home."

"Danki." He grinned and waited until she went inside to step into his wagon. The barn's white paint had faded. He'd offer to paint the building for them. Helping her family would give him an excuse to spend more time with Anna.

Chapter Five

Anna guided the horse out of the barn Monday morning and harnessed the docile animal to the buggy. The breach between Mamm and Leah had begun to heal sooner than she'd expected. The weekend had passed quickly. On Saturday morning at breakfast, Mamm had mentioned rotted wood siding needed replacing on the barn. Sunday afternoon, Daniel stopped by their haus and Mamm had mentioned it again in conversation. Daniel offered to repair and paint the building for them starting Wednesday. Anna enjoyed chatting with him on Sunday while they sipped fresh-squeezed lemonade. She was glad they had services every other week to allow them a full day of rest at home or to visit with friends on their day off from attending church.

Each day had gotten easier without Noah in her life. For the past several months, she'd not enjoyed her time with Noah. She put a hand to her heart. She suspected Daniel's kind gestures and friendly conversations had something to do with healing her bruised heart. He was interesting to talk to and a good listener.

Beth waved good-bye and scampered to Mrs. Hochstetler's. Leah and Mamm joined Anna in the buggy, and they headed to town to work.

Leah pressed her lips primly and glanced at Anna. "In my opinion, Daniel is suggesting repairs at the shop and here to spend time with Anna. Do you agree, Mamm?"

Mamm looked at the road ahead as a small smile played across her lips but said nothing.

Clicking the reins, Anna rolled her eyes. "Daniel's a kind Amish man helping his neighbors. Don't assign ridiculous intentions to his actions."

Leah sniffed. "God's got a plan for each one of us. He may have brought Daniel here for you, Anna. Time will tell."

A hot blush rose to her cheeks. Daniel's big brown eyes and strong build were attractive. *Soothing* described his voice, and his talent to fix anything and willingness to defend them were attributes hard to ignore. "Let's change the subject."

Leah chuckled. "All right, I'll stop teasing you."

Arriving in town, Anna dropped Mamm at the General Store on the way to the livery. Some shop owners were busy sweeping the boardwalk outside their places, and others unlocked their doors in preparation for receiving customers. She and Leah left the livery and opened for business. Two Englisch women walked in. The bent-over, frail older woman moved slowly and depended on her knotty pinewood cane to support her with each step, but she had a sparkle in her gray eyes and a beautiful smile. The younger woman's swollen stomach stretched her cotton dress, as if her boppli might appear soon.

Leah leaned close to Anna's ear. "I'd guess her age is close to mine. Her thick, shiny, brown ringlets and hazel-green eyes are beautiful. Let's go meet them."

They wilkomed the new customers.

"Are you shopping for anything special?" Anna folded her hands in front of her.

The younger patron rubbed her stomach. "I'm April Cooper, and this is my grandmother, Rosetta Cooper. Please call me April." She smiled and took a breath. "My child is kicking up a storm today."

Leah dragged a chair to the elderly Mrs. Cooper. "Please sit and relax. I'll be happy to bring dry goods to you that interest you."

"Much obliged." The feeble woman trembled as she took a seat.

"I'm Anna, and Leah is my schweschder. It's a pleasure to meet you."

April walked over to the row of quilts hanging on the wall. "These are lovely. I would love to learn how to stitch a patchwork quilt. The Jacob's ladder, pinwheel, and wedding quilts are gorgeous designs. Why do they have pockets sewn on them?"

Leah explained the reason for the pockets. She lifted a pinwheel-patterned coverlet from two wooden pegs. "Anna's a wonderful teacher. She taught me how to make them."

Anna couldn't resist the wonder and excitement in April's eyes and voice. She delighted in teaching her schweschders how to sew, cook, and clean. "I'd be happy to teach you how to stitch quilts."

April put a hand to her open mouth. "I would be so grateful for your time. When can we start?"

Leah eyed the young customer's middle. "You may want to wait until after your boppli is born."

Mrs. Cooper spoke in a weak tone. "April, sweetheart,

listen to these kind ladies. You've got enough to do taking care of me and overseeing the property."

She smiled and fluttered her hand. "I'll be fine."

Anna raised her eyebrows. Even if the property wasn't large, the maintenance would be a lot for a young woman to manage, especially in her condition. "You manage the property yourself?"

"We have a neighbor who takes care of the hay fields. He also helps me plant and maintain the garden. I enjoy feeding and caring for the animals. Grandmother cooks and does light cleaning. We're a good team." She winked and smiled at Mrs. Cooper.

What a relief! The young woman had some assistance. April showed such enthusiasm for wanting to learn to quilt. She would work her schedule around Leah's. "You're wilkom to kumme to the shop whenever you're ready."

"Would Wednesday morning be a good day?"

Anna touched April's arm and smiled. "Wednesday morning is fine, but kumme in before eleven to give us enough time to get in a good lesson, and you can practice while I assist customers."

"Thank you so much!" April chose fabric. "This will allow me enough material to make the sheets we need. They are beyond mending." She paid for her purchases.

She tucked her package under one arm and offered her other one to Mrs. Cooper. The older woman grasped her arm and they waved and smiled before the door shut behind them.

Anna came alongside Leah at the counter. "April didn't mention a husband."

"Maybe she's married or widowed and failed to mention him. We'll have a chance to learn more about her on Wednesday."

* * *

Daniel whistled and pushed Grace's Dry Goods Shop door open Tuesday morning. "I hope I'm not disturbing you. We had a soft rain late in the night. I wanted to check my handiwork on your roof." He'd find any excuse to speak to Anna, gaze into her eyes, and have her warm smile brighten his day. She dominated his mind from morning to night.

She shook her head and waved him in. "No, not at all. Kumme in." She grinned and pointed to the dry ceiling. "I'm pleased to tell you we haven't had any leaks."

"Good." He held her gaze a moment.

Leah lifted a mug off the shelf. "Coffee?"

"Maybe after I check the roof. Danki."

He went outside and climbed up the ladder and onto the roof. Inspecting his repair, he smiled. "Looks good."

Crash!

What happened? He climbed down the ladder and rushed inside the shop.

Anna and Leah stood in front of a shattered window. Anna picked up a rock.

"Who threw the rock?"

Red-faced, Anna trembled. "We had our backs turned to the window when the rock broke through the glass and landed on the floor. By the time we turned around, the culprit was gone. He must have gotten lost in the crowd filling the streets. No one looked suspicious."

Daniel examined the damage. "Who would do such a thing?"

Hands on hips, Anna sighed. "I have no idea."

"Do you think Butch is responsible?" Leah's voice trembled and her cheeks glowed scarlet.

Burying her face in her hands, Anna shook her head. "I hope not."

Daniel paced in a tight circle. "I wouldn't rule him out."

Leah grimaced. "What should we do?"

"We can't prove he is the one responsible. There's nothing we can do for the time being, except be vigilant."

He wanted to protect them, but how? He couldn't be here every minute. Going to Butch at his home and confronting him wouldn't accomplish anything. They had no idea who threw the rock. Mischievous kinner could be responsible. He scratched his forehead. "I'll go buy a new window and take out the old one. Be mindful of anything or anyone suspicious. The sheriff's office is two buildings away. Don't hesitate to notify him with the slightest concern. We can't risk you or Leah getting hurt." He had to stifle the urge to reach for Anna's hand to reassure her he would do whatever he could to shield her and Leah from harm. "I'll kumme by and check on you both when I'm in town."

"Danki, Daniel. I don't want to trouble you. You've done enough for our family."

"It's no bother. I find any excuse to enjoy your company." He held his breath a moment and shoved his hand in his pocket. Had he said too much? He coughed and covered his mouth. "I'll go buy new glass and replace the window."

"Let me give you the money first." Anna pulled out the cashbox.

He positioned his hat on his head. "Let me replace the window for you. I'll cover the cost."

"Daniel, I must pay you for the window."

"You can repay me with cups of coffee when I stop by." He rushed out the door before she could protest further. Her petite nose wrinkled in frustration brought a grin to his face. She was pretty no matter her mood. He couldn't bear it if anything happened to her.

He dashed to the hardware store and scanned the crowd on the way for Butch. He didn't find him. Hopefully, the rock had been thrown by an unruly child. Shrugging his shoulders, he pushed the store door open and picked out the window, paid for his purchase, and left.

Leah met him. "I'll hold the door for you. I saw you approaching the shop through the window."

Anna had moved a shelf of aprons away from the damaged area and swept up the shards of glass. "I cleaned the floor as best I could. Is there anything I can do to help you?"

Daniel leaned the window against the wall and adjusted his tool belt. "No. Danki. I'll be fine."

Anna and Leah assisted customers while he repaired the window. He could've stayed all day to hear Anna's chipper voice answering the women's questions. She and Leah were good at selling the shop's offerings.

Less than an hour later, he stood back and scrutinized his handiwork. "Good as new."

Anna handed him a cup of coffee. "Daniel, how generous of you."

He accepted the cup and nodded. "Glad to oblige." If Butch was responsible for the damage, he might not limit his evil activities to the shop. He wanted an excuse to check on Anna at home, too. He had an idea. "I'm glad I'll be working at your place on the barn. While I'm there, I'll keep a lookout for Butch."

Leah showed a customer a wedding quilt and greeted another.

Anna glanced over at her. "I should help Leah. Danki, Daniel. I don't know how we are going to properly pay you for all the help you've given us."

He was happy to steal a few minutes alone with Anna. Her soft eyes and shyness sent a jolt through him like a clap of loud thunder. Her body language was unmistakable. The spark between them was there. He was certain. "I'm glad I can help. You befriended me the first day I met you. The evening I spent with your family was the best time I've had in a long while." His mouth curled in a grin. "I wouldn't turn down another meal or two if I were asked."

Leah bid the two customers farewell and joined them. "You can count on Mamm feeding you, and we'd all like you to join us for supper Wednesday and any other time you're available."

Anna smiled. "She's right. We would all like having you over anytime you're free, not just to work."

His heart soared. Fixing up the barn had been a subtle way of showing his interest in Anna. He wouldn't push or mention his intention to pursue her. She might need more time for her heart to mend from Noah's departure. The sparkle in her eyes and her pink blushed cheeks told him he was making progress. He couldn't quell his growing excitement. "Then it's settled." He waved good-bye and whistled as he left.

He crossed the street. The Englischers had so many conveniences to make life easier. Electricity, inside washrooms, and much more. Using handmade tools and his muscles to accomplish tasks didn't bother him. Hard work satisfied him. Building and repairing things provided healthy exercise.

Stetson hats, colored shirts, pants, and fancy leather shoes hadn't piqued his interest either. Motorcars were another story. He'd always wanted to read and learn about how they were constructed and drive one. He'd prayed about his worldly desire and asked God for help in putting these notions out of his head. He was devoted to God and the Amish customs, and he wanted to shield himself from the temptations of the Englisch world. It wasn't always easy.

What he did want was time with Anna. She'd captivated him with her melodious voice and gentle ways. She cocked her head to the side a little when she smiled. She played with her kapp string and stared at her shoes when she was nervous.

The town was busy. Horses, buggies, and a few motorcars filled Main Street. He moved his wagon to the front of the store, went inside, bought the paint, and loaded all but the last can into the wagon. He returned to the counter and grabbed the last one. Leaving, he bumped into a slender blond Englisch woman he guessed was close to his age. "I apologize."

She waved a dainty hand and batted her dark eyelashes. "I'd pay you to do it again." She had a Southern accent. "You're so handsome, even in your plain drab shirt and pants."

In his way, she had him blocked from the crowded boardwalk. "Excuse me, miss. I need to get by."

She gently pushed him out the door and against the wall. She flattened her hand on his chest and held her nose inches from his. Her rose-scented perfume suffocated him. "Buy a girl a cup of coffee, and let's get better acquainted. My name's Tammy Whitewater. I'm from the East, visiting my aunt. I need a little excitement. With an up-to-date haircut and clothes, you'd be the best-looking man I've been with for a while. I could show you a thing or two."

"No, danki." He stepped sideways and hurried past her.

The woman had been shockingly forward and persistent. He shouldn't have noticed, but he wasn't blind. Her low-cut and tight-fitted dress outlined her perfect figure, but he had no interest in Englisch women. Her flirty behavior appalled him. The encounter was awkward and infuriating.

Amish women were modest, reverent, and soft-spoken. His mamm had been a full partner in his parents' marriage, often advising his daed on family and financial matters. He'd taken her advice more often than not. It was no secret in their haus how much Daed admired and loved Mamm. His parents respected each other for their wisdom, strength, trust, and faith in God. If he could find a woman with the same attributes and share a relationship with her similar to what his parents had shared, he would be happy. Anna reminded him of his mamm. She showed strength in managing the shop and working at home. He'd observed her deportment with her family at dinner. Their camaraderie was comforting. Something he sorely missed having, without his family.

Driving home, he passed familiar neighbors he'd met since moving to Berlin. He nodded and waved. The cornstalks had grown knee-high and if the weather held, it would provide a good crop this year.

Pulling into his yard, he spied a man sitting on the high-backed rocking chair on his porch. Squinting, he couldn't place the man. Who was he? Halting his horse, he climbed out of the wagon and tied it to the hitching post. The tall, broad-shouldered Amish man stood. "I'm Josiah Petersheim." He pointed to the east. "My property is the fourth farm on the left on your way to the church barn."

"Daniel Bontrager." He opened the door, and Otis ran out to his favorite spot for taking care of business. His pet trotted back to them.

"Jah, I was acquainted with your bruder and his fraa. I'm sorry they passed." He let Otis sniff his hand. "Beautiful dog."

"Danki. Would you like to kumme in? Would you like something to drink?"

Josiah removed his hat, rubbed his bald head, and sat in a rocker. "No, danki. Do you have a few minutes? I have a proposal for you."

Mr. Petersheim's jolly dimples, rosy cheeks, and potbelly relaxed Daniel.

He sat in the other weathered rocker. "What may I do for you, Mr. Petersheim?"

Otis jumped up and rested his chin on Daniel's lap.

"Call me Josiah. I came to wilkom you to the community and to run a proposition by you." He chuckled. "Jonathan's single Amish bruder moving to town has been big news. He and Adele held you in high regard. I'm here to ask you to consider an arranged marriage with my dochder, Cora. She's nineteen and would make any man a good fraa. Kumme to our haus and meet her. She baked a delicious sugar cream pie before I left."

He had no intention of meeting Mr. Petersheim's dochder. He'd found the woman he'd be pursuing. Considering how fast news spread in this town, he didn't want his interest in Anna to travel in the gossip circle. "Danki for the invitation. I'm going to have to decline. I have a few items to collect for tomorrow's jobs. I'll be cutting wood here until late. My schedule is full of repair jobs, and I must keep up with maintaining my property."

Josiah rolled up his sleeves. "I'll help you so you can have time to meet Cora."

Josiah wasn't taking no for an answer. He was determined to have him meet Cora. No way would he go with the man out of obligation. More importantly, he didn't want Anna to find out. She would get the wrong impression, and his answer would remain the same even if Cora was the most talented and beautiful woman he'd ever met. Anna had already taken up residence in his heart. "I would've been honored to meet your dochder, but I have a woman in mind already."

Arching his eyebrows, Josiah scratched his beard. "May I ask who she is?"

Having his and Anna's names added to the gossip chain could be disastrous. Taking slow steps to build a friendship had worked well so far. He didn't want anything or anyone to ruin their newfound companionship. "I haven't revealed my interest in her yet, so I'd prefer to not tell you her name."

"I shouldn't have been so nosy. Danki for your honesty and your time." He tipped his hat. "Wilkom to Berlin."

Stretching out his arm, Daniel nodded. "Pleasure meeting you."

"Likewise. Have a productive evening." Josiah stepped off the porch toward his wagon.

Daniel rolled his shoulders and sighed. Josiah seemed kind. He hoped declining to meet the man's dochder wouldn't hinder a friendship between them. Berlin was a tight-knit community.

Would Amish men ask Mrs. Plank if they could arrange a marriage with Anna? News of Noah's departure had to have become a major topic among the women. Noah had been a spiritual, kind, and talented man for any of the single women in the community to consider, if he and Anna hadn't been planning a future together.

He scratched his dog's nose. "Hopefully, my friendship with Anna will grow before another man approaches her. I am taken with her."

Otis rubbed up against his leg. His companion carried a book in his mouth and dropped it at his feet.

Daniel picked up the dusty hardcover and patted the dirt off the cover. "What did you find, Otis?"

Otis barked and stared at him.

Daniel chuckled. "I wish I knew what you were thinking." He slumped in the porch swing and opened the book.

Otis joined him and lay beside him.

His eyebrows raised. "Adele kept a journal." He flipped through the pages and scanned the words. "She thanks God for introducing her to Jonathan, the love of her life." He ran his hand along Otis's back. Skipping through the book, he focused on the middle section. "Here she writes she loves Jonathan even more than the day they married. She mentions his infectious laugh, the sparkle in his big eyes, and his loving touch." He closed Adele's journal and leaned his head on the back of the swing. "Otis, I want my fraa to say those loving thoughts about me someday."

Otis lifted his head and barked twice.

"I'm glad you agree." He laughed. "Soon I'll introduce you to Anna, the woman I've befriended. She has a delightful family, too. I'll take you with me to paint their barn. Maybe Beth will keep you busy. You'll have a wonderful time with her and her family."

Otis wagged his tail and licked Daniel's hand.

He'd never been happier, and he hoped nothing would happen to interfere with the progression of his friendship with Anna.

A snake slithered up the porch steps.

Otis jumped down and barked.

"No, Otis!" Daniel rushed to the shovel behind the maple chair against the wall and grabbed the handle. The snake reared to strike.

Otis jumped back and whimpered.

Daniel slammed the shovel and killed the unwilkom intruder. He shivered. "Life is full of surprises, and not all of them good, Otis."

Chapter Six

Anna greeted Lydia Keim Wednesday morning. "What a wilkom surprise! Kumme in. How's Jonah? Your son captures the hearts of everyone in Berlin with his friendly personality."

"He's sad. He misses Noah." She rested her hand on Anna's arm. "I told Noah before he left I thought you two would marry. He said he asked you to wed him and you said no. Why did you not want to go with him?"

Anna's hands flew to the warm heat on her cheeks. Lydia didn't mean any harm and Anna believed the woman cared about her, but she was inquisitive. Anna opened her mouth, but no words came to mind.

Leah joined them. "Anna doesn't want to talk about Noah. He's a sensitive subject at present. I'm sure you understand." She walked around the counter and gently took Lydia's arm. "Let me show you the new star-patterned quilt I put out for display earlier today." She glimpsed over her shoulder and winked at Anna.

Anna barely spoke above a whisper to Leah. "Danki." Most of the women in the community wouldn't ask her about Noah, out of common courtesy. Lydia had no problem blurting out what was on her mind. The woman cared for the sick and had a big heart, but she had no discretion and enjoyed spreading gossip. Anna's precious schweschder had intervened on her behalf.

Daniel stepped inside the shop. "Good morning, Anna. I bought supplies at the hardware store and thought I'd stop in. How are you and Leah?"

His big smile diminished her awkward moment with Lydia. "We're fine. Danki for checking on us."

Lydia rushed to Daniel. "Good morning. I'm Lydia Keim. I've noticed you in church, and my son, Jonah, has mentioned you. He said you were sitting with Noah in church one Sunday. My neighbor Phyllis Petersheim told me her husband, Josiah, stopped by your haus. They have a lovely marriageable dochder, Cora. She bakes the best sugar cream pies. She would make any man a wonderful fraa. You really should reconsider her daed's offer." She darted her eyes to Anna and Leah. "Wouldn't you agree?"

Smiling, Anna nodded. Lydia never ceased to amaze her. The woman knew no bounds in asking direct questions. She was the most forward of all the Amish women. Her friends in the community gossiped among themselves and with their husbands but not with any men.

Leah put a hand on the small of Lydia's back and guided her to the counter. "You are right. Cora is a sweet woman. Kumme with me to the counter, and I'll wrap your quilt for you. I've taken up enough of your time dragging you around the shop to show you our new things."

"I've enjoyed my visit, but I better get home." She

smiled and darted her eyes to each one of them. "Good day, everyone."

"Give Jonah my best." Daniel grinned.

"Will do." She paid for her purchase and waved as she left the store.

Leah crossed her arms. "I love Lydia, but she is quite the busybody."

Putting a fist to his mouth, Daniel chuckled. "She is direct. News travels fast." He shook his head. "Mr. Petersheim did ask me to meet his dochder." He gazed into Anna's eyes. "I politely declined."

Anna hadn't thought about a man asking Daniel to consider marrying his dochder. She shouldn't be surprised. He was handsome and kind and would provide a good living for a fraa. She would miss their conversations if he agreed to marry a woman in the Amish community. She felt a stab of regret. Their timing was off. If she'd had more time to get over Noah, she might have considered him as a prospective husband. "Lydia doesn't mean any harm, but she should hold back from asking personal questions. She makes people uncomfortable with her inquiries." She brushed a thread from her apron. "How's Otis?"

Daniel told them about the snake crawling on his porch and almost biting Otis.

Anna and Leah gasped and shuddered.

"I killed the serpent before it could bite Otis."

"What a relief!" Anna pressed her hands to her open mouth.

Leah's eyes widened. "You should bring Otis to the haus when you kumme over to paint. We'd like to meet your dog, especially Beth. Mamm already told you she doesn't mind."

"I will. He's well-behaved. You'll enjoy him." He bid them good-bye and left.

Leah grinned and stowed the cashbox under the counter. She pulled the curtain below to shield its existence. "Cora Petersheim is a dark-haired beauty. If Daniel met her, he wouldn't visit us as often. She would be a good catch for a young Amish man. She follows Amish law to the letter, never says a harsh word, and she's always baking and giving away her pies and cookies to the less fortunate Amish families. All are reasons why we love her."

"I suppose many unwed women will ask their daeds to approach Daniel about an arranged marriage. Any Amish woman would consider him a good catch for her husband."

Leah tapped her finger on Anna's hand. "Including you?"

Daniel had surprised her with his cheery moods and friendliness. He'd made it clear he was rooting himself in Berlin, Ohio. "I'd be lying if I didn't admit he piques my interest, but it wouldn't be appropriate for me to entertain thoughts of friendship with another man since Noah left such a short time ago."

Slapping her hand on the counter with fire in her eyes, Leah glared at her. "Like you said, Noah chose to leave rather than marry you and stay here. I'm sorry Noah chose to leave Berlin and not marry you, but you can't waste your life away pining for him. You have a chance to build on our friendship with Daniel and find out if it turns into something more. Don't put restraints on yourself where Daniel's friendship is concerned. You said your struggles with Noah began way before he left. He was too critical of you, and you and he had been arguing for months before then."

"There were a lot of traits I loved about Noah. Those are hard to forget, but I agree with you. I'm wasting time dwelling on him." She wrinkled her nose. "Have I ignored or been rude to Daniel?"

"No, but I'm warning you not to so you don't make the mistake of shying away from his kind gestures. He's not repairing the shop roof or our barn for fun. There's no doubt in my mind he wants any excuse to be near you."

April muscled open the door against the strong breeze. "I meant to come in earlier, but my grandmother had an upset stomach this morning. I offered her tea and bread, and she was doing much better an hour later."

Leah ushered her to a chair. "You're fine. Kumme join us."

Anna slid two more chairs next to April's to form a semicircle, and she sat between them. "May I offer you anything to eat or drink?"

She fidgeted with the red button on the cuff of her sleeve. "I had a big breakfast before I fed the animals. Our neighbor has been taking care of the garden and the corn and hay fields and cutting wood. We're splitting the profits with him, and he's generous and kind to look out for us. My husband left the day he found out I was carrying this child. He left a note saying he was moving to Wyoming to work for a friend's daed who owned a big ranch. He said our marriage was over and he wanted no further contact. He sent me signed divorce papers."

Anna sucked in a breath. "You must've been brokenhearted."

Red-faced, Leah huffed. "How could a husband abandon his fraa and unborn boppli?"

"I ask myself the same question often." April's sad gaze met Leah's.

April had a lot of responsibility with expecting a

child, taking care of her grossmudder, and managing their home and property. Anna wanted to help her. "If there's anything we can do for you, please ask." She covered April's hand.

Wiping her damp eyes, April looked at them. "Learning how to stitch quilts is something I've looked forward to since meeting you. Women have shied away from me since my husband left. Thank you for welcoming me here."

"My pleasure." Anna wiped a tear from the young woman's cheek.

April's simple plaid dress was worn and faded. Her brown leather shoes slid off her heels when she walked. The young maedel must have been having a hard time making ends meet.

Mrs. Zook came in. She waved to Leah and Anna.

"I'll be with you in a few minutes. Please look at our new quilts on the wall." Leah grinned.

Leah patted April's arm. "You stay as long as you like. I'll wait on customers so you can have Anna's undivided attention."

April nodded and gave her a shy grin.

Leah pushed a small stool and lifted April's swollen feet on top of it. "Relax and enjoy your time here with us. Anna, I'll take care of Mrs. Zook. You stay here with April."

Anna grinned. Leah was taking good care of Mrs. Zook. Her schweschder was thoughtful to give her time with April. "I've got material swatches the size you need in dark blue and white already cut for a pinwheel pattern. You're wilkom to rummage through a box of leftover fabric for anything else you'd like to stitch. I'll bring it to you." She went to the back room and brought the extra-fabric box over to the young woman and set it in front of her.

April dug her hands into the colorful material. "I could sew the larger pieces together and make some dresses! Thank you."

"Help yourself." The young woman's excitement lifted Anna's troubled heart. She waited for her to finish making her choices, bagged April's selections, and set them aside. Grabbing a handful of three-by-three-inch squared swatches off a small table, she snatched a clean flour sack off a shelf with the other hand. She put the bundle in the sack. She opened a maple box and selected a needle and thread. "Watch me stitch these two pieces together." Anna wove the threaded needle in and out of the material.

"Your stitches are so perfect."

"Making stitches tiny and straight takes practice." Handing her the threaded needle, Anna smiled. "Try a few stitches."

April did as she was told. "I was able to make them small and in a straight line!" She drew in her eyebrows. "What should I use for a filler?"

"I have cotton batting I'll send home with you." She studied the young woman's handiwork. "You did a good job." She smiled. "Put your practice material aside and I'll explain how you'll pin and sew the clean flour-sack backing to your quilt." Anna instructed April step by step on how to construct the entire keepsake pocket quilt. The young woman's face grew serious. Her determination and attentiveness touched Anna's heart. She was delighted to teach this young woman with child how to sew. "Let's go to the front where Leah and I can watch your progress. If you want to bring your finished quilt to us, we can sell the coverlet in the store and give you a percentage of the profit."

"I'm fearful I'll forget everything you've taught me."

Anna jotted instructions on paper. She handed them to the young woman. "Refer to these steps if you get confused. You're wilkom to stop in and ask questions anytime. Stay as long as you like to work on it."

"It might be a difficult decision putting the quilt up for sale once it's finished. I'm thinking of giving the coverlet to my grandmother with a letter tucked inside telling her how much her love and support has meant to me. My parents and my husband's mother and father died young, and my grandmother took me in. My grandfather died two years ago. We miss him."

Leah pulled a basket out from under the counter. "Our grandparents passed before we were born. Our daed died soon after we moved here from Pennsylvania. God took good care of us. The community folk have helped us with our land and animals. Grace King and Sarah Helmuth owned this shop, and Grace hired Anna. Grace is the sole owner now. Then Anna hired me. Mamm works at the General Store.

"Do you have any other siblings?"

Anna grinned wide and circled her arm around Leah. "We love our younger schweschder, Beth. She entertains us with her inquisitive and cheery personality. She stays with our neighbor while we are working, until school starts in September."

After biting the end of her thread with her teeth, April stabbed her needle in the small, quilted, cotton-stuffed pillow Anna had given her. Tying the thread off, she cut the end with scissors and rethreaded her needle. "I'm an only child. I've often wondered what life would've been like to have brothers and sisters."

Anna couldn't imagine growing up without Leah and Beth to play with, tease, and work alongside. She could tell Mamm some things, but she and Leah talked about everything. Beth's outspokenness and innocence were refreshing and exasperating. She'd sit close, listen, and then ask questions. There was never a dull moment in life with Beth around. "We do enjoy one another. We also have our times of frustration."

Leah's mouth upturned in an impish grin. "Beth and I fuss over doing the laundry, feeding the animals, and other tasks. Anna and Mamm get annoyed with us."

April gave them a reassuring smile. "I'm sure the good outweighs the bad."

Anna nudged Leah. "Jah, it does." Her family's encouragement and support since Noah left soothed her hurt and lessened her anguish. They pitched in to earn money and take care of maintaining their property. How did April and her grossmudder fend for themselves with food and supplies? She got the impression from the worn clothes they might not have much money. "Are you in need of food or supplies? I hope I haven't offended you by asking."

Leah nodded and handed her a ham sandwich, jar of lemonade, and clean, light blue cloth napkin.

"Thank you. Since I've been with child, I'm hungry most of the time." April put her needle and thread aside, placed the jar on the small table next to her, and took a bite of the sandwich. Talking with her mouth half full, she said, "The neighbor who farms our land and tends our garden provides us with meat and vegetables. He splits the money from the corn with us for supplies and other food. Grandmother and I knit mittens and scarves and sell them in the neighborhood. We get by."

April's life had been filled with hardship and tragedy. She must be close in age to Leah, and she would soon care for her grossmudder and a boppli.

The child would add to their expenses. "Please visit and let us help you with food or whatever else you need. We always have plenty of dry goods we've sewn or food we've canned to share."

Leah lifted the basket. "I've got extra sandwiches and ginger cookies you can take home." She passed Anna a sandwich and water-filled jar and took one of each for herself from the basket.

"You're both so kind. I'm blessed to have met you. God has supplied all my needs. I have no complaints. Our crops and garden have flourished the past few years, and the man helping us has been generous. His wife provides us with meals sometimes. Grandmother is diligent in praying and reading her Bible three times a day. I pray and read my Bible, but not as often as Grandmother. God has definitely been good to us."

Anna prayed for God's will in her life whenever she was baffled about something. Through Scripture and prayer, God had given her a peace about staying in Berlin. She trusted Him to guide her through life. She hadn't always made the right decisions, but she got back on the proper path after prayer. Human, she had let her Heavenly Father down often. She kept tight-lipped about most information she'd overheard concerning others' lives, but she'd participated in gossip, gotten angry at her schweschders, and been selfish at times. "God cares about every detail of our lives and forgives us whenever we fail Him, and we can trust Him in every aspect."

Leah sighed. "I don't always jump for joy at our Heavenly Father's answer to my prayers, but it soon becomes clear His answer was best for me in every situation. I get in trouble acting first and thinking about the consequences later." She gave Anna a small shrug and remorseful grin.

"Do you have names picked out for the boppli?" Leah swiped the crumbs from her lap.

"Daniel or Augustus for a boy, and Daisy for a girl."

Leah raised her eyes to Anna. "We have a new friend named Daniel. If you met him, you'd probably choose his name. He's a kind and gentle soul, although strong. Don't you agree, Anna?"

Her cheeks flaming, Anna put her hands in her apron pockets. "I do agree. Daniel is all those things."

"Are you interested in Daniel, Leah?" April had her back to Anna.

Leah shook her head. "No, *I'm* not the one he's interested in. I have a suspicion he does have his eye on someone, but I'd prefer not to say." Leah glanced at Anna and grinned.

Putting a finger to her lips behind April's back, Anna shook her head at her schweschder.

"I'm sorry. I'm asking too many questions."

Anna's cheeks warmed again. "Let me check your stitches." She accepted the material from the young woman and studied her project. "You catch on fast. Your handiwork will turn into a beautiful quilt when you're finished. You're off to a good start." She passed the fabric back to April.

April pushed her threaded needle through the fabric. "I want to finish a full-size quilt first, but I wish I had time to stitch a boppli quilt before my little one is born."

Anna breathed easier. The tension released from her body. April hadn't pushed the topic of Daniel. She was relieved.

Tapping her chin, Leah patted the young woman's shoulder. "I've got a boppli quilt in the back I made last year that I was keeping as a spare for the next friend of the family who found out she was with child. You can have the blanket. I'll make another one." She dashed to the back room before April could protest and returned carrying a green-and-white patchwork quilt. "Here you go."

"You are so generous. It's lovely. I've really had a good time with both of you today. After my husband left, a lot of the women treated me like I had leprosy. They acted as if his leaving was my fault. I'm glad I've had a chance to fellowship with you." She glanced at the wood clock on the counter. "I should get home. I've got chores to do, and I need to check on my grandmother." She gathered her things and hugged Anna and Leah. "Thank you for everything."

Anna had enjoyed getting acquainted with April, and she hoped the pleasant young woman birthed a healthy boppli. Anna touched her shoulder. "After you have your newborn, please bring him or her into the shop."

"I will." She grinned and left.

"I hope she does bring in her boppli." Leah nudged Anna's shoulder. "I'm curious to find out if she has a boy and names him Daniel."

Chapter Seven

Wednesday evening, Daniel sat next to Anna at their favorite spot behind the barn and near the pond. He patted his stomach. "Your mamm outdid herself on supper. The stew and peach pie were excellent."

"Two weeks have passed, since you said you were going to paint the barn, and you've not only completed that task, you've also repaired our fence, corral, and chicken coop. We appreciate all you've done for us. The least we can do is feed you." Anna smiled shyly. "She's flattered you enjoy her cooking."

He would do anything for Anna and her family. Any chance he got, he found a way to spend time with her. He'd run out of things to fix. Maybe she would suggest something. "I'll be glad to do any repairs you might need. Don't hesitate to ask."

"You're spoiling us, Daniel." She nudged his arm and grinned.

Her little nudge sent a thrill through him. Encouraged she might consider him more than a friend. "I enjoy doing things for you and your family." She hadn't mentioned Noah, and she seemed to relax and smile more often. He hoped he'd had a part in making her happier these days.

"I'm happy you chose to live in Berlin. You've become a good friend to me and my family." She pulled up her legs, wrapped her arms around her knees, and rested her chin.

He swallowed. *Friend?* He had to tell her what was in his heart. He couldn't stand to wait another minute. "Anna, I want more than friendship with you. I'll not rush you, but I'd be honored if you would consider me for your future husband. We can take all the time you need to feel comfortable." He covered her hand with his.

She met his gaze and didn't move her hand. "I'd be pleased to consider you, Daniel."

His heart skipped a beat, and he wanted to jump and shout. Jonathan had gushed about meeting Adele and falling in love at first sight, and he'd thought it was doubtful he'd ever experience such a connection. Until he met Anna. Her overall beauty caught his attention. Her soft voice and kind ways touched his heart. Since he'd met her, she'd been joyous, humorous, and a little flirty with him. They'd discussed their childhoods, deep faith and trust in God, and importance of living close to family. Values they shared.

She shooed a bumblebee buzzing around her head. "My family has been pushing for something more than friendship between us since you came to supper the first time. They'll probably spread the news to everyone in the neighborhood."

Delight soared through his veins. Her mamm and schweschders had wilkomed him with open arms. He missed Anna and her family on days he hadn't visited or shared a meal with them. He glanced at Beth playing with Otis at the other end of the serene pond.

"You and your family have filled a void in my life. I've grown accustomed to spending time with you and them. Beth brought me sandwiches and lemonade for lunch on the days I worked. I tossed a ball with her several times, and we had a chance to get better acquainted."

Anna smiled. "I hope she didn't pester you too much."

"No, she's a sweetheart." He paused. "She's curious about us."

"What did she say?"

He wanted to discuss Noah, and the time seemed right. "She said you hadn't mentioned Noah lately and you smiled more when you were around me."

Chuckling, she hugged her knees to her chest. Her long dress covered her legs to her shoes. "She's correct. I've thought less of Noah and more of you."

"Discussing Noah shouldn't be an awkward subject for us. I want you to talk to me about whatever is on your mind." He hoped Noah would become a distant memory as they grew closer. But he understood she had history with him, and she might need a little more time to get over him.

"He's not kumming back, and I'm ready to move on with my life. Do I think about him? Now and then, but you've taken up residence in my mind more than Noah." She tilted her head with a reassuring smile.

Beth and Otis joined them. Her schweschder plopped on the grass next to Daniel and Otis settled on her lap. Beth scratched the dog's ear. "I'm sorry you've finished repairing everything around here. We're afraid you and Otis won't visit us as often."

Anna leaned forward and grinned. "Daniel and I will be spending a lot more time together."

Eyes wide, Beth clapped her hands and squealed. "Yippee! You finally told her you liked her, didn't you?"

His heart soared at Beth's delight. "Jah, I did, and thankfully, she likes me, too."

"Well, of course she does." She stood and bounced on her toes. "I've got to tell Leah and Mamm." She skipped to the haus.

Anna watched her. "I hope Beth spreading the news of our friendship growing into something more won't embarrass you."

Embarrass me? He couldn't wait for everyone in town to find out. He'd been afraid she'd decline his offer and find ways to avoid him. Thankfully, she'd been receptive and open to his suggestion.

He stood and offered Anna a hand. "I'd better get going, as much as I don't want to." He glanced at the orange hue coloring the sky. "The sun is setting, but its beauty doesn't compare to you."

She clasped his fingers and got to her feet. "Danki."

He brushed her fingers with his lips and gently squeezed her hand. "You've made me a happy man, Anna Plank." He walked her across the yard.

Leah came running toward them. "Beth told Mamm and me the news. When can we plan the wedding?"

Mamm joined them and pulled Anna close. "I'm overjoyed!" She changed her smile to a stern look. "Don't rush them, Leah. They've got a lot to discover about each other."

Beth and Otis joined them. "Why wait?"

He and Anna laughed. She playfully yanked on Beth's kapp string. "We have more to learn about each other, and we'll tell you when we're ready to make plans."

He would've married her the next day, but he

understood she may need more time letting him into her life after Noah's departure. Their attraction had grown fast, and their conversations had progressed with ease. Each time they were together, his love for her had grown.

They went inside, and Anna loaded him up with food to take home. She walked him to the wagon and breathed in the warm air. "We are fortunate to have met you, Daniel Bontrager, especially me."

He grinned. "Our time together has been brief, but I'd marry you tomorrow. You decide when you're ready to get married, and I'll set the date with the bishop." He wanted to pull her into his arms, hold her tight, and kiss her lips. He would wait for the right moment, but he could hardly contain himself. He held her hand for a few seconds. "I love you, Anna."

Her cheeks flushed, and her eyes sparkled. She rubbed her thumb over the top of his hand. "I have strong feelings for you, Daniel, but I need time to let them grow. Is that all right? Our friendship has progressed at a rapid pace. I don't want our friends to think I'm jumping from one man to the next."

He moved closer to her and softly caressed her cheek. "You make a good point. We can wait to announce our news. I just want you happy."

He bid her farewell and left. The clouds darkened, thunder clapped, and a bolt of lightning hit the ground yards from him. Raindrops pelted his hat. The weather had changed in minutes. The rapid change in climate reminded him life was uncertain. Hairs prickled on his neck. He hoped nothing ruined the progress he'd made with Anna.

* * *

Anna dragged a puzzle off the shelf, and she and her schweschders chatted and finished piecing the picture of a squirrel in an oak tree in an hour. She yawned and stretched her arms. "Time for me to go to bed."

Mamm stood. "I'm ready to say good night too. Beth and Leah, say your prayers and tuck yourselves in tonight. I'll put the puzzle away."

"Danki, Mamm." Leah and Beth hugged Mamm and Anna and went to their room.

Anna washed her face, changed her clothes, and rested her head on the pillow. Daniel had finally told her he loved her. She and her family had no doubt he'd been working to get her attention. There wasn't one thing left he could possibly do for them. He had worked a lot at their place over the last two weeks. The wood was stockpiled high and their property had never looked better. They'd enjoyed their time together in their special spot by the pond. Putting a hand to her heart, she smiled. She was falling in love with him.

The man had a calmness about him. He loved God, and he worked hard. Enjoying a steady routine, he was comfortable with the ebb and flow of country life. Confidence, strength, and self-assurance, but not arrogance, were attributes she found attractive about him. Daniel was satisfied and content, and his lifestyle matched hers. How many kinner did he want? Would she still work in the shop until they had kinner? She had so much to learn about him.

Thursday morning, Anna and Leah waited on customers. Two Englischers strolled into the shop.

The tall woman wearing an ankle-length pink cotton skirt and high-collared crisp white blouse wandered in, whispering to her friend. The friend was almost the same height as her companion.

"Doreen, do you remember me talking about the Winter family?"

Anna bid her present customer good-bye and moved closer to the Englischers. Eavesdropping on their conversation, she paused and straightened towels on a shelf. She stood close enough to overhear what they were saying.

"I remember. You said the couple was delightful but the son was quite rude. Am I right, Tilly?"

"Yes, and my neighbor is friends with Mrs. Winter. She told me the Winters' son had been out of town to pick something up for his father. He got in trouble and thrown in jail. He'd been released from jail, and he returned to Berlin last night. He went straight to the saloon, and he's already in jail here for getting into a fight and breaking her cousin's arm. They drank too much, and their behavior got out of hand. She mentioned Butch has a temper and is always getting into trouble."

Anna shuddered. The man was dangerous. They hadn't encountered him lately, but this got her stomach churning. Had he stayed away from Leah because he'd spent most of his time in jail?

"How much time will he be locked up, Doreen?"

Anna glanced at Leah. She was oblivious to the women's discussion about Butch. The patron her schweschder waited on had her cornered in the back room, asking endless questions about keepsake quilts.

"I don't know."

"Does his father care about what his son is doing?" Tilly picked up an apron and examined the stitching.

"Butch's parents are sorely embarrassed. George, Butch's father, is a kind and considerate man, and he is the opposite of his son. He's spoken to the young man about his behavior, but Butch won't listen. It's a shame they have to contend with such a disorderly son." Tilly strolled over to her friend. "The last time I saw you in your apron, it was showing wear. You should buy a new one."

Anna rubbed her temples. Her head began to pound. She hoped Butch wouldn't harass or harm them, but she couldn't convince herself this would be true. She approached the women. "May I help you?"

Tilly unhooked the wedding quilt. "The workmanship and pattern are exceptional. I'll buy it."

"Your daughter will be grateful for the gift." Doreen ran her hand over the top. "I'll buy this larger apron. I've had a terrible time finding one to provide enough material to cover my expanding stomach. I've got to put my fork down and quit indulging in too much dessert each night."

Anna motioned them to the counter, wrapped the purchases, accepted payment, and thanked them for their patronage.

Leah wrapped her patron's dry goods order and bid her farewell. She stretched her back. "The store is finally empty. We've had a lot of customers today. I'm exhausted."

Anna glanced at the ceiling and frowned. "Did you happen to overhear any of my last customers' conversation?"

"No, I didn't." Leah shook her head. "Why?"

"I'm afraid I did, and what they had to say was disturbing."

Leah straightened and frowned. "Anna, you're scaring me with your worried look. What did they say?"

"They said Butch Winter has been out of town and in jail. He came back to Berlin last night, got in a fight, and is back in jail here."

Wringing her hands, Leah furrowed her brow. "I hoped we'd seen the last of him because he decided to leave us alone, not because he's been locked up."

Anna paced the floor. "I'm nervous and frightened. I don't trust him. The women didn't mention when he was being released. You've got to keep a watchful eye and be careful."

Leah hugged herself. "Don't worry. I'll be cautious."

Daniel came in and set a paper bag on the counter. "I brought you and Leah a treat."

Like the sun shining through a soft rain, Daniel's kind face lifted her mood. She breathed in the sweet scent. "Gingerbread cookies! Danki." She passed one to him and one to Leah.

"How is your day going?"

"Good until a few minutes ago." Leah pulled three chairs together.

Alarm crossed his features. "What happened?"

Anna's cookie crumbled in her tight grip. She caught the pieces in her apron. "Butch has been in jail for getting into a fight and breaking a man's arm."

Daniel frowned and rubbed his chin. "I'm not confident he's forgotten about you, Leah." His jaw tensed. "In jail, he's been unable to get to you."

"Leah and I were thinking the same thing. The Englischers said he served additional time in jail for resisting arrest, which doesn't surprise me. He's been nothing but belligerent and rude to us."

Daniel remained calm the first time they encountered the defiant young man, and he was calm now. She hadn't hesitated to discuss difficult subjects, such as Noah and Butch with Daniel. She could depend on him to speak about these situations in a thoughtful manner. Another trait she found attractive about him.

He stood. "I'm going to go to the sheriff's office and ask him when he plans to release Butch. I'll kumme back and tell you what I found out."

Anna and Leah nodded.

He dashed out.

Leah slumped in the chair. "What would we do without Daniel? He's been a lifesaver. Having him in my life is akin to having a big bruder I can depend on. I'm glad you're considering making him an official part of our family."

"He is pretty wonderful." Anna closed her eyes a moment, lifted her shoulders, and grinned wide. "I am falling in love with him."

"How could you not? The man's a devout believer in God and kind, and he can't take his eyes off you."

Anna and Leah spoke quietly a little while longer. The door opened.

Daniel rushed in and paused to catch his breath. "I asked the sheriff about Butch and I told him about his rude behavior toward Leah in the shop. He said Butch will remain in jail until Sunday, but he's worried he may cause trouble when he gets out. The sheriff said his temper hasn't improved. We need to keep a watchful eye out for him."

She quivered. "I hope he's done badgering Leah."

Leah gripped fistfuls of her apron. "Danki for

checking on Butch's whereabouts. You're like a big bruder to me, Daniel. I feel much safer when you're around."

"I'm flattered you consider me a big bruder."

An Amish couple strolled into the shop.

"I'll wait on them. You and Daniel visit." Leah approached them. She greeted and waited on the elderly man and woman.

Anna led Daniel to the back door and they stepped outside. "I'm concerned about Butch pursuing Leah."

He held her hand, his eyes reassuring. "The sheriff is going to walk by the shop and drive by your haus to keep a lookout for Butch after he is out of jail. I'll kumme by and check on you and your family, too, once he is released." He caressed her cheek. "Hopefully, he'll not want to go back to jail and keep his temper under control. Try to put him out of your mind. We may never deal with him again."

Sunday, Anna sat under the big oak tree after the church meal and passed Daniel a blueberry tart and a jar of lemonade. "I'm glad the weather cooperated today. The cloudless sky and bright sunshine lifts my mood. I've missed you the last few days."

He stuck out his bottom lip. "Here I thought it was me putting a smile on your face." He gazed at her and grinned. "I missed you, too. I had two difficult roofs to repair. They took a lot more of my time than I'd anticipated. It cost me time with you, since I also had to catch up on working in the hay field and garden."

"I forgive you." She winked. "You deserve the most credit for my cheery disposition."

His expression serious, he held her gaze. "You light up my life, Anna Plank."

"I'm happier since you walked into mine, too." His pleased smile warmed her heart.

A ball rolled in their direction, hit Anna's foot, and bounced away.

Anna shifted her gaze to the child running toward the jagged stick. "Be careful of the stick, Sheila!"

Sheila stumbled, her leg landing on the sharp piece of wood. "Ack!"

Anna ran to her, with Daniel on her heels. She knelt next to Sheila. "Are you hurt, sweetheart?"

The child rolled onto her side, pushed herself up, and sat. Blood dripped down her leg. "My leg is bleeding. It hurts." Her lips quivered.

Leah and Beth approached Anna. "How bad is it?"

The child nodded and swiped a tear from her cheek.

Anna pulled Sheila onto her lap and stroked her arm. "She scraped the skin and the wound is bleeding, but I doubt she needs stitches."

Frowning, Leah circled her arms around Beth. "Our little schweschder has a stomachache. Since you're busy helping Sheila, I'll drive her home. Will you tell Mamm? I couldn't find her, and I didn't want to make Beth wait."

"Beth, I'm sorry you're ill." She kissed Sheila's hand. "I'll find Grace. I'm sure she has her medical bag with her. Being a midwife, she carries it with her for emergencies. We need to wash and bandage Sheila's leg. As soon as I find Grace to help Sheila, we'll hurry and catch up to you."

Pressing a hand to her middle, Beth nodded and huddled to Leah's side. "I want to go to bed."

Daniel knelt in front of Beth. "Is there anything I can do for you before I go find Grace?"

Beth moaned and shook her head. "No, danki."

Leah turned to Daniel. "I'm leaving to take her home. She's miserable from eating too many sweets."

"Anna, I'll find Grace while you stay with Sheila." He waved to Beth and Leah. "Be careful."

Soothing the child, Anna held her as Daniel walked away. He was dependable and always there when she needed him. He didn't hesitate to jump in and do what was necessary before she asked.

Grace and Daniel approached Anna and little Sheila. She knelt and opened her bag. "What happened, little one?" She winked at Anna. "It looks like Anna is taking good care of you."

Sheila nodded, swiped her wet nose, and squeezed Anna's hand.

"Grace, I'm so glad you're still here. Beth's stomach is upset, and Leah took her home. Do you mind tending to Sheila? I would like to fetch Mamm and catch up with my schweschders. Where's Joy?"

Grace removed a bottle of clean water and washed her hands with a clean cloth. "You go ahead. We'll be fine. Mamm's holding Joy and showing her off to the other ladies."

Ellen Troyer ran, knelt beside her dochder, and caressed Sheila's cheek. "How did you hurt your leg?"

She scrambled from Anna's lap to her mamm's, straightened her leg, and pointed her chubby finger to her injury. "I fell down on a stick. Anna helped me, and Grace is going to fix it."

"I'm so sorry." Sheila's mamm pulled her little one close.

Anna watched the child embrace her mamm and her stomach fluttered at the endearing picture. "The stick was against a stone and upright, and Sheila tripped over it. Her leg grazed the stick enough to cut her leg."

Grace waved her hand to Anna and Daniel. "I'll take care of Sheila. You two head home and tend to Beth."

"Danki, dear friend." Anna pressed a hand to her throat. "Daniel, have you seen Mamm?"

He scanned the sea of Amish men and women. "She's not anywhere in sight. Let's go search for her."

They bid Sheila, her mamm, and Grace farewell and scanned the crowd for Mamm.

Out of the corner of her eyes, Anna spotted Mamm leaving the outhaus and pulled her aside. "Mamm, Beth is sick. Leah suspects she devoured too many desserts. I don't think it's serious, but I'm uneasy leaving them alone. Butch is being released from jail today."

Mamm stiffened and gently clasped Anna's wrist. She nodded to Daniel. "Let's get going. I'll feel better when Leah and Beth are home safe."

Daniel carried her basket to the wagon and waved to friends fetching their buggies.

The women scooted on the bench next to Daniel and waved to them too.

He flicked the reins and drove them in the direction of their haus. He noticed a buggy turned over a few yards from the entrance of the Planks' lane. "Someone's had an accident!"

Anna pointed. "Oh no, the buggy is ours! Where are Beth and Leah! The horse is gone, and the harness is broken!"

Daniel halted his horse, jumped out, and scanned the area. He pointed. "Over there!"

The three of them ran to the ditch.

Mamm peered over the embankment. "Leah! Beth! Are you hurt!"

Leah yelled, "We're banged up, but no broken bones."

Anna held her breath for a moment. "Please be careful, Daniel." She hoped he didn't fall. He stepped sideways and made his way down the bank. He reached them. "Beth, are you too sick and shaken to make it up the hill?"

"I don't feel good, but I can make it."

"I'll take you and return for Leah." He put her in front of him, held on to her waist, and guided her where to step.

She reached the top, and Mamm pulled her close.

Daniel climbed back down the hill and did the same routine with Leah.

Anna reached for her schweschder and hugged her. "What happened? Your hands are scratched. Are you in pain?"

Leah huffed and puffed. She put a shaky hand to her chest. "I'm out of breath from fright. I'll tell you when we're in the wagon and on the way home so everyone hears the story at once."

Beth groaned.

Daniel lifted her. "I'll carry you. You sweet maedel. I'm sorry you're sick and had an accident. We'll get you home and to bed."

She buried her face in his shoulder. "Danki, Daniel."

Anna hugged Leah, and Mamm climbed in the back and Daniel passed Beth to her.

Mamm stroked Beth's cheek. "I'm so thankful you didn't break any bones. I was terrified when we pulled up to the buggy. I have some aspirin powder at home. I'll make you some tea." She patted Leah's back. "Leah, are you sure you don't have any other injuries?"

"My dress is torn and I've got some minor cuts, but nothing serious. We fell over the side and down the hill." She gripped her dress. "I didn't get a good look, but the person responsible for our wagon going over might have been Butch. He had the same color hair and body build. He fired his gun at close range and spooked the horse just as the buggy wheel hit a deep rut in the road. The horse jerked and rattled the buggy hard, breaking the harness as he bolted away."

Anna held her fists to her chest. "What should we do, Daniel?"

"After we take your mamm and schweschders home, I'll have you go with me to fetch your buggy and find your horse. Later, I'll tell the bishop our suspicions. I'll suggest he and I pay Butch's daed a visit and enlist his help. Without proof, the sheriff won't arrest him, but he's already agreed to pass by your haus and shop often once I told him about Butch's rude comments and our suspicions the troublemaker threw the rock through the shop window. If your family doesn't mind, I'll stay with you for several days. I don't trust Butch."

Mamm squared her shoulders. "You'll get no argument from me, Daniel. We have no idea what this man will do."

He nodded, drove down the lane to their haus, halted the horse, and tied him to the hitching post. He carried Beth inside and lowered her on the settee. "You get some rest."

"Danki, Daniel." She closed her eyes and rolled on her side.

"You rescued us again." Leah's lips quivered. "I'm grateful, Daniel."

"God watched over you, and I'm glad He's allowed me to help you." He faced Anna. "Let's go take care of the buggy and horse. I'll bring you back, leave to visit the bishop, and go get my things."

Mamm carried water and a spoonful of aspirin powder to Beth. "I'll rest much easier with you here. Danki."

Anna followed him outside. Her heart thumped in her chest. She'd never been so afraid. The Amish had guns to hunt for their game, but they wouldn't raise one to a human. How were they going to stop Butch? The man's anger had escalated. He'd shown he wanted to harm Leah. Would he actually kill her? She shuddered in fear. They had to stop him, but how? "Do you think Butch was aiming the shotgun at Leah?"

"No. If he'd meant to shoot her, he wouldn't have missed. Kumming up behind them unaware, he had ample time to aim and fire. He wanted to scare her."

"I should be relieved, but I'm not. They could've been killed. What if the buggy hadn't righted itself and rolled down the hill?"

"Anna, don't let your mind go there."

His words ignited an angry flame within her. How could she not let her mind go there? Her schweschders were in obvious danger. She frowned and pinched the bridge of her nose. "I'm offended by your condescending tone."

Daniel stepped back and held up his hands. "I didn't mean to insult you. I meant to comfort you. I want to save you from any more anxiety over Butch."

She had no reason to lash out at him. Anna hung her head. "I apologize. I'm taking my frustration out on you." She paused and bit her bottom lip. "I've heard it said you take your frustration out on the one you're closest to."

"I like being the one you're closest to." He kissed her cheek and helped her into his wagon.

The kiss thrilled her. Anna studied Daniel. She could no longer imagine her future without him. In such a short time, he'd become an intricate part of her life. He'd taken charge and was doing his best to protect her and her family. The love in her heart for him had grown to new heights.

Daniel pulled up next to their buggy. "Don't get out. I want you to rest. You've had a terrible day. I'll assess the damage."

Two men pulled to a stop on the road next to them. "May we help you?"

Daniel raised his hat. "There was an accident, and the horse broke the harness when he got spooked and ran. I could use an extra pair of hands. Do you mind?"

The two Englischers helped him right the wagon and repair the harness. "Looks like you were lucky." The stockier man patted the sturdy wooden wheel. "Your wheels are fine." He pointed to the deep rut.

"We're blessed the buggy didn't topple over. The damage could've been much worse."

Anna glanced at the Englischers' wagon. Her eyes wide, she held a hand to her open mouth. "You found our horse!"

The young man pulled a rag tucked in the waist of his pants and dabbed at the sweat on his upper lip. "We found him grazing along the side of the road not far from here. We were asking the farmers along the way if he belonged to one of them. I'm glad you're the owner and we can quit searching."

"I'm grateful for the unexpected blessing. Danki so much."

Daniel and the men secured the horse to the Planks' buggy. He shook their hands. "Daniel Bontrager. Nice to meet you. You've been kind."

"I'm Alfred Rollins, and this is my brother, Walter. Glad to help."

Anna and Daniel waved good-bye to the thoughtful men.

Daniel flicked the reins. "Anna, I'll follow you home. Stay on the lookout for anything ahead and on either side of the road, and I'll keep watch in the rear. I'm afraid to let my guard down where Butch is concerned."

She kept a watchful eye out on the way home. Her haus in sight, she blew out a heavy sigh of relief. She hoped the menace would turn his life around and behave.

Pulling alongside her, Daniel halted his horse, got out, and accepted her animal's reins. "Anna, I'll stow your horse and buggy. Is your shotgun hanging on the sitting-room wall?" He tied his wagon to the hitching post and guided her buggy inside.

She nodded and followed him to the barn. "Mamm keeps it there in case we need to shoot twice in the air to alert the neighbors if there's a fire or danger. The shots are a signal the community put in place to notify one another for assistance."

"Good. If you notice anything while I visit the bishop and fetch my bag and Otis, alert the neighbors immediately."

"I will." Every nerve she possessed was on high alert.

"Tell your mamm not to worry about accommodating me in the haus. I can stay in the barn."

"Absolutely not, Daniel Bontrager. Mamm will insist you sleep inside. I'll arrange a cot and bedding for you in the sitting room."

Daniel pulled her close and kissed her softly on the lips.

Her heartbeat raced against her ribs. Their first kiss would be a memory she wouldn't forget.

He gazed into her eyes. "I've been waiting a long time to kiss you. It isn't proper, but I didn't think you'd mind."

She blushed and smiled. She was glad he'd kissed her. It was one of the happiest moments of her life. "I have no objection." She accompanied him to his horse.

He kissed her gently. "I'll be back soon. I'll go to the bishop's haus and then return and tell you what he says." He got in the wagon and drove toward Bishop Weaver's haus.

She savored his kiss. His soft and gentle lips on hers had sent a thrill through her. She touched her mouth. The warmth of their kiss lingered. The taste of his lips was as sweet as honey.

Chapter Eight

Daniel arrived at the bishop's haus and knocked on the door. How would Bishop Weaver react to his news?

"Greetings. What brings you here? Is something amiss?" The man pushed his spectacles on top of his head and ushered him to the front room.

"Jah, I'm afraid so." He recounted his story of Butch's rudeness and aggression toward Leah in the shop, and his suspicions regarding the young man causing Leah and Beth's buggy accident. The bishop went out of his way to avoid confrontation with Englischers. Daniel hoped the bishop wouldn't ask him to ignore Butch's threatening behavior toward the Planks. "Discussing Butch with his daed might help."

The bishop scratched his neck and stared at the ceiling in deep thought. "Speaking with Mr. Winter about his son is a delicate matter. Both men might get angry with us."

The bishop's reluctance sent his pulse racing. Maybe he should've gone to meet Mr. Winter alone and suffered the bishop's consequences later. He hoped Mr. Winter would have a strong, positive influence on his son and be able to reason with him. "Butch presents a danger to the Plank family. I believe we are in dire need of finding a way to protect them. I'm hoping his daed can have a positive impact on him."

"I see your point. Pray with me before we head out." The bishop prayed and lifted his head. "Do you mind if we go together in your wagon?"

"No. I'd planned on taking you with me and bringing you home."

The bishop lifted his hat off a knotty-pine empty coatrack and headed out the door.

Daniel took a deep breath. *Here goes.* The bishop might not relish his informing the sheriff of his concerns about Butch. "I spoke to the sheriff before the accident happened. Anna overheard two Englischers gossiping in her shop about Butch. Apparently, he was in jail for fighting and injuring a man. According to these women, his release was scheduled for today. The same day Beth and Leah had their buggy accident. The sheriff agreed to pass by Grace's Dry Goods Shop and the Planks' property each day."

"Do you think notifying the sheriff was necessary, especially before the accident?"

"Jah, Butch is reckless. I suspect he's the cause of what happened to Leah and Beth and I believe him to be a threat. The sheriff is aware of his temper and bad behavior pattern. If he commits another crime, the sheriff will put him in jail again. In the meantime, the Plank family is at risk. Starting tonight, I'm staying with them and driving the women to work each day until Butch calms down or is put away in jail for good."

On the way to the Winter farm, Daniel noticed the bishop's frown, clenched jaw, and arms crossed so tight against his chest it would take an ax to separate them. Daniel blamed the ache starting in his head for the bishop's awkward silence.

He didn't regret notifying the sheriff, but he had hoped the bishop wouldn't object to his decision. He had run out of anything else to say on the matter. He wished he could bridge the distance between them.

Maybe speaking about Anna with the bishop would give them something enjoyable to talk about and smooth things over between them. He cleared his throat. "Bishop Weaver, I've asked Anna Plank to consider marrying me, and she said she would. We've known each other a short time, but I'm confident she's the fraa for me." He stared straight ahead and gripped the reins. He hoped bringing up Anna would cut the tension between them.

The bishop's elbow bumped his. His frown turned to a smile. "I'm glad to hear it, son."

No mention of Noah, and no lecture on waiting for a period of time before scheduling a wedding date. Relieved, he relaxed his grip on the reins. "I'm grateful for your support, and Anna will be too."

"She's a sweet and kind woman. I'm thrilled for both of you. Do you think you'll wait till November?"

The tense moments they had experienced earlier melted away. The man's happiness about his news had lightened Daniel's mood. "Anna and I haven't discussed a date yet. We're still getting acquainted."

"It's wise to spend time together and ensure you're both well suited for each other. You tell me when you and Anna are ready, and we'll announce the date to the members in church a month beforehand."

As soon as Anna agreed to marry him, he'd not waste any time setting a date for their wedding. He hoped Butch would calm down and they could get on with their lives.

The bishop was quiet for a few minutes. Another awkward silence loomed. Was he going to mention his displeasure about Daniel speaking with the sheriff about Butch Winter again? Daniel thought he'd smoothed this over with the bishop.

Daniel stole a glance at the man. His face serious, he had his arms crossed against his round middle in deep concentration. Daniel would endure the silence and wait for the bishop to speak.

"You *were* in a bad position with Butch, and you had to tell the sheriff your concerns. I understand you had to act quickly. Your decision was right this time." He drummed his fingers on his knee. "Hmm . . . maybe Mrs. Plank should consider sending Leah to live with Noah's aunt and uncle in Lancaster for a couple of months until Butch settles down."

Daniel's stomach churned. He didn't want the Planks to have ties to Noah and his family. "I would rather we not ask Leah to leave. She's a big help to her family and to Anna at the shop, and they are close. We have no guarantee Butch wouldn't travel there and harm her. How would Noah and the Schwartzes protect her?"

The bishop shrugged. "I just thought putting distance between Leah and Butch Winter might discourage him and he'd tire of tormenting her."

Daniel turned down the lane to Mr. Winter's haus. It would be hard to miss on the edge of town with its big sign WINTER'S FARM out front, many rows of tobacco plants, beautiful garden, and impressive hay field. He had no trouble finding the property.

Relief eased through Daniel's shoulders. He halted the wagon and tied the horse to the hitching post. Mr. Winter ceased sweeping his front porch and propped his broom beside the front door. He walked across the yard to greet them. "I don't believe we've met. How may I help you? I'm George Winter, and please call me George." The tall, robust man resembled his son's physical appearance, but not his arrogant demeanor. He had kind eyes and a cheerful voice.

They shook hands with George. "I'm Bishop Weaver, and with me is Daniel Bontrager."

Daniel smiled and tipped his hat. "Call me Daniel."

Winter made a sweeping gesture toward the house. "We can sit on the chairs on the porch."

The bishop and Daniel went to the porch and settled in shiny new maple high-backed chairs. "Danki for your time."

"Lemonade?"

"No, we're fine." The bishop told George of Butch's aggression at the shop and their suspicions about the accident with Beth and Leah and their wagon on their way home from church.

George groaned and shook his head. "I'm sorry. Our son's a bully, and he's been a problem for my wife and me for a while. His crimes are increasing in seriousness, and I'm worried he'll hurt someone real bad. I've disciplined him in every way possible, and nothing works." He sighed and raised his arms. "I'll have a serious conversation with him. I pay him well for the work he does for me. When I threaten to throw him out, he behaves for a few weeks. I'll do what I can."

Daniel shook the man's hand again. "Danki for your help."

The bishop nodded, and they bid George Winter farewell.

Climbing into the wagon, Daniel jerked his head to the lane. Butch's horse raced toward them.

The bishop got in. "Let's get out of here!"

The angry young man yanked his horse to a rearing

stop, blocking their wagon. He glared at them. "What are you stinking Amish doing here?"

"Son, leave these men alone."

Butch stood his ground.

"Bishop Weaver and Daniel were leaving. Let them go. Come inside. We have important matters to discuss."

Butch sneered and beetled his brow. "What did you tell my father?"

Daniel didn't flinch at the man's angry gaze.

The bishop swiveled toward the scowling young man. "We mean you and your family no harm. We have stated our purpose to your daed and he will explain to you why we are here. Please let us leave in peace."

Butch snatched the leads from Daniel. "You're not going anywhere. Get out of the wagon."

George threw open the front door, reached in, and retrieved his rifle. He fired off two shots toward the sky.

The young man jumped and scowled at his daed.

Daniel grabbed the leather leads from the troublemaker and flicked them hard. The horse bolted and the wagon bounced over the ruts down the lane. He held his breath for a moment and hoped the dangerous young man wouldn't pursue them. He yelled at his horse. "Go boy, go!"

The bishop shuddered. "I owe you an apology. You were wise to notify the sheriff. Butch Winter *is* a dangerous man."

Daniel respected the bishop, but the man had set his teeth on edge questioning him about alerting the sheriff. Weighing the facts, he'd proceeded quickly to avoid the Planks' being harmed. There hadn't been time for Daniel to consult with the bishop before alerting the sheriff. Butch's threatening actions had been unfortunate, but he wasn't sorry the bishop witnessed the man's reckless anger firsthand. Bishop Weaver now had a clearer picture of the evil troublemaker's violent nature. Mr. Winter had his hands full. Sighing, Daniel shook his head. The incidents today had been sad and frightening.

The bishop's hands trembled as he rested them on his knees. "The young Englischer is a menace. He had his eye on you. I fear he'll seek to harm you and Leah."

"The sheriff will be keeping a watchful eye, and I'll be alert. I'm a light sleeper. If he kummes to the Planks', I'll hear him. Otis has a keen ear. He'll bark at any hint of an intruder."

Daniel stopped in front of the bishop's haus. "Danki for talking with Mr. Winter, Bishop Weaver. On a happier note, I can't wait to tell Anna I spoke with you about our growing interest in each other. She'll be delighted we have your blessing."

"Jah, you most certainly do have my blessing. You've impressed the men in the community. Doing repairs for many of them has given you a chance to get acquainted. I've observed you in the services every other Sunday, and I'm happy with what your friends say and what I've observed." He sighed. "Be careful, son, and keep me informed."

"Will do. Good night." Daniel turned the wagon around, drove home, packed a bag with clothes, and grabbed his toolbox and threw them in the back of the wagon. "Kumme on, Otis."

Otis jumped in and settled on the bench next to him. He hurried to the Planks' and told them what had transpired with Butch and Mr. Winter.

Anna handed him a ham sandwich on a plate with

cut cubes of cheese on the side. "You must be starved. I'll sleep better with you here tonight." She filled a bowl with table scraps and offered it to Otis. "Here you go, you good boy. It will be a comfort having you here too." She petted the dog's head.

Otis put his nose in the bowl and didn't look up until he'd polished off every last morsel.

Beth wiped milk from her upper lip. "I like having Daniel and Otis here too." She poured Daniel a glass of water and passed it to him.

"Danki, little one."

Leah moaned. "I'm to blame, and I'm so ashamed. The bishop must hate me."

"Nonsense." Mamm covered Leah's hand. "He doesn't hate you. He cares about you."

Daniel bit his lip. "The bishop suggested you inquire if Noah's aunt and uncle would consider Leah staying with them in Lancaster until Butch simmers down."

Anna splayed her fingers on the table. "We'll not abandon her by handing her off to another family. Noah chose a life away from us. Sending Leah to live with his family would be awkward for everyone. Leah's leaving Berlin isn't an option I'm willing to consider!"

This was a side of Anna he hadn't observed. She was upset. He didn't blame her. The bishop had raised the hairs on his neck when he mentioned Leah leaving Berlin. He would keep silent.

Mamm stamped her foot. "Anna Plank, you calm down. The bishop has her best interest at heart. I've forgiven Leah, but she is responsible for her error in judgment. We, as a family, have to deal with the consequences. I agree we won't send her away. We will stand our ground and ask God for His protection and guidance." She refilled Daniel's water glass. "Daniel, we are blessed we have you here to watch over us."

"I will do what I can to keep your family safe. I'm confident the sheriff will too."

Otis wagged his tail and barked.

Beth laughed, knelt on the floor, and petted the dog. "Otis is trying to get my attention." She petted his head. "You're a good boy." She gave Mamm her best puppy dog expression. "Can Otis sleep in my bed? Please, Mamm?"

Leah raised her sad face to her Mamm's. "I'd rest easier if you'd let Otis stay in our room tonight."

Scratching the dog's back, Mamm looked at Beth. "He can stay in your room if Daniel agrees." She rolled her shoulders and stretched her arms. "I can hardly keep my eyes open. Let's go to bed."

Daniel grinned. "It's fine with me if Otis sleeps in your room."

Beth bounced on her toes. "Danki, Daniel!"

Mamm, Leah, and Beth bid Daniel good night and left him and Anna alone at the kitchen table.

Otis stayed close to Beth.

Anna's face softened and she slumped in her chair.

Daniel fought to reach out and gently cover her hand. She had a fierce love for her family. Noah should've understood leaving them would've ripped her heart in two. His family had been close, but the Planks had a tighter bond. It hadn't taken him much time to recognize their bond. He enjoyed being accepted into their snug, warm circle. "I'll get up early and help with the morning milking and feeding the animals before I take you to the shop."

He followed Anna to the sitting room and watched her unfold the clean set of sheets and blankets and make the bed. She fluffed the feather-stuffed pillow and put it on the cot. "Is there anything else I can get you?"

She spoiled him by fixing his bedding and serving him food. Her eyelids were heavy and her shoulders slumped. He longed to kiss her good night, but he wouldn't dare. "No, I'm fine." He threw her an impish grin. "I had an interesting conversation with the bishop about you."

Anna lifted her eyebrows. "Me?"

"Jah. I told him I asked you to consider marrying me when you were ready."

A mischievous grin crossed her lips. "You didn't actually ask me to marry you."

"Anna Plank, asking you to consider me for a husband is the same as asking you to marry me." He wrinkled his nose and shrugged. "Am I right?"

She lifted her left shoulder and raised her eyebrows. A coy smile tugged the corners of her sweet mouth.

He'd mishandled asking her to marry him. He should make his proposal a formal one. Kneeling on one knee, he took her hand in his. "Anna Plank, I love you. Will you marry me?"

"Why, Daniel Bontrager, I'd be thrilled to!" She clasped his hand. "Do you mind keeping our news a secret for a while? I'm not ready to set a date. I'd like us to continue spending time together and to wait until the unpleasantness with Butch is over. Surely he'll soon leave us alone." Daniel's proposal had sprung happiness in her soul, put a bounce in her step, and had met all her expectations. They didn't have any problems between them putting her nerves on edge, unlike when Noah had proposed before he left. She looked forward to building a life with him, becoming the mamm of their kinner, and couldn't wait to share her life with him.

Daniel clapped a hand to his chest. His heart raced. He and Anna were getting married! "We can wait, but I'd marry you tomorrow if I could!" He lowered his voice barely above a whisper. "I'd kiss you if I didn't think your mamm or schweschders might walk in on us."

She chuckled. "I wouldn't object if it wasn't so risky." She tapped his nose. "I love you, Daniel."

"You've made me the happiest man in the world tonight." He brushed her fingers with his. "Get a good night's rest."

She left him and shut the door.

Daniel got on his knees and folded his hands. "Dear Heavenly Father, please forgive me where I have failed You. Please protect me and the Planks from Butch Winter. Guide me to the right decisions. Danki for Your love and mercy. Amen."

After rising, he went to bed in his stocking feet and clothes. He didn't want to worry about being indecent if something happened during the night. He got comfortable in his cot and stretched the soft covers to his neck. Staring at the ceiling, he patted his racing heart. Bursting with excitement, he doubted he'd sleep a wink tonight. Mrs. Anna Bontrager. His fraa. He couldn't wait to have her by his side.

Crash!

Otis ran to the door and barked.

Daniel leapt to his feet, opened the door, and scanned the grounds. There was quiet in the dark night. The only light came from the full moon illuminating the barnyard. A gray tiger cat scurried off the porch. The animal had knocked an old, empty metal water pitcher off a small oak table.

Otis sailed past him and shot off after the cat.

He whistled sharply. "Otis! Kumme back to the haus!" He and the Planks didn't need any further commotion from these rascals tonight.

Tail between his legs and head down, Otis padded reluctantly back inside.

Anna poked her head out her door. "What caused the noise?"

Her long, beautiful braid hung over her shoulder, and he blinked in surprise. His breath caught at the sight of her, radiant, even when sleepy. "A stray cat. Go back to bed. Everything is fine, sweetheart."

She yawned, nodded, and closed the door.

He got back in bed. For the first time since he'd met her, Anna didn't have her kapp on. Her braid had been much longer than he'd thought. *She is so pretty and sweet*. He would do everything in his power to protect her.

He swallowed the lump in his throat. Tonight the intrusion was an animal. What if the noise had been caused by Butch? He squeezed his eyes shut in anger. He'd never encountered a man as mean as Butch Winter. The bully was determined to inflict harm on him and the Planks. He doubted talking sensibly to the troublemaker would dampen his resolve to punish them because of Leah's rejection of him. His Amish vow to remain nonviolent would be sorely challenged if Butch raised a hand or gun to someone he loved. Most especially Anna.

Monday morning, Anna cooked eggs and pancakes with Mamm while stealing glances out the window. Daniel was feeding the hog notorious for escaping the pen the minute the door opened. He had a close eye on the animal. Her schweschders were feeding the chickens. It was as if she'd known him all her life. Yet she looked forward to learning more about his life before he came to Berlin. They had finished the early morning milking, feeding the animals, and collecting the eggs. Daniel had completed most of the chores and he played hide-and-seek with Beth and teased Leah, chasing her with a little white mouse. They laughed and enjoyed him. She'd relaxed and been comfortable, unlike the unrest she'd experienced with Noah the last several months before he left. Even with Butch's threatening behavior, she was assured Daniel would handle whatever problem came their way. His staying last night in the next room had been a great comfort to her.

He, Otis, and her schweschders scrambled in the door chuckling, their faces flushed, and smiling.

Leah gasped, bent, and held her stomach. "Daniel chased me around the yard, while Otis followed and barked for him to stop." She pinched off a piece of bread and fed the morsel to the dog. "Good boy."

Beth giggled. "I think he peeks when I go hide. He finds me right away!"

"I'll never tell." Daniel grinned and shook his head at his faithful companion. "Otis is a traitor. He loves Beth and Leah more than he does me." He pouted his lips and scratched Otis's back. "You fickle boy."

Otis barked, nudged his leg, walked over to Beth, and flopped at her feet.

Sitting next to Daniel, Anna buttered her pancake. "Your dog keeps an eye out for his master at all times, even when he's playing with Beth. It's sweet."

Leah scratched Otis's ear. "He snores, but I'm not

complaining. I slept soundly having him near to protect us last night."

Mamm served freshly scrambled eggs. "Daniel, don't be shy. There's plenty of food here. Eat up." She set a steaming bowl of grits, a plate of hot bacon and ham, a small bowl of butter, and a basket of warm, fresh-baked bread on the table.

"I never have a big breakfast at my haus. What a treat!" Daniel placed a snowy-white cloth napkin on his lap.

Leah forked a slice of ham and slid the pork onto her plate. "I read the front page of the newspaper the other day about the Ford Model A. It was quite interesting."

Mamm set her coffee cup on the table and heaved an aggravated sigh. "You shouldn't be reading the newspaper or dwelling on motorcars."

Beth wiped butter from her mouth with the back of her sleeve. "May I ride in a motorcar someday, Mamm?"

"Where are your manners, Beth Plank? Use your breakfast cloth." She sighed. "If we need to travel a long distance, we may pay an Englischer to take us by motorcar or we may go by boat or train. As you've already been told before, we Amish are not to drive or purchase motorcars. We don't allow ourselves to get caught up in worldly things. We need to maintain our simple life and concentrate on things of God."

Anna waited for Beth to argue. "Do you understand what Mamm is saying?"

"I do. I'm happy with Amish life too. I don't want to do anything to make God unhappy. Besides, I enjoy riding in our buggy and wagon. Our horses are my friends. I wouldn't want to hurt their feelings."

Leah choked on her water. "I'm surprised you didn't put up more of a fuss. You're growing up, little schweschder."

Grinning from ear to ear, Beth snapped a piece of bacon in two and stuffed it in her mouth.

Anna grinned. Daniel fit together with her family as well as a soft, snug glove. It was as if she'd known him all her life. She'd wait until their problem with Butch was resolved to consider a wedding date.

She cleaned the kitchen with Mamm, while Daniel got the wagon and horse ready.

Beth waved good-bye and scampered to Mrs. Hochstetler, complaining she wished school would start soon.

Anna glanced out the window. Daniel was watching Beth go next door.

She followed Mamm and Leah outside and climbed in next to them. They all enjoyed the slight breeze and warm air on the way.

Daniel dropped the women off at the General Store and Grace's Dry Goods Shop. "I'll pick you up at five."

Anna grinned. "Danki."

She studied him scanning the area before he guided the horse away to go to his first job. She darted her eyes around town. No sign of Butch anywhere. The sheriff waved to them from across the boardwalk. She returned his wave, nodded, unlocked the door, and went inside the shop with Leah.

Throughout the day, Charity Lantz and other Amish friends brought in quilts for her to sell in the store. She and Leah enjoyed visiting and catching up on their news, grateful the store was slow and allowed them time to chat. Five rolled around fast. She hooked her arm through Leah's after locking up. They met Mamm at the General Store.

On time, Daniel halted the wagon and waited for them to settle. Again, she watched him survey the area for any signs of danger on the way home. She did the same. Nothing. She relaxed and sniffed the honeysuckle to the left of them.

She and Leah told Daniel and Mamm about their stock of new quilts and all the good things happening in their friends' lives.

They pulled into the lane leading to the haus. Anna gasped and pointed to Beth. "Mrs. Hochstetler doesn't have a dog. Beth's playing with a fluffy white one in her yard. It looks like a tiny fur ball."

Daniel laughed. "Otis is taken with his new friend. He's on the dog's heels."

Beth ran to them, carrying the white dog. "Isn't she beautiful? Pet her. Mrs. Hochstetler said I can have her if you grant me your permission. Oh, can I keep her, Mamm? Please let me keep her. Otis and Cotton are good friends already. I've had so much fun with them today."

Mamm scrutinized the dog. "Where did you find her?"

"She wandered into the yard. Mrs. Hochstetler thinks the owner didn't want her anymore and abandoned her here."

Leah reached for the animal. "The sweet little dog must've been scared and hungry. May I hold her?"

"Mrs. Hochstetler poured water in a bowl and put food in another for my new little friend. She gobbled up both fast. Otis and I named her Cotton." She petted Daniel's dog. "Didn't we, Otis?"

Otis barked and licked her arm.

Daniel joined them. "She is a pretty little dog." He scratched Cotton's ear.

The white dog licked his hand and wagged her tail.

Leah nuzzled her nose in Cotton's neck. "She's adorable."

Mamm chuckled. "Who could resist her pug nose, chubby little body, and bouncy white hair. Cotton is a perfect name for her."

Anna pointed her finger at Beth's chest. "Listen, you will have to take her outside to do her business, feed, and bathe her. She isn't a toy you can put aside."

Mamm crossed her arms against her chest. "Anna's right, Beth. Will you commit to taking care of Cotton?"

She bobbed her head and snuggled the dog close. "I'll take care of whatever she needs. I promise."

"All right, you can keep her." Mamm smiled.

"Yippee!" Beth snuggled the dog.

Leah petted her. "It will be fun to have her around."

Daniel stepped to his wagon. "Sounds like Otis has a new friend." He glimpsed at Anna. "I'm going home to feed the animals. I'll be back soon."

"Take your time." Anna waved to him, along with the rest of her family.

Leah and Beth separated outside to milk the cow, feed the animals, and muck the stalls, while she and Mamm cooked supper.

Two hours later, Anna greeted Daniel coming in the kitchen, and they enjoyed a hearty meal with her family.

Leah emptied her leftovers onto two plates. "We can feed these to the dogs. I'll wash the dishes, and Beth, you dry them."

Beth shrugged and took heavy steps to the sink. "Oh, all right."

"I'm off to fold a basketful of laundry." Mamm left the kitchen.

Daniel leaned close to Anna's ear. "Would you join me for a walk?"

Nodding, she followed him out the door. Breathing in the warm evening air, she stepped alongside him and they strolled to their spot. The pond's water stood as still as a pane of glass, and the lush green grass and straight tall maple and oak trees painted a serene picture across her family's property. She sat and leaned back against an old oak tree and waited for Daniel to sit next to her. "Are you happy you chose to live in Jonathan's haus?"

He plucked and toyed with a tall blade of grass. "I'm comfortable and making the haus my own." He met her gaze. "When you marry me, we'll live there first. If you'd prefer a larger haus, I'd build you one. You can arrange everything inside. You do a wonderful job with your displays in the shop."

Anna pressed a hand to her heart. Daniel accommodated her at every turn. Their relationship was easy. He'd complimented her on her displays, cooking, and so many things. She felt loved and adored. "Your haus is perfect for us. I'd be content to live there indefinitely." It was exciting to discuss their future. "Have you considered how many kinner you want?"

"Five would be ideal, but I'd settle for whatever number of kinner you have in mind. Hopefully, God will choose to bless us with kinner."

Her breath caught and she hugged herself. She'd assumed she'd have kinner. The thought hadn't occurred to her she might not. Whether she had a male or female boppli didn't matter to her. She would be thankful if they were healthy. And if they had a physical handicap, she'd love them more. Noah had wanted only one child. She'd reconciled to having one boppli to please him, but she'd struggled with wanting more kinner if they married. Daniel had removed that worry. "I hope we're blessed with kinner. Five would be a good number."

"The more we communicate about what we want out of life, the more excited I am to start a future with you. We haven't disagreed on anything yet."

Her throat constricted. She hesitated to broach the subject of working after having her first boppli. Working was out of the question for most women. Of course, she'd not manage the shop after her second boppli, but she achieved great satisfaction managing Grace's Dry Goods Shop. "What's your opinion about me working at the shop after our first child is born? I could ask Mrs. Hochstetler to watch the child."

His cheerful expression turned stern. "Our child and home should be your first priorities rather than working. I'd prefer you quit your job after you find out you're with child. We will have enough money to live comfortably. There's no need for you to work."

Heat rose to her cheeks. She studied the gray clouds forming above them. They matched the new tone their once-cheerful conversation had taken. "Running the shop is something I enjoy, Daniel. Ordering supplies, keeping the records, meeting and waiting on customers, displaying the quilts and dry goods are things I do well. I'd prefer to remain there for as long as I can. I'd quit when I was with child the second time."

His tone firm, Daniel crossed his arms. "Managing our household and caring for a boppli will be difficult enough without adding the responsibility of managing a store. I would have to insist you stay home."

Most fraas stayed home with or without kinner. Her mamm worked after their daed passed because they needed the income. Keeping her job was important to her. Why couldn't he be more understanding? "I wish you'd take time to consider my request."

He stood and swiped one palm over the other. "I stand firm on my decision. Kinner need their mamm's full attention. You don't have a sufficient reason to deny your kinner your time." He offered her his hand to help her to her feet.

Rising, she grasped his fingers, her heart heavy with disappointment. Silently they returned to the haus. Her family had gone to their separate rooms, and they were alone. She bowed her head and whispered, "Is there anything I can get you before I go to my room?"

His soft and loving gaze met hers. "No, danki. Sleep well."

She squeezed his hand gently, turned, and padded away. She turned up the flame in her lamp, removed the pins from her dress, shrugged out of it, and put on her nightgown. After climbing in bed, she rested her head on the pillow and tears of sadness wet her cheeks. It was early to discuss having boppli with Daniel, but she wanted to know his opinion about kinner and her working as a new mamm before they wed. She didn't want to disappoint Grace and quit any sooner than she had to. She rolled her eyes. Who was she fooling? Her friend would most likely agree with Daniel. Grace had asked her to manage the store after she'd discovered she was with child. She'd not hesitated to stay home.

The shop had given Anna a sense of accomplishment. Managing a business before she'd met Grace had never entered her mind. The colorful and perfectly stitched quilts displayed on the walls, and the shelves filled with beautiful-patterned dry goods, provided a pleasant environment to work in. She'd miss every little thing about managing the shop.

Twinges of guilt pricked her conscience. She rubbed her temples as a dull ache throbbed in her head. She sat up, relit the lamp, and reached for her King James Bible. Flipping the pages to Isaiah Chapter Thirty, Verse One, she read in a whisper, *"'Woe to the rebellious children, saith the LORD, that take counsel, but not of me; and that cover with a covering, but not of my spirit, that they may add sin to sin.'"*

She had allowed her selfish desire to take hold of her. What had she been thinking? Guilt riveted through her. God would never be happy with her choosing to put work over and above her family. She'd been prideful and ungrateful. Daniel loved her and wanted to provide for his family. What more could she ask? She'd apologize to him tomorrow and tell him she'd had a change of heart and would quit the shop whenever he wished her to.

After crawling out of bed, she dropped to her knees, rested her elbows on the bed, folded her hands, and pressed them to her bowed forehead. "Dear God, forgive me for my prideful attitude and for pursing my selfish desires with Daniel. I'm sorry for being selfish and stubborn. Danki for bringing him into my life. Please protect Daniel, my family, and me from harm. Danki for Your mercy and grace. Amen." She rose and got back in bed. She turned out the flame and pulled the sheet up over her. The summer air was warm.

Thunder clapped and she startled. Regret trickled from her head to her toes. Had she put shadows of doubt in Daniel's mind about marrying her?

Chapter Nine

Anna got up Tuesday morning and milked the cows. Her mamm and schweschders fed the rest of the animals. Daniel had gotten up before them and left a note saying he'd gone home to tend to his animals. He would return in time for breakfast.

She had to get Daniel alone and ask his forgiveness for her rash behavior, but the task wouldn't be easy with her family around. Finished with chores a little while later, she went to her room. She peeked out the window. Daniel was kumming down the lane. She dressed into her work clothes and joined her family in the kitchen in time to greet Daniel coming in the door. "Good morning." She glanced at the handsome and protective man and her heart beat faster.

"Good morning." Daniel gave her a half grin.

Mamm served them, and Leah and Beth smiled and turned their attention to Daniel's amusing story about chasing the sow back in the barn earlier at his haus.

Beth and Leah told about the hens fighting over their breakfast.

Daniel carried his empty plate to the dry sink. "Take your time. I'll hook up the horse and buggy and wait outside. The weather is perfect today. It's hot and sunny with a slight breeze."

Her stomach churned. She swallowed two bites of buttered bread. "I'm not hungry. Beth, are you interested in the rest of my breakfast?"

Leah pressed a hand to Anna's forehead. "You're not warm. Are you ill?"

"I'm fine. It's nothing." She hurried to the pump outside and filled a pail of water to rinse the dishes. Scanning the yard, she spotted Daniel. *Time to talk to him.*

The door banged shut. Beth ran out. "I'm going to Mrs. Hochstetler's. Have a good day." Her schweschder skipped off.

Anna went inside and helped Mamm and Leah wash the dishes. She followed behind them outside to join Daniel.

The opportunity to approach him alone was lost. She shut her eyes for a moment. Not apologizing to Daniel would prick at her mind throughout the day if she didn't get a chance to resolve their dispute before he dropped them off in town.

"Anna, we're running late. Leah's got your dinner to take to the shop."

Leah held up a basket. "I packed cold chicken sandwiches and ginger cookies."

Leah and Mamm sat in the back and left the front seat for her. She got in beside Daniel.

He smiled at her, flicked the straps, and drove them to town. Leah laughed about Otis and Cotton snoring while sleeping in her and Beth's room. Anna struggled to sit still. She bumped Daniel's elbow with hers when the wagon wheel hit a rut in the road. She'd hurt and confused him. She doubted he considered her the perfect fraa. Tonight, after supper, she'd ask him to go for a canoe ride. It would be the perfect place for her to apologize for her impulsive words last night.

Daniel halted the buggy in front of the General Store for Mamm to get out.

She glanced at him and grinned. "Leah and I can get out here. The shop's close."

"No. I'll take you." Daniel coaxed the horse forward, and he dropped them off in front of the dry goods shop.

Leah handed Daniel a clean flour sack. "Here's cold chicken, an apple, and oatmeal cookies for your dinner today."

"Oatmeal cookies! I'll eat those first. Danki."

Anna and Leah got out of the buggy.

She waved. "Have a good day, Daniel. I'll look forward to seeing you at five."

He tipped his hat. "Me too, Anna."

Anna unlocked the door, pushed it open, and stepped inside.

Hand on her hip, Leah faced her. "Out with it. What's wrong between you and Daniel? You and he were cordial, but strained. Not giving each other endearing glances and engaging in cheerful conversation. You fidgeted with your kapp string all the way here."

"I don't want to have this discussion. Do you mind?"

Leah waggled her finger. "Jah, I mind. I'm not moving until you tell me what's going on. Daniel is the perfect Amish man for you. I care about you and him. You're guilty of something. You won't look me in the eyes. Tell me what happened."

Anna crossed her arms. "Daniel and I discussed

kinner. I asked him if we were to get married, if he
had any objection to my asking Mrs. Hochstetler to
care for our first child while I worked. He is firmly
against my idea. I pursued the matter by expressing
how much I enjoyed working here. He wouldn't
budge. We walked in silence to the haus and we were
cordial, but there was an uncomfortable silence between us."

Leah slapped the counter. "Anna Plank, why would
you suggest working if he wants you to quit? He's offering to care for you. Why would you risk losing him
to have your way? God would not honor your request.
You're being stubborn and ungrateful."

Her schweschder's words struck her remorseful
conscience. Family came first. It was the basis of Amish
teaching. She wished she hadn't spoken to Daniel
about her ridiculous notion to work. "I wanted to
apologize to him earlier, but I couldn't catch him
alone to speak in private. I prayed and asked God to
forgive me, and I'll ask Daniel to do the same."

Hand on hip, Leah narrowed her brows. "As soon
as we get home, you find time to tell him you're sorry.
He loves and adores you."

The shop door clanged against the wall. She gasped
and froze. *Noah.* Her heart beat wildly in her chest.
What was he doing here? Visiting? She stared at him
in disbelief and stepped back.

Leah clasped Anna's hand and bristled. She glared
at Noah. "What are you doing back in Berlin?"

Noah removed his hat, raked his fingers through
his sandy-blond hair, and curled the corners of his
mouth in a cheerful smile. "I've kumme home to stay."

Anna stared at him and swallowed. Her heart
raced. She couldn't kumme to grips with the fact he
was standing right in front of her. She had no words

to say to him. His declaration muddled her mind. *He is staying in Berlin permanently?*

Noah took one step, paused, and then took another step closer to her. He spoke one notch above a whisper and twisted his hat in his hands. "Anna, say something. Aren't you happy to see me?"

Leah stepped between them, raised her chin, and took a defiant stance. "You left her behind, broken-hearted, to move to Lancaster. She's moved on with her life. How dare you show up to rip her heart open again!"

Gripping his hat, Noah lifted his pleading eyes to Leah. "I understand why you're frustrated with me, Leah, and I'll answer any questions you have once I speak to Anna. Please let me have a few minutes alone with her."

Leah put her hands on Anna's shoulders. "Are you ready to talk to Noah?"

She nodded and bit her bottom lip.

"I'll mind the shop." She motioned to the back. "The two of you should go behind the store to talk."

"I'll be quick." Anna motioned for him to accompany her outside. She stepped out the door, blinked, and hugged herself tight. He'd left her in Berlin to pursue his selfish desires. She'd never expected him to return. A bundle of joy, confusion, and frustration swirled through her.

He reached for her hands. "Anna, I should've waited until your workday ended and you were at home to show up unannounced, but I couldn't wait to speak to you. I've missed you. My life is incomplete without you. I made a terrible mistake leaving you, and I beg your forgiveness. If you'll grant me another chance, I'll stay in Berlin and we can raise a family like you asked."

She blinked back tears. "Your desire to wander wasn't our only problem. You shrugged off my concerns when I said we no longer fit together, and you didn't think they were worth your remaining here and working them out. Why now?"

Gazing into her eyes, he clasped his hands to his chin. "I love you and I believe we can solve whatever problems we may encounter. You still love me, right?"

Doubt, fear, dread, and love clouded her mind. She was confused. Noah was her first love, and she had good memories with him before their relationship turned sour. She had no doubt she loved Daniel. Her heart ripped in two. "Love isn't enough to build a firm foundation for marriage. Before you left, we argued more than we enjoyed pleasant conversations."

Noah paled. "Are you saying you won't give me a chance? Please, Anna, don't give up on us."

"You're the one who gave up on us, Noah." Her head throbbed. She must consider Daniel. "I've had a lot of changes in my life since you left."

"What do you mean?"

She clasped a fistful of her apron and focused on her feet. She must tell him she'd fallen in love with Daniel. Gossip spread like a knocked-over pail of fresh spring water. She took a big breath and blew it out slowly. "Do you remember Daniel Bontrager?"

He raised his eyebrows. "Jah, what would Daniel have to do with you and me?"

"Daniel is a good friend of our family. He's helped us in numerous ways. I've invited him to suppers, and we've taken walks and had conversations about life, our hopes, and our dreams. Our friendship has grown more serious. I've agreed to marry him." She kept her chin to her chest and waited. The silence awkward, she closed her eyes for a moment. *Why doesn't he say something?* She glanced at him.

His damp cheeks and pale face hurt her soul. Noah had been the love of her life. The man she'd envisioned becoming her husband until they had argued more frequently about their differences and he'd chosen to leave Berlin.

"Is it a marriage of convenience or are you in love with him?"

"I love him very much." Her words were true. She had no doubt about her love for Daniel.

He gasped and his face paled. "Do you still love me?"

"I don't know how I feel about you. I opened my heart to him because you and I no longer had a future."

"I beg you." He stepped closer to her. "Please tell him to step aside. Give us time to heal." He tucked his chin to his chest and stared at the ground. "Please, Anna, may I kumme to your haus later? I must apologize to your family and ask them to forgive me. Getting back on good terms with them is important to me, no matter what happens between us."

Her family loved Noah and Daniel. They would voice their opinions, but they would abide by her decision and accept whoever she chose with open arms. She would have to tell Daniel about Noah and this conversation. She needed time to sort out her emotions. Would Daniel understand and give her time or would he withdraw his proposal? Her stomach clenched. She'd upset him with her request to work after the birth of a boppli, and she hadn't had a chance to recant. She had to right this wrong between them. She couldn't imagine letting him go. Would he listen and try to understand? "Noah, I'm shocked you've kumme back. I'm confused, anxious, and happy, all at the same time. I need to tell Daniel about this conversation, and I'll need time to think."

He gently lifted her chin with his forefinger to meet his eyes. Those same captivating blue eyes she'd fallen in love with three years ago. "You've had little time with Daniel compared to the three years we were together. Those years must mean something."

He was right. Their time together had created precious memories of laughter, fun, and serious plans for their future before they encountered their differences and he left Berlin. Those years loving him did mean something, whether she wanted to admit it or not. She and Daniel hadn't needed much time to fall in love. They were compatible and comfortable with each other. They shared the desire for the same lifestyle. He hadn't attempted to change her or the way she did things. She owed it to herself, Noah, and Daniel to sort out her feelings before she could commit to either one of them. She gazed at him in silence.

He touched her forehead with his. "I'm going to pray you choose me."

She stepped back and rubbed her arms, scanning the grounds for anyone within earshot. A man fetched water from his pump and went back inside. "If there would be any chance for us, and I'm not saying there is, you have to be content with me the way I am and stop trying to change me."

"I regret not taking your concerns more seriously. I shouldn't have nagged you to alter your ways. I'll try my best not to change you to fit my mold."

She didn't want the man she married to constantly be annoyed with her choices. She questioned when he left and again now whether they were well matched. Had he matured and discovered he loved her for the way she was? She pressed her hands to her face. Confusion, memories, and mixed emotions rumbled in her mind.

Part of her wanted to believe Noah, and the other part said marry Daniel. Noah had scarred what they once had together. Daniel had introduced her to a future of comfort and security. Reuniting with Noah would be fraught with uncertainty and risk, but he'd been her first love. Should she give him a second chance? He'd left her. She groaned. She couldn't have any lingering doubt about Noah. She had to kumme to a clear conclusion. Choosing Daniel or Noah would be one of the hardest and most important decisions she would make in her life. "I need time, Noah. There's much to consider. I should get back inside."

"I'll leave you alone, but only for a few days. I'm not giving up until you tell me I no longer have a place in your heart." He brushed her hand with his, flashed her a sad grin, and disappeared around the corner of the building.

The rush of happy memories she'd once had with him returned with force again. The brush of his hand on hers sent a flurry of excitement through her. The same flutter of excitement she enjoyed when Daniel touched her hand. She had crucial matters to discuss with Daniel tonight.

Leah met her at the back door. "Kumme inside. It's been like walking on jagged stones waiting for you to tell me about your conversation with Noah. And don't skirt the details."

Anna went into the shop and closed the door behind her. "Noah wants immediate forgiveness. I'm frustrated with him, and I need time to unravel my feelings, and I love Daniel. Oh, Leah, I am so confused."

Leah rubbed her shoulder. "Noah is funny, kind, smart, and adventuresome. His downfall was leaving you and trying to change you the last several months you were together."

"He claims he'll stop trying to change me to fit into his mold. I question if he's matured and time away from me has given him clarity about us. It would take time to find out. I'm not sure where my heart is with Noah. I love Daniel, but I can't marry him while my mind is muddled about Noah."

"Daniel is calm and settled, but he's also humorous, intelligent, and kind. He hasn't tried to change you, but you don't have a longer history with him like you do Noah. You have a difficult choice to contemplate."

Slam. Clang. Anna whirled around to face the open door. She froze. *Butch Winter.*

Leah trembled and gripped Anna's hand.

The bully barged in. "Your friend and the bishop showed up at my house complaining I'd been threatening you, Leah. They upset my parents."

The man's eyes glittered with resentment. His bold demeanor was threatening and fierce. Staring at the rifle in his hand, Anna quivered and moved in front of Leah. "Please leave. We don't want any trouble."

"Me and Leah got some catchin' up to do. Don't we, little lady?" He shoved Anna against the wall.

Her heart racing, she stumbled but pressed her hand against the wall to right herself.

"Let go of me!" Her schweschder jerked her arm from his grasp and rushed to Anna.

The bold Englischer came between them and

reached for Leah again. "You come here, Leah, or I'll shoot her and drag you outta here!"

Anna elbowed her way in front of Leah again. "Get out!" She eyed the rifle and sucked in her breath for a moment. Would he shoot her? She shuddered.

The shop door slammed open. Anna pressed a hand to her chest. "Daniel! Be careful! He has a rifle!"

Butch scowled and spat tobacco on the floor. "You shut your mouth, or I'll shoot all of ya." He turned and waved the rifle at Daniel. "You get over here with them where I can keep an eye on ya."

Daniel rushed to Anna and Leah, turned his back to them, and shielded them with his widespread arms. He faced the menacing young man, spread his legs in a confident stance, and crossed his arms against his chest. "Leah has told you she's not interested in you. You were in jail for a while. I'm sure you're not anxious to return."

Pointing the rifle at Daniel's chest, Butch scoffed. "You don't tell me what to do. Get out of the way, or I'll shoot you." He pushed the rifle hard into Daniel's chest.

Anna's eyes widened. Her heart pounding, she clasped Leah's hand and, with the other, gripped the back of Daniel's shirt. He had stood fearless and confronted Butch. His courage was admirable and frightening. Butch might kill them.

"Please leave us alone!"

The sheriff and Butch's daed charged into the shop.

The lawman aimed his sidearm. "Put the gun down, Butch!"

Mr. Winter got between Daniel and his son. "You don't want to do anything you'll regret. You'll be put to death! Think of me and your mother. You're our only child. We don't want to lose you."

Butch lowered the rifle but raised it again. "Step out of the way. I aim to teach these simpleminded people a lesson."

Daniel put his arms back and huddled the women behind him. "Don't pull the trigger, Butch!"

Grabbing the barrel of the rifle, Mr. Winter struggled with Butch.

Bang!

Wide-eyed and mouth open, Mr. Winter crumbled to the floor. He groaned and pressed his hand against his shoulder. Blood spread from the wound through his dark green shirt.

"Oh no!" Butch knelt next to him. "Dad, look what you made me do!"

"Ack! Mr. Winter!" Anna put her hands to her cheeks and stared at the blood forming a puddle on the floor around Mr. Winter's shoulder.

Leah pressed fisted hands to her cheeks. "He needs help!"

The young man dropped the rifle and wrung his hands. "I'm sorry. I didn't mean to hurt you, Dad. Why'd you have to get in the way?"

The sheriff kicked the rifle away. It slid across the floor and landed at Daniel's feet. The lawman grabbed the back of the criminal's shirt, forced him facedown on the floor, and handcuffed him. He yanked the young man to his feet. "I'm sorry, folks. Butch's father noticed his son riding out fast from his place with a rifle. He saddled a horse and took off after him but couldn't keep up. When Butch headed into the shop, George came to fetch me." He nodded to Butch's daed. "You did the best thing. I'm holding Butch in jail to wait for the circuit judge, but you can stop and talk to him when you're strong enough."

"Thank you, Sheriff." George Winter winced and moved his head. "Don't cause any more trouble, Son. Do what the lawman tells you."

"I'm sorry, Dad. I didn't mean to shoot you, but you shoulda stayed outta my way."

The sheriff kept a firm hold on his prisoner. "Your dad saved you from making a big mistake, you ungrateful brute." He turned his attention to Daniel. "Will you run over to Dr. Rogers's office and ask him to tend to George?"

"Jah, I'll be glad to."

Anna threw a handful of towels to Daniel. "You can use these to slow the bleeding."

He knelt next to Mr. Winter and applied pressure to the wounded man's injury but held his other palm out to Anna and Leah. "Don't move from where you are until the sheriff leaves with Butch."

Butch squinted and sneered at Anna, Leah, and Daniel. "I wish I'd shot every one of you."

The sheriff shoved him toward the door. "Shut your mouth." He lifted his chin to Daniel. "He'll be locked up for a long time. You won't have to worry about him. The judge will be disgusted Butch brandished a gun and threatened lives in the short time he's been released from custody. I'll leave Butch's rifle. George can take the weapon home. Take care."

Daniel placed Mr. Winter's hand on the towels covering the wound. "Press your hand firmly on the towels to slow the bleeding." He hurried to open the door.

The sheriff gripped Butch's cuffs and the back of his shirt and pushed him toward the door.

Butch planted his feet and spit in Daniel's face. "You're lucky to be alive!"

The sheriff growled and thrust him over the threshold. He leaned back and glanced over his shoulder at Daniel. "Sorry. This one is rowdier than most."

Daniel swiped the sputum from his face with his sleeve. "Good day, Sheriff. Danki again for your help." He ignored the dangerous culprit.

Anna's love for Daniel swelled. He remained calm under immense pressure. She snatched another handful of towels and sat at Mr. Winter's side. "I'll take over while you fetch Dr. Rogers."

"I won't be long." He pointed to their store sign. "Do you want me to turn your sign to show the shop is closed?"

"Please do, and danki."

Watching him turn the sign and leave, she couldn't believe his resolve to stand strong with a rifle pointed at his chest. Daniel had been willing to give his life to protect them. She hadn't doubted he would, but his fearlessness and protective stance surprised her. She had gripped his shirt, and he hadn't trembled during the horrifying experience.

"Leah, lock the door and don't open it until the doctor gets here." She applied more pressure to the gunshot wound.

Mr. Winter groaned and blinked a few times.

"Try to relax. The doctor will be here soon."

Leah stood over them. "I'll lock the door and get water from the pitcher." She hurried to the door and locked it, went to the stand, poured water in a pot, and brought it to Anna.

"How are you doing?" Anna dabbed sweat from Mr. Winter's forehead with a clean cloth.

Opening his eyelids halfway, he winced. "I'll be

fine. I'm worried about my son and my wife. She'll be wrought with grief over our son's violent behavior." His eyes moist, he gazed at her. "I'm so sorry for the trouble he's caused your family. I hope you can forgive him."

Leah returned and sat next to Anna, near Mr. Winter, and passed the pot to Anna. They exchanged a sympathetic glance.

Mr. Winter's sad face pricked her heart. He loved his child and, no matter what his son had done, he wanted the best for him. Anna couldn't imagine the pain the man must suffer watching his child struggle with such a fierce anger and need for control. It had been apparent Butch didn't need much of a reason to fuel his temper. "We forgive him, and we don't hold you responsible for his actions."

Leah wiped a tear from her face and nodded. "I'll get the empty flour sack from underneath the counter. We can use the sack to put the bloody cloths in." She got the bag and accepted the soiled ones from Anna. After plunging them in the sack, she dropped the soiled bag behind her.

Anna leaned way over and reached for a small flat pillow from a chair. "Can you raise your head?"

Mr. Winter raised his head and moaned.

She slid the pillow beneath him. "Does the pillow make you more comfortable?"

"Much better."

Dr. Rogers and Daniel tried to open the locked door. Leah jumped to her feet and let them in.

Anna rose and stepped back.

"We'll get out of your way, Dr. Rogers." Anna relaxed her tense shoulders.

The doctor would help him better than they could. "Thank you. I'll take over. George and his wife have come to me for minor things from time to time like you and Leah, so we're already acquainted." He smiled. "Good afternoon, George. Looks like you've had better days. Don't worry. I'll take good care of you." He lifted the soiled towels. "Anna and Leah, you've done a fine job to control the bleeding."

"Danki, Doctor." Anna's cheeks warmed.

Leah took a step back from Mr. Winter, tucked her chin to her chest, and smiled.

Dr. Rogers removed the bloody towels. He studied the wound. "Let's check the bullet entry and exit. I hope the bullet went clear through." Carefully he lifted Mr. Winter's shoulder to check the other side.

The man groaned.

"I'm sorry. I had to find out if the bullet was lodged in your body. I'm relieved to report it went clean through. We won't have to dig the projectile out of you." Dr. Rogers sprinkled antiseptic powder on the wound.

Mr. Winter grimaced. "I'm relieved. Digging a bullet out of my shoulder sounds awful."

Dr. Rogers threw his bag open and tended to his patient. "You need stitches, but your wound should heal fine if you change the bandages and keep the injury as clean as you can to prevent infection." Dr. Rogers removed his supplies. He drew up a syringe.

"What a relief. I'm grateful for your help, Doctor." Mr. Winter winced as the needle penetrated his skin.

Daniel came alongside Anna. "How are you?"

"We're shaken up but fine. Butch's daed is a sweet man. I feel sorry for him." She clasped her hands in front of her. "I'm so relieved you came in when you did. I can't believe how you stood up to Butch Winter."

"I'd never hesitate to give my life for yours or Leah's."

"You're a brave man, Daniel Bontrager. You're the calmest man I've ever met." She patted Leah's back. "Do you mind if Daniel and I talk behind the store outside?"

"No, go ahead."

Dr. Rogers glimpsed at Leah. "I would like a few more clean towels."

"I'll get them." Leah passed him some from a small display table.

Anna motioned to Daniel to follow her to the back of the room out of everyone's earshot. With all the commotion, she'd forgotten about telling Daniel about Noah. He could've run into Noah in town before he came here. She hoped not. She would prefer he found out about Noah's return from her first. "What brought you here early?"

He shoved his hands in his pockets. "I needed more paint to finish a job. I've been nervous about Butch and thought it best if I checked on you and Leah." He met her gaze. "I would be lost if anything happened to you."

Staring at him, she inhaled his woodsy scent, and admired his thick, brown hair and structured jaw. The calm sound of his voice and the protectiveness he'd displayed during their scary time with Butch reminded her how much she loved him.

"I feared you'd be shot. I couldn't stand to lose you." She fumbled with her kapp strings. "I've had time to ponder my asking your permission for me to manage the shop after having a child, and I'm sorry. It was selfish and foolish of me. I would quit whenever you asked me to without hesitation."

"Anna, sweet Anna, I'm so relieved we can put our dispute behind us. I love you so much. Are you ready to set a wedding date yet? With Butch's arrest, there's nothing else standing in our way."

Dread shot through her. Her throat dry, she dropped her chin to her chest. "I've got some troubling news to tell you. Noah is back in Berlin. He came to the shop, and I couldn't believe my eyes. He said he came back for me. He's asked me to forgive him and pick up where we left off."

Stepping back, Daniel sucked in a loud breath. "What did you tell him?"

The anguish in his voice hurt her heart. "My mind circled with joy, frustration, and confusion. I told him I needed time to sort out my emotions."

"Anna, what about us? Did you tell him about us?"

"Jah! Jah! Of course. I told him I love you very much and we plan to marry." With watery eyes, she gazed at him. "Daniel, I must take time to digest his return and request." She brushed his hand with hers. "I'm sorry I've upset you. Noah's return is shocking for both of us. I'm begging you, please don't walk away from me. Please give me time to think."

He held her hands. "I'm disappointed his return has confused you about us. I'm stunned, but I love you. I'll wait for now."

Leah approached them. "Daniel, Dr. Rogers would appreciate your tying Mr. Winter's and his son's horses behind your wagon and taking him home. He could take himself home, but he's a little shaky and pale."

Daniel nodded to Leah and gave Anna a weak smile. "I'll take him home first. Later, I'll return to take you, Leah, and your mamm home."

She wiped her damp cheeks and, lips trembling, smiled feebly.

His heart heavy, he bid Dr. Rogers good day, went to the livery, returned to the shop, and went inside. He escorted Mr. Winter to the wagon.

Daniel's thoughts ran rampant. Noah had kumme back to Berlin to win Anna's heart again. He could hardly comprehend her revelation. Anna's asking for time to contemplate this new turn of events was more difficult. Noah's history with her held more weight than he'd understood.

He had to put his problems aside and take Mr. Winter home. Butch's daed must be bereft with having to tell his fraa their son had shot him in a scuffle to prevent him from killing Daniel, Anna, and Leah. The pain in the man's shoulder probably paled in comparison to the agony in his heart. He secured the horses and climbed in beside Mr. Winter. "Our ride home isn't a smooth one. Are you in pain?"

"A little but not too bad. I'm weak but capable of making the trip." He winced. "I dread discussing my son's actions with my wife even more than the physical pain. Butch's going to jail again and for a more serious crime will turn her world upside down. We agonize over what we have done wrong in raising him."

Clicking his tongue, Daniel coaxed the horses onward. "You and Mrs. Winter aren't to blame for your son's transgressions. I'm certain you taught him right from wrong. He's responsible for his choices."

Hanging his head, Mr. Winter pressed his arm tighter against himself to minimize the movement of his shoulder on the bumpy road. "I love my son, but I'm relieved he's in jail. I worry each night his temper will escalate and he'll seriously harm someone. I'd hoped he'd learned his lesson while he was there, but he's as unpredictable and dangerous as ever. My wife is a wonderful woman. She's nurturing, loving, and gentle. It's heart-wrenching to watch her suffer because of our son. He'll spout off to her, and she'll make excuses for him. It's her way of coping with him.

"Did your son disrespect you when he was younger?"

"He helped me in the fields and garden, but he kept his distance. After our evening meal, we played board games with him, hoping to lighten his dark moods. He participated and laughed with us, but if he didn't win, he got angry and stomped off to his bedroom. I believe he's not right in the head. I've never met a person so unhappy most of the time for no apparent reason."

"Have you asked Butch if something is bothering him?"

"Many times. He shakes his head 'no 'and apologizes for his bad behavior. Soon after, he shuts me out."

Daniel yearned for a close relationship with his kinner. If he encountered such a dilemma, he'd pray to God for guidance and search the Scriptures for answers. "Have you asked God for help concerning your son?"

The man scratched his neck. "We stopped going to church a while ago. We were too embarrassed about Butch's rabble-rousing in town. We attended the Methodist church where the bell rings each Sunday at nine thirty in the morning. I miss going there."

"If I'm going through a difficult time, I ask God to direct my path. He doesn't always provide the answer I want, but I trust Him to do what's best for me. I read my Bible in search of answers to my problems. I find comfort in Him. I trust He will provide you and Mrs. Winter with the strength and comfort you need. I'm so sorry for your pain and sorrow you're experiencing with Butch."

The man nodded, hanging his head. "Our pastor

and friends have visited us many times and pleaded with us to come back to church. When I did pray, God provided me with a peace I can't explain. I need to get back to praying and attending church services." He glanced at Daniel. "I admire the Amish. You keep your focus on God at all times."

Daniel had his faults, and he hadn't always taken his own advice. He questioned why Noah had returned to take the woman he loved away from him. Why would God allow this turmoil in his life? He rubbed the knot in his neck. It might have nothing to do with him. Could God be using him to teach Anna or Noah something? He didn't want Anna to have any doubts about him for her husband, nor did he want to be used by God to teach them anything. Should he withdraw his proposal or wait? In the meantime, he wouldn't rest easy. "We have our downfalls and problems, too." He brought the horses to a standstill, jumped down, tied the animals to the hitching post, and helped his passenger to the front door.

Mrs. Winter met them. "You're hurt! What happened? Where's Butch?" She helped her husband sit in a cushioned maple high-back chair and knelt beside him. "Are you all right, dear?" She turned her head to Daniel. "Thank you for bringing him home." She stood and wrung her hands. "One of you must tell me what is going on."

Mr. Winter's fraa hadn't taken a breath between asking her questions. They hadn't had a chance to answer them. He knew he best let Mr. Winter explain his injury and Butch's part in it.

Daniel held his hat. "I'll leave and let you have privacy."

Mr. Winter grasped his hand. "Again, I'm sorry for

the trouble my son caused you and your friends. Thank you for all your help."

Mrs. Winter gasped and her mouth fell open. "What trouble has Butch gotten himself into, George? Is he hurt?"

"I'll tell you after Daniel leaves, dear. I've taken up enough of his time."

Mrs. Winter crossed the room and opened the door. "Oh my! I'm so sorry for my outburst. I'm worried sick about my son. Again, I'm grateful to you for bringing my husband home."

"Don't apologize. I understand. Good afternoon." He tipped his hat and left.

On the way home, he had a heavy heart. He resented Butch for treating his parents with disrespect. Missing his mamm's love, hugs, and encouragement, he couldn't relate to the way the wrongdoer acted with his parents. The rage in Butch's eyes suggested something was off about him. Maybe he did have something wrong with him mentally. Why did Butch have such a strong desire for power, dominance, and control?

He went and finished painting the fence he'd repaired for a neighbor and collected payment. He checked the clock on the neighbor's mantel. The women would be waiting for him to pick them up and take them home. He gathered his tools and put everything in the back of the wagon but left enough room for Leah and Mamm to sit in the back. There was enough room for three up front, but he'd leave where to sit to them. He'd gotten used to practically living at the Planks' haus to protect them from Butch. He'd have no good reason to stay at night any longer. He drove to the shop. Would Anna invite him to her haus? Would their time together be awkward? How would her family react to Noah's return and declaring his love for Anna? Would Noah be invited for suppers? He didn't want to compete with Noah for her hand in marriage. He needed a fraa sure of him and only him.

He stared ahead, instead of enjoying the rolling hills and farmland on the way. He shouldn't act in haste. She might conclude she loved him, and not Noah. He'd wait for now. What choice did he have? His heart wouldn't let him walk away from her.

Daniel waved to Leah and his lovely Anna standing outside, waiting on him. Anna's sad eyes and tentative smile showed she wasn't in her usual chipper mood. Noah's return must be burdening her. He'd rather she be sad than giddy with excitement about having Noah in Berlin. He wanted to go back to the way his life was with Anna before Noah's return. He put on a smile and greeted them. "How was the rest of your day?'

Anna sat next to him, and Leah climbed in the back. Anna turned to him. "We reopened the shop, and we had a steady flow of customers but sold only two quilts. Most of them witnessed the sheriff taking Butch to jail, and they were curious about what happened."

Leah asked, "How did your day go, Daniel?"

Shrugging, he said, "I took Mr. Winter home, painted a fence I'd repaired for a neighbor, and he paid me a fair sum." He glanced at Anna. "I've had better days."

Anna met his gaze, her gaze rife with empathy.

He needed to speak to her in private. Would he have a chance to speak with her tonight? He stiffened.

Noah could be taking his place at their table. Squinting, he clutched the reins and clenched his jaw.

"Whoa, boy." He coaxed the horse to halt in front of the General Store. "Good afternoon, Mrs. Plank."

Mamm hoisted herself into the back of the wagon. "Daniel, I'm so relieved you are all safe. I heard about what happened at the shop. I couldn't get away from the General Store to check on all of you, but the sheriff stopped by and assured me you were all fine. I was the only one managing the General Store for most of the day." She rubbed her arms and shuddered. "Butch Winter is a dangerous man. He needs help. Danki for protecting my Anna and Leah!"

"I'm happy to oblige."

"Of course, you'll join us for supper." Mrs. Plank settled next to Leah.

Rolling his shoulders back, he loosened his grip on the reins. "Danki, Mrs. Plank." He glanced at Anna.

She smiled and nodded. "I'm delighted you're kumming over."

He grinned and this time it was genuine. "Me too. Will you take a walk with me later?"

"I'm looking forward to it."

His mood lifted. She'd met his gaze and her sincere eyes reflected joy at his acceptance of her mamm's invitation. He listened as Leah recounted to Mamm her version of Butch barging in and threatening them and shooting his daed.

Mamm said, "The sheriff came to the General Store for tobacco and told us what happened just now. I'm sad for Mr. and Mrs. Winter. It must break their hearts to have their son back in jail, but it's also a relief to know he is safe and unable to hurt anyone. Maybe he's learned his lesson."

Anna shook her head. "His temper is out of control.

I wish he'd turn from his evil ways, but he's so full of anger. We'll have to remember him in our prayers."

Leah said, "Mamm, Noah came to the shop today. He's returned to Berlin to stay."

Mamm touched Anna's shoulder. "You must've been stunned when Noah came to the shop."

Anna fidgeted with her kapp string. "Please, I'd rather not talk about him right now."

"Jah, of course. I should've waited until later to ask you about him."

Daniel heaved a breath. "I don't mind, Mrs. Plank. Anna told me she needs time to sort out her emotions about Noah." He scooted back in the seat. "I love your dochder, and I asked her to marry me before he returned. We kept our plans to marry to ourselves because Anna was afraid friends might think she had jumped from one man to another too quickly. In light of Noah's return, please understand you're like family to me and you should be aware of where I stand with Anna." He exchanged a loving look with Anna.

"I've noticed the way you look at her, and she's been giddy and all smiles around you. My heart goes out to you, Daniel. You have my blessing should Anna choose to marry you." Mamm cleared her throat. "We're fond of you and Noah. I'm sure Anna will ask God to give her direction."

Anna blushed and wiped the tear dripping onto her cheek. "I am praying for God's guidance, and I'll search the Scriptures for answers. I don't want to hurt Daniel or Noah." She glimpsed at Daniel.

He swallowed around the lump in his throat. He'd ask God to steer Anna toward him. Noah had abandoned her. The man hadn't cared enough about her wishes to stay and marry her. It would take the force of a tornado to remove him from Berlin, away from Anna, if he'd been in Noah's place. "I'm glad we're talking about Noah and me openly."

Leah sighed. "Butch's interference in our lives would've been a lot scarier without your protecting us. It seems as if you've always been a part of our lives. No matter what happens, please don't walk out of our lives, Daniel."

Anna lowered her chin to her chest and wiped her damp face.

He wished he could hold and soothe her. Leah's plea touched him. He'd miss them if he had to back away because Anna chose Noah. "I care for all of you, but I can't make any promises when we don't know what the future holds. I may not be able to remain in Berlin if Anna isn't a part of my life. Running into her in town and church would be too painful for me." He halted the wagon in front of the haus and climbed out. He tied the horse to the hitching post.

Beth embraced the squirming Cotton, and Otis stood at her side as she ran to them. "I watched you coming down the lane. I've been playing outside at Mrs. Hochstetler's. I'll tell her you're home, and then I'll kumme back to help with the cooking." She skipped away.

Mamm touched Anna's arm. "Leah and I will be inside. Take your time kumming in and speak with Daniel."

"Danki, Mamm."

Leah frowned. "I should have waited to tell Mamm about Noah. I'm sorry, Anna."

"I'm not upset with you. By telling her in front of Daniel, you allowed him the opportunity to speak his mind and bring our plans out in the open."

Daniel grinned. "One of my favorite things about being with your family is the openness you share. I'm thankful you include me in these conversations and permit me to make clear where I stand."

"I agree. I'll leave you and Daniel to talk in private and go and help Mamm." Leah left them.

Beth said, "I had the best day! Thomas's mamm came to visit Mrs. Hochstetler. Thomas and I played checkers. I let him win. He still won't agree to marry me someday, but I'll keep working on him."

Anna and Daniel chuckled.

Daniel grinned. "Give Thomas time, little one. You both have a lot of growing up to do before you need to worry about getting married."

Anna smiled. "Beth, do you mind if Daniel and I chat alone?"

Her little schweschder shrugged her shoulders. "I don't mind. I'll go help Leah and Mamm." She picked up Cotton. "Kumme on, Otis."

Anna twisted her hands. "I'm shocked and confused Noah is back. I need to get used to the idea and sort out my feelings. I love you, Daniel. Please try and understand. I need time to put all this in perspective."

He held her hands. "I'm hurt Noah's return interfered with your firm commitment to me. I wish you were as certain of me as I am of you. His return and effect on you is confusing for me, too."

Beth came out and interrupted them. "I can't find the sugar cookie recipe. Mamm said I could make a batch."

Anna shrugged. "I'll have to search for my note. I don't remember where I put it." She tilted her chin. "We'll finish our conversation after supper, Daniel?"

"Of course." It would be wonderful if he and Anna could put their troubles behind them and be happy. When would she make up her mind? She wouldn't have an answer to his question, so he wouldn't ask it. His patience was waning, and a full day hadn't passed yet.

Steam rose above the carrots and green beans Mamm placed in the center of the table. Thick slices of ham arranged on a platter made his mouth water. His stomach growled, and he couldn't wait to taste the pork. Daniel joined hands with Anna and Leah, prayed, and asked God to bless their food.

Beth passed him a dish of steaming hot vegetables. "Take all you want. There are more in the pan on the stove."

"Danki." He plopped a heaping spoonful of carrots and green beans onto his plate.

Forking a small piece of ham, Leah cleared her throat. "Beth, we have some news."

"What?"

Anna told Beth about Butch. "We can put him out of our minds. He's in jail, and he's likely to stay there for a good long while. I don't want you to worry."

Beth swiped her forehead with the back of her hand. "I'm thankful you, Leah, and Daniel weren't hurt."

They discussed Butch and the scary event for a few minutes.

Leah waved a dismissive hand. "Enough about Butch Winter. We have more news. We had a visitor at the shop you might be interested in."

Beth wrinkled her forehead. "Who?"

Anna stared at her plate. The room silenced. Each of them had ceased eating. Hearing Noah's name and talking about him sickened Daniel, but Beth should learn Noah was back in town from family.

Leah lowered her chin but met Beth's gaze. "Noah."

Bobbing her head up, Beth leaned forward. "Is he here for a visit?"

Sucking in her top lip and toying with the corner of her white cotton napkin, Anna stared at her hands. "He's staying in Berlin. He's asked me to forgive him and he wants to marry me."

Daniel stifled the urge to cover Anna's hand and comfort her. Her sagging shoulders and defeated look softened his heart. Hurt at the notion she might choose Noah over him, he wanted her happy.

Beth set her fork down with force. "Forgive him, but don't marry him!"

Biting his tongue, Daniel delighted in her reaction. He couldn't agree more.

Leah choked and caught the water spewing out of her mouth with a cupped hand.

Anna swallowed her sip of water. She opened her mouth to speak, but Beth stood and interrupted her.

Beth crossed her arms, as if ready for battle. "Daniel, what do you have to say?"

Mamm put her hand up. "Beth Plank, I'm ashamed of you. You are being rude. It is none of your business how Daniel stands on this matter. Furthermore, you are to address Daniel with respect."

He was fond of Beth. She spoke her mind, and she had no problem voicing her support of him. Smiling, Daniel motioned for Beth to sit. "As difficult as this conversation has been, I prefer we discuss Noah's return together. I appreciate being included and having an opportunity to answer your questions. I love Anna, and I've asked her to marry me. She agreed but requested we wait a little longer before telling anyone other than the bishop. She was concerned people would think she'd chosen another man too soon after Noah's leaving."

Beth grinned and took her seat. "You had me worried. You don't need to wait. You and Daniel should set a date for the wedding."

Groaning, Anna sat back. "I'm seeking guidance from God on what He would have me do."

Beth swung her head closer to Anna and gripped the edge of the table. "What?"

Mamm rose and gathered the dirty dishes. "Beth, anything else you have to say to Anna, you need to tell her in private."

Leah lifted the platter and a vegetable dish. "Beth, you've said enough."

Daniel carried the water glasses to the dry sink. "I'll wait for you outside, Anna. Take your time."

Beth ran to him. "I need to tell you a secret."

He bent to her level.

Beth cupped her mouth and whispered in his ear. "I'm rooting for you."

"You're sweet, little one." He wanted to twirl her around and tell her she was the best little schweschder he could ever hope for, but he refrained. He couldn't feed into her support of him. Her family wouldn't approve, and conspiring to have an edge on Noah wasn't his way.

Ten minutes later, Anna joined him. "Would you care to take the canoe in the pond?"

He nodded and grinned. After turning over the canoe, he grabbed the paddles from the barn and threw them inside. They carried it to the pond. He held her hand until she got seated on the wooden slat serving as a bench. He shoved off, jumped in, and sat opposite her. He then paddled them out to the middle and threw over the tin can sealed with heavy rocks to anchor them. He waited for her to speak.

"I'm so sorry for Beth's outburst, and for my family's discussing my dilemma in front of you. You were gracious to allow them to talk about Noah's return in your presence."

He held her hand. "I've grown close to your family. Conversations aren't always pleasant. Sometimes difficult problems must be discussed. If we marry, it would be so. I'm thankful they are willing to speak freely in front of me."

"Daniel, I don't have the right to ask, but I beg you for your patience."

"I won't lie and tell you I'm comfortable with your confusion about Noah and me. This is an awkward predicament we're in. I'm seeking God's guidance and His will for our lives too." He released her hand and gazed at the fish jumping for insects. "Will you invite Noah to your haus for meals and walks with you?" He gazed at her with worried eyes.

Hands on either side of her neck, she squeezed her eyes shut for a moment. "Noah wants to ask my family to forgive him for causing me heartbreak. He'll kumme to the haus and talk to them at some point, and he and I will need to have private discussions to help unravel my turmoil.

"Please don't shy away from me, Daniel. My love for you hasn't changed. I promise. I have to sort this out to do what's best."

He paddled the canoe back to shore, helped her out, and stepped onto land. He pulled the canoe far enough away from the pond, turned it over, and tied it to the tree. He joined her, and his eyes drifted to two deer frolicking on the other side of the pond. Noah had wilkomed him and been kind. Under any other circumstances, he'd have been glad to have him back in Berlin. He'd have enjoyed spending more time with him. But Daniel loved Anna, and he didn't want to lose her.

He rubbed the ache in his neck. He would treat Noah with respect and be kind if they ran into each other. Seeking God's will for his life, he would trust Anna to do the same and accept her decision either way. He wasn't comfortable having the woman he loved confused about her feelings for another man from her past. He rolled his head and closed his eyes for a moment. He loved her too much to let her go yet. He'd be patient for now. "Maybe time apart from me will help you arrive at a decision sooner."

"No, Daniel, please don't change our routine."

"I'm uncomfortable you are considering him. He was your first love. I'm not sure if I'm doing the right thing keeping my hat in the ring."

"I love you, Daniel."

"I love you, too." He looked deep into her eyes, willing her to perceive the depth of his love. "Have no doubt, I'm praying you'll wed me."

She broke their gaze and glanced at the two hummingbirds fighting over the sugar water hanging from the handcrafted tin feeder.

He stared at the tiny wonders. The birds resembled him and Noah vying for her attention. He bid her farewell and drove down the lane. What would he do in Anna's situation? Decisive, he doubted he'd have to contemplate which woman to choose. Had a woman he loved left him to move for no good reason, he would surmise she didn't care enough about him in the first place.

Noah had invested so much time in his and Anna's relationship. If he'd been Noah, he couldn't have walked away from the woman he loved. Would her history with Noah change her mind about him?

Chapter Ten

Trembling, Anna bid Daniel farewell and waited until he disappeared heading home. She had no idea what to say to her family about what she was feeling inside for Noah and Daniel. Confusion reigned. She loved Daniel and she had mixed sentiments about Noah.

Mamm sat knitting mittens and Beth and Leah teased Cotton with a ball of yarn. Mamm set her wooden needles in her lap. "How are you holding up? I'm sorry you're going through a difficult time."

She covered her face and sobbed. Mamm, Leah, and Beth circled her and wrapped their arms around her. Their tenderness and compassion meant more to her than at any other time in her life. Minutes later, she raised her head from her mamm's shoulder. "Danki for your love and support as I go through this difficult period."

She plopped on the high-backed maple chair.

Cotton bounced over to her and jumped on her lap. She petted the dog's soft, fluffy white hair and enjoyed her pet's snuggle. "Daniel's gone home. Let's get your questions out of the way." Discussing her emotions and thoughts about both men with her mamm and schweschders may help her find answers. They loved her and knew both men.

Beth slapped the dish towel against her leg. "Why you are considering Noah? He chose Lancaster. He didn't care enough about you to stay."

"I'm not sure if I love Noah for more than a friend. I've forgiven him for leaving, but I'm hurt he left. He was my first love, and we've created good memories together. I was happy to marry him until the last few months before he left. His constant suggestions about my cooking and baking, not wanting to take long walks, how I throw my fishing line, and so many other things got on my nerves. He wasn't satisfied with anything I did. His relocation demand on such short notice left me no choice but to refuse to marry him. I had too many doubts. He declares he's in love with me and will stay in Berlin and stop his complaining. Has he matured and realized he loves me the way I am? I need time to decipher my feelings for him first, and if what he says is true."

Leah settled in the settee next to Mamm. "I expect you to forgive him, but can you trust him? He chose Lancaster not you."

Her schweschders made this complex situation sound simple to solve, and it wasn't at all. "I trusted him until he left me. He's saying to give him a chance to prove I can trust him again. The Noah I fell in love with is what I'm having a hard time letting go, but maybe it's the past I'm holding on to and there is no present for us." She threw her head back, exasperated. "I don't disagree with either of you. Noah's showing up in my life again is confusing and my heart has been ripped wide open. I have to make sure I have no regrets where Noah's concerned."

Mamm folded her hands in her lap. "Pray and read your Bible. God will direct you to the man He has chosen for you to marry. Be patient."

Leah knelt before Anna. "Let's pray."

Beth slid next to her middle schweschder. They held hands.

Mamm joined them.

Anna bowed her head and closed her eyes. God didn't promise life would be easy, but she wished He'd hurry and shout out His answer.

Leah's sweet voice calmed her. "Dear Heavenly Father, we kumme before You today and ask You to forgive us when we've disappointed You. We're asking You to provide a clear answer to Anna about whether she should wed Noah or Daniel. Help us as a family to encourage and support her in her decision. We love You. Amen."

Mamm gestured to the Bible on the table near her. She bent one finger at a time reciting each word of the Book of Philippians, Chapter Four, Verse Thirteen. "*I can do all things through Christ which strengtheneth me.*'"

Anna's lips quivered. "My favorite verse. You taught me this verse when I was a child, and it calmed me." Her mamm always knew what to say in good and bad times.

Beth raised her eyebrows. "I'm fond of Noah, but I'm hoping you marry Daniel. I don't believe Daniel would've ever left Anna. He loves her too much."

Puzzled, Leah asked, "You sound so grown up for a maedel your age. How can you be sure?"

"In my heart, I am certain. It's the way he's cared for us. He's always put our needs before his."

Leah glanced with a raised eyebrow and small grin. She reached out to her schweschder. "You've got a

point, little one." She yawned and motioned to Beth.
"Time to go to bed."

Anna bid her family good night and went to her
room. Changing into her bedclothes, she rolled her
neck from side to side to relax. A warm breeze cooled
her through the open window. Innocent, Beth hadn't
experienced falling in love with a man yet. She'd
been a decisive child from the time she could reason.
There were no gray areas for her schweschder.
Beth's and Leah's questions and opinions held a
truth she couldn't ignore. She trusted Daniel. Did
she trust Noah?

Cotton jumped on Anna's bed early Wednesday
morning. She grabbed him before his wet, rough
tongue licked her face. "Good morning, you fluffy
pile of fur." She nuzzled his neck. Minutes later, she
coaxed him off the bed and onto the floor. After
quickly dressing for milking the cows and feeding the
horses and sows, she padded outside and joined her
schweschders in the barn. "Good morning, everyone.
Sorry I slept late." She lifted a dented pail and carried
it to a small stool. Sitting on the three-legged, wobbly
pine seat, she milked the cow.

Beth and Leah smiled at Anna. They offered food
and water to the animals.

Leah said, "You needed the extra rest. You're going
through a hard time with having Noah back in town."

Mamm came to the barn. "I've got grits, warm biscuits, and fried eggs for breakfast. I have milk out of
the icebox and warm coffee."

Anna took the milk inside and strained it. She
washed and dressed for work and joined her family. At
the kitchen table, she mashed and pushed her eggs

around the plate. Breakfast didn't appeal to her. "Does anyone care to have my breakfast?"

Mamm rapped her fingers on the table. "Anna, you need your strength."

"I'm sorry. I can't swallow a bite without gagging. My stomach's in knots. I'm hoping the shop will take my mind off things."

Beth pulled Anna's plate to her. "I'm hungry. Danki, Anna."

Leah stood and poured Anna a cup of hot tea. "Drink this. It will help settle your stomach." She rested her hand on Anna's shoulder. "I'm not rushing you, but how long will you keep these men waiting for an answer?"

"I don't intend to take long. I'll talk to Noah again in more depth. Hopefully, I will gain some clarity."

Beth spooned grits. "I'll be nice to Noah, but I'm still rooting for Daniel."

Mamm shook her head. "You've made yourself clear on your support of Daniel, Beth. I'd argue you should keep your preferences to yourself, but you always speak your mind before I have a chance to warn you."

Beth turned her chin up to Anna. "Anna cares about what I think."

Anna laughed and patted Beth's head. "I do care."

Beth hurried to swallow the last of her breakfast and scampered to her room. She returned in minutes, dressed and ready to begin her day. "I'm going to Mrs. Hochstetler's." She lifted Cotton. "Kumme on, friend, it's time to go."

Cotton wagged her tail and licked Beth's chin.

Anna and her family bid Beth good-bye, dressed for work, and harnessed the horse to the buggy. Anna drove them to town. After dropping Mamm off, she left the horse and buggy at the livery and walked with Leah to the shop. She paused. *Noah and Daniel!*

Hooking her arm through Anna's, Leah leaned close to her ear. "Are you prepared to face them at the same time?"

Tongue twisted and beads of sweat forming above her lip, she nodded. "I better get used to running into the two of them in town and at church."

"They aren't smiling."

She opened her clean flour sack she used for carrying her things and removed her keys. She approached them and shoved the key in the lock. "Good morning, would you like to kumme in?" She stared at the door and hurried inside. Stowing her bag under the counter, she closed the curtain to conceal her belongings. Slowly, she glanced at them.

The men stood staring at her.

Noah tipped his hat. "I wouldn't mind a cup of coffee."

Leah pulled a container from her bag and poured the coffee in a pan over the stove. She lit the wood, already in the compartment, to warm the coffee. "Shouldn't take but a few minutes to warm." She smiled and stowed her bag next to Anna's under the counter. "Would you like a cup, Daniel?"

"No, danki. I intended to say good morning and be on my way. Have a good day." Daniel nodded to them and left.

Leah winked at Anna. "Why don't you and Noah go out back and talk in private. I'll manage the store."

"Danki, Leah."

Anna and Noah crossed the room, and she pushed the back door open. Stepping outside, Anna faced him.

Noah grazed her hand with his. "Daniel told me

what happened with Butch Winter. I'm sorry I wasn't here to protect you."

A spurt of annoyance took her by surprise. She touched her hot cheeks. "I wish you would've been here too. A lot has taken place in my life since you left."

"You can't blame what happened with Butch and Leah on me. I would've done everything I could to help you had I been here." Noah held her fingers. "Anna, I'm thankful none of you were harmed. Daniel's a good man. He told me about Butch and Mr. Winter and how he and the sheriff helped you."

Anna sighed. Noah couldn't understand the depths of her reaction to Butch, since he wasn't here when she encountered him. Their trouble with Butch wasn't his fault. She was taking her lingering fear out on him, and she shouldn't resent him for leaving. Her anxiety did them no good. "I'm sorry, Noah. I shouldn't have gotten terse with you." She shook her head. "I was surprised Leah agreed to meet Butch alone. She's usually an intelligent and obedient young woman. We all make errors in judgment. She had no idea of his true character."

"I'm glad it's over and you don't have to worry about him anymore."

"Me too." She tilted her head in question. "What will you do for work now that you're back?"

"Mark has rehired me to manage his property, and I can use his workshop in the evenings to build things to sell in his store."

"What about the young man he has working for him?"

"He's been offered a job with his uncle to help with additional property he's bought. I'm thrilled to have my old job back."

Noah and Mark had been close. Mark must be overjoyed he'd returned to town. They shared a lot of the same interests. "Your mamm must be ecstatic to have you home."

"She's cooking and baking for me. She and I stayed up late last night and talked. I missed her. Our reunion has been a good one."

Jane was cheerful and easygoing. She would never have asked her son to give up his dreams for her personal well-being. She put Noah's happiness before hers.

Anna had seen how she'd cooked, cleaned, and doted on him. They shared a close bond. "Wasn't leaving her difficult?"

He gently squeezed her arms. "Leaving you, Mamm, and my friends was difficult. I realized my mistake not long after I arrived in Lancaster. My aunt and uncle understood. I told them I had to win you back and return to Mamm. God spoke to me through prayer and the Scriptures. He pricked my heart, and showed me I'd been selfish to satisfy my desires." He shuffled his feet. "I was miserable and, even though I met interesting people and had plenty of work, I couldn't take my mind off you."

Anna stared at her hands. "I should go back in and help Leah."

"I'll go with you." Noah opened the door, and they went to the front of the shop.

An Englischer, a short and round man dressed in a blue shirt and linen tan pants, shiny leather shoes, and a fancy straw hat, approached them. His fraa matched his body type and stood by his side, blinking and smiling, her cheeks pink and her eyes twinkling.

The woman said, "A friend visited your shop and

showed us the most beautiful wedding ring quilt. We came to purchase one."

Anna pointed to the quilts on the wall. "Please take a look around. I'll be with you shortly."

The man and rosy-cheeked woman studied each quilt.

Noah clutched the doorknob. "May I kumme by your haus later? We could grab our fishing poles and catch up on our news by the pond." He rearranged her washcloths and placed them next to the towels on the lower wall shelf. "Customers will notice these better there. You've got them hidden." He unhooked her aprons hanging on a peg and moved them to another peg next to a small table containing folded boppli blankets. "These colors go better displayed next to each other."

Anna folded her hands in a tight clasp. She wouldn't ask him to leave her dry goods alone. She had customers to tend to. "Please do kumme by later."

He gently tapped her nose and whispered, "I love those big hazel eyes and sweet little nose of yours. I've missed everything about you. You're more beautiful than I remembered. I'll be at your haus later."

Anna closed the door behind him. He had a sparkle in his eyes and a lilt to his step she enjoyed. He made the most of every minute, always exploring, and his mind swirled with ideas constantly. What she once thought was exciting she now found irritating. She felt herself tensing around him like she had before he left Berlin the first time. She missed the calm she enjoyed with Daniel.

Leah was showing the couple the various quilts they had for sale. They oohed and aahed at each one. Glancing out the window, Anna watched Noah leave Mark's store and head to the livery. Dinah Yoder, a strikingly pretty Amish woman, stopped to speak with Noah. They laughed, and she handed him a container. Had she baked or cooked something? He handed the container back to her. She appeared disappointed. Had Dinah found out he was in town? Was she interested in Noah? She'd batted her eyelashes at him a time or two before he left Berlin.

Jealousy reared its ugly head. Picturing Noah with someone else sent a wave of nausea sailing through her. Dinah and Noah had much in common with their adventuresome ideas, overabundant energy, and desire for change. Her chest tightened with guilt. She liked and admired Dinah, and they were having an innocent conversation. What was wrong with her? She forced a smile at the couple and darted her eyes back to the brown paper on the counter.

Anna wrapped the quilt the couple had chosen. "You made a wonderful choice."

The sweet woman beamed. "We're buying the quilt for our daughter. She's getting married and moving far away from us. I'm going to write a letter to her and place it in the pocket. The letter will remind her each day how much we love her."

Leah accepted payment. "What a thoughtful gift. Your reason for buying the quilt is what gives us such joy to sell them." She took the wrapped package from Anna and passed the purchase to the couple. "Danki for shopping with us today."

Searching outside the window, Anna noticed Noah and Dinah were gone. She'd been silly to jump to conclusions.

Leah stretched her neck. "I caught a glimpse of Dinah and Noah outside. She and Noah have similar personalities, and I wouldn't be surprised if she's interested in him. I don't think she'd take a second glance at Daniel."

"Why not Daniel?"

Leah reached for her clean flour sack of goodies from under the counter and pulled out a bag of lemon drops. She held out the bag to Anna. "Want one?"

Shaking her head, Anna waited for her answer.

"Daniel's calm, reserved, predictable, and safe. Most important, Daniel is dependable. Noah can't sit still, and he's unpredictable. His mind is working non-stop. He gets bored easy, and he craves change. I can understand Dinah loving those things about him. She's like him in many of the same ways."

Leah's observations hit a sore spot. She and Dinah couldn't be more different. She worked hard, but she enjoyed planning her day and going to bed early. Noah's opposite personality had challenged her and livened up her life. She'd delighted in being around someone unlike herself, until the last months before he left. Irritable and annoyed with his constant plans to interrupt their lives by moving away from Berlin and his determination she needed to change her way of doing things, she was so frustrated with him. Was he better suited to a woman with a personality matching his? If Dinah had given Daniel food and batted her eyelashes at him, she would've been more jealous. She moved closer to her decision.

Hours later, Anna rocked on the porch in the white maple chair gazing at the horses at Mrs. Hochstetler's place. The brown horses whinnied and danced playfully in the corral. Noah pulled into the lane and galloped his horse to the hitching post.

She stood and went to greet him. "You're on time." She raised her eyebrows and grinned.

He laughed. "Being late to everything isn't something I've overcome. I'm working on being on time."

"I'm teasing you." She patted his arm.

He surveyed the property and windows. "No one's looking." He leaned in, and she turned her head. "I'm sorry. I shouldn't have presumed I could kiss you." He hurried to tie his horse and gently clasped her hand. Lifting fishing poles and a small rusty metal box from his wagon, he gestured. "Let's go to the pond."

"I'm sorry, Noah. I'm having a hard time overcoming the awkwardness of being with you again. I'm not sure where we stand." *Oh no*, he was leading her to the spot she and Daniel favored.

She cringed. Tugging his hand, she hurried to another thick green patch of grass still behind the barn but a few feet away. "Let's fish here." She prepared to cast her line.

"Throw your line harder. You never bring your arm back far enough to make a good cast."

She swallowed the aggravation welling in her. "I'll be right back." She ran into the barn, snatched a horse blanket, and spread the coverlet on the ground. "I'm not in the mood for fishing." She didn't want to endure a list of instructions on fishing tonight. "I'll sit here and watch you. We'll talk after you're finished."

She drew up her knees and clasped them with her arms. "I saw you and Dinah having a conversation when I peeked out the shop window today."

"Yes, Dinah offered me a container of cookies she'd bought from my mamm at the bakery for herself. I handed them back and told her to enjoy them. She's a sweet woman, but you have nothing to worry about."

"She is a sweet woman, and she reminds me of you."

He opened a can of red worms and baited his hook. "Dinah isn't the woman I love. I love you." He paused and gave her a long stare. "I'm scared of losing you, Anna."

She looked away from him and stared out over the sun dancing on the water. "Can I trust you to settle here and not become resentful?" She sighed. "You challenge me, but do I challenge you?"

"Jah, you can trust me. I wish you were more spontaneous, energetic, and carefree like me, but our differences don't hinder my love for you. I'll love you forever." He pulled his line out and set it in the grass alongside the blanket. He sat next to her.

"Noah." She gazed into his eyes. "I'm content and happy with my routines, and I'm worried you're too often annoyed with my way of doing things. Your constant suggestions upset me. I don't rearrange your wagon bed of tools or criticize your handcrafted products, or ask you to change anything."

He pulled his knees to his chest and hugged his legs. "You calm me. Something I need. I get carried away and push you to change. I'm sorry." He caressed her hand with the pad of his thumb. "I enjoy sitting here, having discussions, and sharing our thoughts with each other. Again, my suggestions to you are harmless." He grimaced. "I believe you would benefit from not being so set in your ways."

She gazed at two skittish barn kittens rolling and playing on the ground near them. She remembered the time when she'd flutter with excitement waiting for Noah to visit her at the shop or her haus. Sitting here with him, she couldn't deny their good memories, but she had an awkwardness with him now. Her stomach rolled with uncertainty.

He squeezed her hand. "You and Daniel have

gotten serious in a short time. I'm surprised you've fallen in love with him so quickly."

She didn't want to discuss Daniel with Noah. The Amish frowned on competition of any kind. Pitting them against each other for her affection was the last thing she wanted to do. Her choice would be based on what she knew and loved about them thus far.

She rose and dusted off her dress. "The mosquitoes are biting. We should get inside."

Noah rose to his feet and walked with her to his wagon. "I'm sorry if I overstepped my bounds. I should go home."

She nodded and stared at her hands.

He brushed her cheek with his lips. "Sleep well." Touching the lingering warmth of his mouth on her face, she waited until he'd left and went inside. She cherished his sweet and kind heart, in spite of the distress she had with him.

Daniel drove past the Planks'. Jah, there was Anna standing with Noah beside his wagon. His heart plummeted. He could drop in. She had offered him the opportunity. He had no desire to share his time with Anna and Noah. It was painful enough picturing the two of them together.

Driving home, he groaned and slumped forward. He dreaded heating cold potato soup for supper and spending the evening alone. The Planks had spoiled him with hearty home-cooked meals and lively conversation. He'd been accustomed to the quiet eating and working alone until he met them. He loved every minute he'd spent with her family. He missed Anna, but their marriage might not be meant to be. She might want more time with Noah than he was willing to give her. He scratched his ear. He longed to enjoy their courtship again and not carry ~~around this heavy~~ burden of worry.

He stirred his soup in the iron kettle over the fire in the fireplace, enjoying the orange hue and the crackle of the flames. The evening had cooled, but he'd have to extinguish the fire after he heated his food to keep the temperature comfortable inside. The breeze blowing through the windows helped.

Otis had devoured his supper and lay snoring on the floor in front of the hearth.

The clip-clop of horse hooves caught his attention. He opened the door. What was Noah doing here? Earlier they'd spoken at the shop. They'd avoided speaking about the subject of their mutual love for Anna. He waved Noah in. "Kumme inside. Is anything wrong?"

Otis raised his head and barked.

"You stay put."

The dog reluctantly went back to his bed by the fireplace.

Noah got out of the buggy and tied the leads to the hitching post. "We need to have a serious conversation. I've a favor to ask you." He stepped inside.

"Have a seat. Are you thirsty or hungry?"

Noah shook his head. "I'm fine."

"What kind of favor?"

"I'm not comfortable with you and Anna spending time together, and I'm certain you don't relish her and me discussing the future."

"I'm not willing to walk away from Anna if you've kumme here to ask me to step aside."

"I am asking you to step aside for a couple of weeks. Before you met Anna, she and I had nurtured a three-year relationship and planned to marry. I'd hoped she'd join me in Lancaster and stopped at the post office often hoping she'd sent me a letter saying she'd had a change of heart. Time passed and I realized I'd made a terrible mistake. She'll remain confused if she spends time with us both."

"Why should I step aside? Why not you?"

Noah's request set his teeth on edge.

"You've had time with her while I've been away." He smacked a mosquito biting his arm and swiped the dead pest away. "Please, Daniel, allow me this time with her."

Noah nagging him to stay away from Anna was as annoying as a pesky mosquito. Noah was draining him of his happiness with the love of his life. Daniel mulled over his words. He'd justified his request because of the history he had with Anna. It was apparent in his sincere tone and pleading eyes. He was desperate to gain her trust and win her heart again. Had he not fallen in love with Anna himself, he'd have empathy for Noah. But he did love Anna, and he wouldn't honor Noah's request. "I'm not willing to distance myself from her unless she asks me to. It is her decision. Not yours and not mine."

Noah clutched the smooth maple side arms of the comfortable chair. "The day you and I met at the shop before I left, I enjoyed our conversation. We spent a little time together at church and sat together at the meal. I considered you a new friend. You're a good man, but I resent you not respecting what Anna and I had together. You've only been in Berlin a short while." He straightened his spine and thrust his chin forward. "Find someone else to marry."

Fury flowing through his veins, Daniel had heard enough. Noah shouldn't assume he knew what he and Anna had together. He'd had his chance, and he'd ruined her trust in him. "Noah, I'm not stepping aside. I'll decide the length of time I will wait on Anna's answer, and I'll continue to visit her at her haus and the shop unless she asks me to stop. Above all else, I desire Anna's happiness. Do you?"

The man's face paled and his determination wavered. Daniel hoped he'd gotten through to Noah.

Noah removed his hat and twisted the brim. "I was wrong to demand you do anything. Forgive me for presenting my request to you in a rude way. I'm asking because I'm desperate to make this right with Anna. I beg you to consider my request. If not, I won't hold a grudge." He offered his hand to Daniel.

Daniel shook his hand and nodded. "I'll consider your request."

"Danki, Daniel." He tipped his hat and headed outside to his wagon.

Daniel waited until Noah was out of sight to shut the door. He stretched out on the settee and shoved a pillow under his head. Staring at the ceiling, he reached down and idly petted Otis on the floor next to him. He closed his eyes. "Dear Heavenly Father, I have no idea what to do. I'm asking You to intervene on my behalf and speak to Anna's heart. If my request is not Your will, please cover me with the grace to accept losing her. Forgive me for getting angry with Noah. Guide and direct me in the way You would have me go in all matters. Amen."

Should he allow Noah and Anna time to find out where they stood with each other? Would there be such indecision in Anna's heart if God wanted them together? It wouldn't be easy, but he'd distance himself from her for a couple of weeks. It was the right thing to do. God would bring them together if they were meant to marry.

* * *

Two weeks later on a warm and humid Wednesday evening, Anna rested her hand on Leah's arm after replacing loose stitches in her white kapp. "Noah's been over every night this week. Daniel hasn't kumme to the shop or the haus. You and I have driven by his place on the way home from work several times, and there's been no sign of him, but his wagon may be in the barn. He wasn't at church Sunday either. Would you go with me tonight to visit him? I'm worried he's given up on me." She loved Daniel. Her heart ached at the thought of losing him.

"He was probably repairing things for customers when we went by his haus, but I agree. It does look as if he's avoiding you." She squinted. "Are you any closer to a decision?"

"Jah, but I'm not ready to voice it to Noah or Daniel yet."

"Why don't you leave him alone for now? He may need time to think too."

She'd honor Daniel's position, but she had to understand why he'd shied away from her. "I need to ask. Whatever he says, I will abide by his wishes."

They told Mamm and Beth their plan.

Mamm stared at her in awkward silence. She cleared her throat. "You're putting these two men through a difficult time. I can understand if Daniel is having second thoughts. He probably wants a woman who is sure about him. I'm not accusing you of doing it on purpose. I realize how agonizing the choice is for you, but don't tarry too long on telling these men your decision. You and Leah be careful. Give Daniel my best."

"Danki for your advice, Mamm. I'm gaining clarity on my decision."

Beth smiled. "Tell Daniel to bring Otis and kumme over real soon."

Anna nodded and followed Leah out the door and headed for the buggy. She drove to Daniel's. How would he react to her kumming to speak with him? She hoped he would tell her his thoughts and not hold back. They'd not held back on their thoughts thus far.

Leah breathed deep. "Fresh night air is the best. I love summer." She patted her schweschder's hand. "I wish I could provide you with answers and eliminate your worry."

Anna wasn't so sure, but she appreciated Leah's attempt to calm her. In her heart, she knew she was favoring Daniel. The loss of him would be painful if he'd given up on her. "I hope you're right." She drove down Daniel's lane and halted the horse. "A buggy is parked in front." Laughter rang out. She sat on the edge of the seat and poked her head out. Mark King and Daniel sat on the porch.

Turning around, she coaxed the horse into a turn. "I don't want to interrupt his visit with Mark. He's busy, and he doesn't get to enjoy company too often. I'm glad they are getting better acquainted."

Leah gripped the side of the bouncing buggy for support. "Slow down and turn this buggy around! We can visit with them, and we'll stay until after Mark leaves. Take your time. I'll play with Otis in the meantime."

"It's getting late, and I don't think talking to Daniel with Mark there is a good idea."

Leah growled. "You are making excuses, Anna Plank."

"I'm not. I will talk to him. I have to find out why he's avoiding me."

"Noah's buggy or wagon has been outside our place every day this week. Daniel could be passing our property and noticing the two of you together. How awkward this must be for him. No wonder he's giving you a wide berth."

"I've been foolish to assume things would go smoothly while I took so much time to contemplate what to do."

"Noah's got some catching up to do. He's not giving Daniel a chance to steal a few minutes alone with you."

Anna and Leah fed and bedded down the horse and went inside. She nodded at Beth and Mamm playing checkers. Leah sat next to Mamm. She bid them good night and went to her room. As she read the Scriptures, the words in her Bible blurred. She closed the book and slouched inside the covers. She must reach a decision soon. Daniel might be lost to her. Even if he was, she might not choose Noah in the end.

Leah knocked and opened the door. "Do you mind if I kumme in?"

Anna pulled back the covers and scooted over. "I'd love some company."

Leah climbed in next to her. "I had a thought."

Anna smiled at her schweschder. Leah always had a *thought* to share.

"What?"

"Has Noah said anything to you about asking Daniel to step aside for a while?"

Anna sat straight up. "No, but I will definitely ask him.

How would he dare to make such a request without telling me?" She put a hand on her schweschder's leg. "Danki for bringing your idea to my attention. If Noah spoke with Daniel, I'm certain it's why he's staying away from me."

Leah swung her legs off the side of the bed and padded to the door. "I'm always here if you want to talk. Good night."

"I treasure you, Leah. You always provide me with good insight. Sleep tight." She turned down the lantern and snuggled under the sheet. Would Noah take such a liberty without asking her first? She'd learn the truth tomorrow.

Noah walked into the shop Thursday afternoon. "How's my lovely Anna?" He wore a broad smile and moved her two chairs and table to the other side of the room, stood back, and studied them. "The furniture belongs here on the other wall to balance out the room. Don't you agree?"

No, she didn't agree. She had the table and chairs where she wanted them. He seemed compelled to find something wrong every time he came here, but she wouldn't address his interference now. She had a more important issue to discuss with him. "Good morning, Noah. I'm glad you're here." Pulling him aside, she faced him. "Let's talk in private. I've got a question for you." She gestured for him to follow her out the back door to the sunshine. "Did you ask Daniel to avoid me to give us time to work things out?"

Color drained from Noah's face. He hung his head. "I did."

"You were wrong to ask Daniel such a thing without consulting me." He shouldn't have interfered. It wasn't his place to ask Daniel such a thing. On the other hand, he was doing his best to win her back. Daniel shouldn't have agreed to Noah's request if he wanted her in his life. Had he given up on her? She needed to quit speculating. She had no idea what either of them was thinking.

"He's a grown man. He chose to honor my request. I respect him for it."

Leah poked her head out. "I'm sorry to interrupt, but I need your help, Anna. We've got customers."

"I'll be there in a minute." She waited until Leah went back inside the shop.

"I'm so upset with you, Noah."

"Have you considered he has let you go? You and he had a much shorter time together than you and I."

"He may have, but you overstepped your bounds by asking him to back away from me."

"Anna, don't be upset. He chose to remove himself. No one is forcing him to ignore you."

"Noah, don't tell me how to feel, and please don't discuss me with Daniel again."

"I'm sorry." He gently lifted her chin enough to meet his gaze. "Can we put this argument behind us?"

She melted at his lopsided grin. "I forgive you, but I shouldn't be away from the shop. Leah needs help. We'll talk again."

She and Noah went inside.

Leah held her hands up. "The store cleared out in a hurry. Neither customer who came in bought anything. I'm sorry I bothered you."

An Englischer with her golden hair in ringlets pulled back in a silk bow strolled in. She had a fitted print dress with a small belt at the waist. She was stunning with her sky-blue eyes and dainty features.

"Good morning. Do you have any patchwork baby quilts in stock?"

Leah whispered to Anna. "I'll help her. You and Noah go to the back room and finish your conversation." She grinned at the Englischer. "I have three stacked on the shelf on the left. I'll be happy to show them to you."

"My friend is expecting her third child, and I want to give her one for a gift. I bought quilts for her two other children, and she loved them."

Anna grinned as she walked with Noah to the back room. She would leave the door open to watch for customers. "I'm looking forward to having at least three bopplin someday."

His smile faded. "I haven't changed my mind on having more than one. If we have more kinner, we won't have as much time to spend together. I don't have any siblings, and I turned out fine."

Stunned, Anna held her breath. She'd hoped he'd altered his thinking on this subject, since he knew she wanted more kinner. She had assumed wrong. "Would you reconsider?"

"Maybe we could compromise and have two." He raised his eyebrows.

She sucked in her upper lip. She wanted three or more kinner. Her desire had always been to have a big family. Noah's pained expression sent chills through her.

Two more customers sauntered in. Noah glanced in their direction. "I should let you get back to work. Don't worry. We'll reach a mutual understanding about this when the time kummes." He hurried out the door.

He may not have realized it, but he had put even more distance between them. She had more reasons even before this news not to choose him, so what was she waiting for? She had to put her uncertainties aside and concentrate on the elderly patron approaching her. She forced a smile and turned to the woman. "How may I assist you today?"

Two hours later, the shopper finally purchased a red linen tablecloth and left. Anna slumped in a chair. "The woman fingered every tablecloth we have in the shop. I'm surprised she finally bought one." She pressed her fingertips to her temples. "Listen to me. I'm in a terrible mood and talking ill about our customers. God must be disappointed with me."

"We all have our bad days." Leah sighed and leaned against the counter.

They tidied the shop, grabbed their bags when the clock struck five, and headed for their wagon at the livery.

Mamm met them halfway. "Ready to go home?"

Anna and Leah nodded.

On the way home, Anna drowned out Leah and Mamm's chatter about what to have for supper. She couldn't take her mind off Noah and Daniel. She'd been leaning more toward Daniel. She still had to speak with him. To find out what he was thinking.

Whaaaa!

A boppli is crying!

Anna ran on Mamm's heels to a basket on the porch.

Leah tied the leads to the hitching post and joined them.

Anna peeled the blanket back, and hazel eyes met hers. "How long has this infant been on the porch? Who would do such a thing?" She lifted an envelope tucked inside the basket. She removed two pieces of paper and read the signature. "Here's a letter from Mrs. Cooper, April's grossmudder."

"What's does it say?" Leah knelt beside the infant and lifted the newborn out of the basket.

Mamm fluttered her hands. "I can't believe the woman would leave the newborn alone! She must have good reason. Read what she has to say!"

Beth ran from Mrs. Hochstetler's yard to them with Cotton in her arms. She stared wide-eyed at the newborn. "Who does the wee one belong to? Where is the little one's mamm?"

Anna scanned both documents. "We're about to find out." She read the letter to them. *"Dear Anna, I'm sorry to inform you, April passed away giving birth to Daisy. I'm not able to live alone, and I've left to reside with my elderly sister. Neither of us is in good enough health to care for her. I don't have anyone willing to raise Daisy.*

"'I'm sorry to burden you with her, but I have no choice. I wrote to the baby's father, and he sent me a legal document giving me custody of her and a note stating he wants nothing to do with his daughter. I had an attorney draw up another document giving you custody of Daisy. Both documents are enclosed. Blessings, Rosetta Cooper.'"

They gasped. Anna's eyes pooled with tears. She met Leah's eyes. "Poor April. She was such a sweet young woman."

Leah hugged her and swiped a tear from her cheek. "Her passing is so tragic. She was looking forward to becoming a mamm."

Beth frowned. "I remember you telling us about her. You must be sad she died."

Mamm stood next to Anna. "I'm sorry she passed, but we must find out more information. Check the other papers. Does Daisy's daed state he wants nothing to do with her?"

Anna read the documents. "His signature is on this one, and Mrs. Cooper signed away her rights to Daisy to me on the other one. A judge's signature is on both papers. Everything looks in order."

Leah blew out a breath. "We don't have to worry about anyone claiming Daisy later. Do we have to inform the bishop about taking Daisy in to live with us?"

Beth kissed the boppli's cheek. "Poor little orphan. She's alone, except for us." She brightened. "She's got beautiful hazel eyes and the daintiest little nose like Anna's." She chuckled. "Her silky brown hair is standing on end as if someone scared her." She put her finger in the boppli's tiny palm. "Look at her curl her pretty little fingers around mine!"

Leah's eyes filled with tears. "April was such a sweet woman. I can't believe she's passed."

Anna reached for the little maedel. Her tears dripped onto her apron. She searched Mamm's distressed face. "We must keep her. I'll take responsibility for her. I want to raise her for April. She stole my heart as soon as I beheld her."

"How would Daniel or Noah react to raising another man's dochder?"

Panic rose within her. She didn't have any idea how Noah or Daniel would react to her caring for another man's child. She hoped they would wilkom her with open arms and share her enthusiasm to raise Daisy.

Leah rocked the child in her arms. "I'll help you."

"Me too," Beth chirped.

Mamm nodded with resignation. "We'll have to inform Bishop Weaver."

Would he have any objection to their raising an Englischer's boppli? He had shown compassion with Leah. Anna couldn't bear to hand off Daisy to anyone. Everyone had abandoned her, but she refused to do

so. April and Mrs. Cooper had trusted her with Daisy.
She couldn't let her go. The minute she cradled her,
she connected with the child. "When?"

Leah and Beth stared at Mamm.

Mamm raised her hands. "Who will care for her
while we're working?"

Beth pointed at her own chest. "I will, and Marlene
Hochstetler loves kinner. She says she can never have
enough little ones to care for in her haus."

"We could ask her." Leah shrugged.

Anna had to put a plan in place, and she didn't
have time to wait. "I'm going to Marlene's. I'll ask her
if she's willing to care for her while we're working."
She carried her new little bundle close to her chest as
she walked to the neighbor's haus. She stepped onto
the porch and knocked on the front door.

Marlene Hochstetler opened the door wide. "Anna,
what a pleasant surprise to find you here." The woman
stood tall, and her round middle and big smile were
inviting. She had a singsong tone to her voice and a
sparkle in her eyes. She reached for Daisy. "Oh, how
sweet. Are you caring for someone's boppli?"

Passing her to the woman, Anna beamed. "Meet
Daisy. To answer your question, Leah and I met a
young Englisch woman and her grossmudder in our
shop several weeks ago. Leah and I taught her a few
sewing lessons, and we got better acquainted with her.
The daed of her expected boppli fled when she told
him she was with child. The grossmudder left Daisy on
our doorstep in a basket today with a note tucked
inside saying April died birthing Daisy. She's aged and
in poor health and unable to care for her. With no
relatives to hand Daisy off to, she brought her to us
hoping we'd take her in."

Marlene snatched a nappy off a nearby table and changed the little one. "How tragic for the boppli to have no parents. What may I do to help you?" She picked her up and cradled her. "Daisy has worn herself out. She's fast asleep."

"She's been through a lot today. Danki for changing her wet nappy for me. I'll have to bring some nappies home from the shop. Would you take care of her for us during the day while we're working in the store? Beth volunteered to help you."

"I'd be thrilled to have her with me to cuddle and fuss over. Beth will be a big help. She does a lot to assist me with the little ones already." Marlene stood, opened a drawer, grabbed clean cotton nappies, and handed them to Anna. "You'll need them for tonight. From time to time, I take care of infants for young mamms after they've given birth and need to rest. Wait here." She went to the kitchen and returned. "Here are some empty bottles. I don't need them back. I've got plenty." She took the nappies from Anna and added them to the bag of empty bottles. "Here are a few more."

Anna accepted the bag and gently squeezed the woman's arm. "Danki. I'll make good use of these tonight." She laughed.

"She's an angel. I haven't heard a peep out of her while you've been here."

"I'm thankful we didn't stop anywhere on the way home. I'm worried she's been left here for hours."

"God had His eye on her, and you must've made quite an impression on the grossmudder for her to leave her in your care."

"We liked them even though we hardly knew them. Sad, but the woman had no alternative. She mentioned having no living relatives other than her elderly schweschder."

"I'm pleased to have her each day. Beth and I will enjoy her."

"Danki again, Marlene. You're a good friend." Anna bid her good evening and crossed the yard. Why were her mamm and schweschders standing by the buggy?

Mamm met her and reached for Daisy and the bag. "We should go to the bishop's place. I'll hold Daisy, and you can drive."

Anna shivered and passed the bag Marlene had given her to Beth. "Would you mind running these nappies and bottles inside?"

Beth nodded and did as Anna asked. She returned and climbed in the buggy along with the rest of them.

Anna had wanted to feed the newborn a bottle, but she didn't want to argue with Mamm. The infant was resting comfortably. She handed the little one to Mamm and accepted the reins. She drove to the bishop's haus. Would the bishop suggest Daisy needed a mamm and a daed? There were barren couples in their community who wanted kinner. They'd been praying for them. Would Bishop Weaver advise her to hand Daisy over to one of those couples?

Chapter Eleven

Quiet on the ride there, she whispered her favorite verse from Philippians, Chapter Four, Verse Thirteen. The promise calmed the sea of turmoil engulfing her. *"'I can do all things through Christ which strengtheneth me.'"* Was she being selfish if the bishop strongly suggested she hand Daisy to an Amish couple? She would provide her a good home and love her. She planned to marry one day.

At Bishop Weaver's haus, she climbed out and tied the horse to the weathered white hitching post. She accepted the boppli from Mamm and headed for the door with her loved ones.

Bishop Weaver came to the open door and jerked his head back in surprise. "Who do you have in your arms, Anna?" He waved them in. "Have a seat."

Anna told him about meeting April and her grossmudder and finding Daisy on her doorstep. She passed him the legal papers she'd found in the basket. "They are signed by the grossmudder and Daisy's daed and a judge. Mrs. Cooper states in her letter there are no other living relatives to give Daisy a home. She's in bad health and moving in with her aged schweschder.

She gave custody to me. I want to keep her, Bishop
Weaver. My family and I will take care of her together."
She darted her eyes to her family.

They nodded in agreement.

Bishop Weaver scanned their faces. He finally spoke.
"I'm afraid the daed will change his mind as he ma-
tures. I don't want any trouble from the outside world."

Anna cradled the warm, helpless, and precious
boppli in her arms. She couldn't think of anything
else but her strong desire to keep Daisy. She had to
convince him Daisy was better off with her. "Please,
Bishop Weaver. The daed left his unborn child and
signed a document giving away his rights to her. Besides, he has no idea Mrs. Cooper left her to us. She's
safe here."

He glanced out the door as if in deep thought.

She froze. Her heart thumped wildly in her chest.

They waited.

Leaning back against the old oak chair, he slid his
hands up and down the side arms. "Couples in our
community are praying for kinner, and they haven't
been blessed to have them. Don't you think a boppli
needs a mamm and a daed?"

Leah spoke softly. "Mamm does a wonderful job
taking care of us by herself. I promise we'll take good
care of her." She slid to the edge of the settee. She
darted a glance at Anna. "Anna may marry soon, and
she will take Daisy with her when she does."

Anna held her breath for a moment. Leah
shouldn't assume she'd wed. She wasn't sure what the
future had in store for her and the infant. She ex-
haled and kept silent. The bishop was a wise man. He
would understand she couldn't control the future.

Smiling, he nodded. "I understand, but if and
when she should marry, she and her new husband will

need time to adjust to each other. These couples have been married more than a year, and they are ready for kinner."

Beth pressed her fist to her chest and looked at him with pleading eyes. "Please, Bishop Weaver, let us keep Daisy. We promise to love her with all our might. You told us God is our Heavenly Father. Even though our daed is in Heaven, we still have our Heavenly Father, who takes care of us. God must've thought we were best for Daisy, or He would've had Mrs. Cooper put her on someone else's porch step."

Mamm smiled and wiped a tear. "My family and I would love to raise Daisy. Anna's already spoken with Marlene Hochstetler about taking care of her while we're working. She's agreed. I hope you'll grant us your blessing."

Anna exchanged an endearing look with her mamm. Her timing to chime in and agree with Anna couldn't have been better. Beth and Leah had chosen powerful words too. Her body tensed and she stared at him with anticipation.

Bishop Weaver rubbed his hands together. "You all present a good case. Beth, you may be the youngest, but you are not short on wisdom. God doesn't make mistakes, and with what you've told me, I believe He had His hand in giving you Daisy. You have my blessing to raise Daisy and wilkom her into your family. I'll announce how she came to you at the next service."

Anna's knees weakened and her eyes dampened with tears of joy. She kissed the sleeping newborn's tiny forehead. The boppli's eyes opened. Her tongue moved in and out of her sweet lips. "Danki, Bishop Weaver!" She traced the child's face with her finger. "We better get this one home. She's getting hungry."

The bishop laughed and ushered them to the

door. "She's a sweetheart. She slept through our entire meeting. She's blessed to have you in her life. I'm certain she'll be wilkomed with opened arms by all."

Anna swelled with excitement looking at Daisy. "I have a feeling we're the ones who will be blessed. We're grateful for your blessing."

Anna crossed the thick, lush grass to the buggy, passed Daisy to Mamm, and untied the horse. They climbed in and went home. Happiness at the bishop's blessing warmed Anna's heart.

Daisy fussed and cried, and Beth and Leah sang to soothe her.

Rocking the boppli, Mamm snuggled her close. "Daisy needs to be changed, and she's hungry."

Anna pulled in the yard and halted the horse.

Leah jumped out. "Anna, you go inside. We'll take care of the horse and buggy."

Anna marveled at how her schweschders never hesitated to support her. She took the newborn from Mamm, went inside, warmed a bottle, and filled it with milk.

Daisy settled down and suckled the bottle.

Beth entered, dug out a nappy from the bag Mrs. Hochstetler had given Anna, and passed the cotton cloth to her.

Anna waited for Daisy to drain her bottle. She put the empty bottle aside, got what she needed, and changed the delightful child's nappy.

Beth stood close. "I'll take the soiled cloth, rinse it, and put it in a bucket of water like Mrs. Hochstetler showed me." She skipped away.

Minutes later, Beth scampered into the room. "Mamm let me use the cradle we all slept in after we were born for my dolls. I removed them from the cradle, lined it with a clean sheet, and dragged it into your room, Anna." She held up a thin yellow blanket. "We can cover her with this one. It's hot tonight. She won't want much on her."

Mamm patted Beth's shoulder. "You're a good little helper." She went to the kitchen.

Leah followed her. "I'll set the table."

Anna marveled at her little schweschder. Beth had taken the initiative and provided what Daisy needed before Anna had time to think about a proper sleeping place for the child. Daisy would fit into their family fine, and she didn't have to care for her alone. "Tomorrow morning, you'll take the latest addition to our family with you to Mrs. Hochstetler's haus."

"Don't worry. I'll enjoy taking care of Daisy. She'll be fine."

"I trust you, and our new addition is fortunate to have you in her life. Let's go put her in her new bed." She and her little schweschder went to her room and laid the infant in the maple cradle. "You did a wonderful job making her bed cozy and safe, Beth."

They tiptoed out, hoping Daisy wouldn't wake, and headed for the kitchen. After they'd filled their stomachs with the food Mamm prepared, they said good night and headed for bed.

Anna quietly changed into her nightdress, knelt, and prayed a prayer of thanks to God for Daisy. She crawled into bed and turned down her lantern. Wide awake, she tossed and turned. She had to talk to Daniel as soon as possible. She'd waited long enough. What would Daniel think of Daisy? Would it no longer matter? Had he removed himself from her life?

Daniel turned on his side and stared at the dark night sky through the open window. Honoring Noah's request had been difficult. He missed Anna. Two weeks had passed since he'd been at the dry goods shop or her haus. Should he have removed himself to give her time without him around to contemplate her choice? He winced as a twinge of guilt settled in his stomach. He should've warned her he wouldn't be kumming to visit her. He regretted not telling her.

He rolled his shoulders and turned his head from side to side. Stiff and tired, he hadn't slept through the night since the last time he'd seen her. Enough time had passed. He'd go to the shop in the morning.

The rooster's crow woke Daniel and Otis at dawn on Friday morning. A gentle rain pinged the windows. He got up, dressed into his work clothes, and followed his routine of chores. A loud growl roared from his stomach. He tossed his dirty gloves on a rickety wooden table in the barn, and he and Otis strolled to the kitchen. After filling his four-legged friend's water and food dishes, he scanned the kitchen. Pancakes sounded good. Fixing his breakfast, he wondered how Anna would receive him. Would her eyes cast downward or meet his gaze? His heart thumped wildly in his chest. Would she have an answer for him? He finished his breakfast, hurried, and dressed, taking extra care. He harnessed and secured his horse to the buggy, and went to the shop.

Taking a deep breath, he went inside. There she stood, as beautiful and radiant as he remembered. "Anna, Leah, how are you?"

Anna smiled a wilkom greeting. There it was. The smile he'd missed. The assurance he needed. His heart fluttered with excitement.

"I'm glad to see you, and I'm sure Leah is too.

Kumme in, stranger. I've been wondering where you've been."

Leah handed him a cup of hot coffee. "Anna's right. We've missed you. What have you been doing?"

"I've been busy, and I was giving Anna time to think."

Leah gave him an impish grin. "She's had more than enough time. Why don't you two go out back for a bit and chat? If we have customers, I'll assist them. You speak with Anna. I'm sure you have a lot of catching up to do."

Anna nodded and gestured for him to follow her. They stepped outside.

He took a few steps forward and stood close to the woman he loved. "Anna, I've missed you."

"Why have you stayed away?"

The hurt expression on her face made him regret not coming sooner.

"Noah asked me to step away for a couple of weeks. At first I didn't want to honor his request, but later I thought better of it. I wanted to give you time to have a clear mind about all of this. I don't want you to have any regrets. Not one."

"You could've told me your intentions. I didn't understand why you disappeared from my life."

Her tone, laced with pain, struck a nerve. He didn't want to add to her angst. "I should've told you what I was going to do and why. I'm sorry." He grinned and reached for her hand. "I'm here because I couldn't stand being away from you. I've been in a miserable mood the last two weeks."

She ran her thumb over his fingers. "Leah and I drove out to your haus and Mark King was there. I didn't want to interrupt, so Leah and I went home. I was hoping to find out why you were avoiding me."

Her soft voice and her sad facial features pained his heart. He gently squeezed her hand. "I wish you hadn't left." He gazed into her hazel eyes. "Anna, I'm in love with you, but the longer you take to clear your mind, the more confused I am."

Her eyes sparkled and her face beamed. "I love you, Daniel, and I'm not in love with Noah. I'm clear about where I stand with him, but I'd rather we had this serious discussion tonight at home. Seeing you, I couldn't wait a minute longer to tell you how much I love you, and only you."

Her words sent his heart soaring, but the overwhelming relief and excitement didn't kumme as anticipated. She'd hurt him. He loved her with all his heart, but her indecision about Noah had blemished their happiness together. In spite of his muddled mind, he could hardly stifle the urge to wrap his arms around her waist and hold her. "Anna, I'm so happy we can move on with our lives. Your committing to me makes me so happy, but we do need to talk. I'll kumme over later after work, and we'll settle this."

"Oh, Daniel, I can't wait to plan our future!" She pushed two chairs together. "Sit. Something exciting has happened while we've been apart."

"What?"

She reminded him about April and Mrs. Cooper shopping in the store and her giving April quilting pointers and told him of April's tragic death and Daisy. "Daniel, I can't wait for you to hold her."

"What a sad story! I'm so sorry this poor young woman didn't have a chance to raise her child, but I am anxious to hold the boppli." He was amazed how she had accepted the responsibility of raising Daisy without reservation. She had such a nurturing personality with her mamm and schweschders. She'd be a caring and loving mamm. The kind of woman he wanted for his kinner. Sorry for April's passing, he wasn't surprised the love of his life had a deep compassion for the woman and her infant. He loved kinner and would wilkom being a daed to Daisy one day soon, and he hoped he and Anna had many more kinner together.

Anna beamed. "I fell in love with her right away. I have taken on the role of her mamm. Do you have any objections? Would Daisy alter your desire to marry me?"

"Absolutely not."

"I'm relieved. I doubt many men would be so amenable."

"I wouldn't turn away a child in need."

"One more reason to love you."

Leah joined them. "When are you going to bring Otis to visit us?"

He grinned. "So Otis is the one you miss, not me."

The three of them laughed. Leah took his empty cup. "We miss both of you."

"I invited Daniel to meet Daisy this evening."

Bouncing on her toes, Leah grinned. "I couldn't wait for Anna to tell you about her. I've been bursting to tell you about our new little addition. You'll take one look at her and fall in love with the tiny darling. If you didn't know the truth about Daisy, you'd think she was Anna's. Daisy has her same hair and eyes."

Anna hadn't mentioned Noah. Had she told Noah about Daisy or her revelation she wasn't in love with him? What was his reaction to her raising the boppli? He'd find out more this evening. "I'd better get going. I should let you get back to work. What time would you like me to kumme to your haus?"

"Six is good."

* * *

Daniel traveled to three different barns, hammered and nailed more boards than he would have liked to repair roofs and porches, and headed home to change. The clock's hands hadn't moved fast enough to reach six. He hurried to wash and dress into a crisp clean shirt and black pants. He snapped his suspenders over his shoulders and set his hat on his head.

On his way to Anna's, he flicked the leads for his horse to trot faster. He wouldn't take his time and view the gardens, sunflowers, lilacs, and honeysuckle today. Cows and horses grazed on the thick green pastures.

Otis panted next to him on the bench, seeming to sense where they were headed.

The rain had cleared and the sun dried the wet grass. Clothes hung on the Mast family's line and flapped in the gentle breeze. A red fox ran in front of his horse and hid in the thick woods. Honeysuckle scented the air. He hummed a tune, anxious to meet Daisy as he turned down the lane to the Planks' haus.

Anna was in a rocker on the porch, holding the boppli. He waved, tied the horse to the hitching post, and headed for them.

Otis ran to Cotton, who was sitting under a big maple tree.

He reached Anna and peeked at the round, pinked cheeks. "She's pretty."

Anna flipped the blanket back and he got a good look. "She's got long legs."

He gasped. "She's exquisite."

Handing her to him, Anna smiled. "She's a contented child. She cries when she's hungry, tired, or needs a fresh nappy. Otherwise, she's an angel."

Daisy captured Daniel's heart. Her warm body wrapped in the soft blanket fit perfectly into his arms. He was meant to be a daed.

Daisy sneezed and jerked.

They laughed at her scrunched face and wide-eyed expression. She stared directly into his eyes.

His heart melted. "She's captivating."

"And irresistible. I can hardly put her down." She hugged his arm. "You aren't a bit nervous with her, are you?"

"No. I've always been comfortable around bopplin and kinner. The boppli are warm and soft, and the kinner are energetic and full of curiosity, and they ask the most innocent and humorous questions. They're full of wonder."

"Kinner add so much to our lives. Beth is still innocent, but she's growing into a young lady. I'm delighted we'll have a little one to dote over again."

"Getting up at night for feedings and changing nappies will have you dragging some days. Do you have someone in mind to care for her while you're at work?"

"Our neighbor, Marlene Hochstetler, has already agreed to care for her. Beth stays with her in the summer and after school. She's a wonderful, caring woman. Beth loves her."

"You're blessed to have everything work out so well for you with Daisy."

She gazed at him. "I'm relieved you're willing to raise her with me if we marry."

"Did you tell Noah about Daisy?"

"Not yet." She sighed. "I also haven't told him what we had together belongs in the past and there is no future for us, but I will soon."

"I don't take pleasure in his being hurt, but I'm

glad you've concluded you're in love with me." He caressed her cheek. Now wasn't the time for him to tell her about his wounded heart. She was so enthused to have this beautiful little one. He didn't want to spoil her memorable day. He'd tell her later. "Tell me more about your plans for Daisy."

She told him the bishop's response and how they'd quickly made arrangements for Daisy's comfort. "Daisy has inherited the cradle Mamm used for me, Leah, and Beth."

The peaceful infant slept in his arms. He'd held her the entire time they'd been together, and cradling her felt like the most natural thing in the world. He didn't want to part from her.

Beth came outside. "Daniel, I didn't hear you pull in." She pointed to Otis and Cotton chasing each other across the yard. "Cotton's happy Otis is here. It's about time the two of you showed up." She peered at Daisy. "Isn't she precious?"

"I missed you too, Beth." He clasped Daisy's tiny hand. "She is beautiful."

"I hope you're hungry. We have enough to feed the neighborhood. Time to sit for supper."

They rose and went inside.

Leah reached for Daisy. "Daniel, I'm so glad you're joining us. What do you think of our new addition?"

"She's a very good boppli. I don't want to give her up."

"She's a sweetheart." She kissed the sleeping child's nose. "I'll put her in her bed. We'll feed her when she wakes."

Mamm carried a bowl of boiled potatoes slathered with melted butter to the center of the table. "Daniel, we've missed you. Have a seat, son."

His heart warmed. She called him "son." He hoped

to hear her endearment over and over in the years to kumme. "Danki for having me. This table is as pretty as a picture decorated with colorful food. Would you like me to pray?"

"Please do."

Waiting until everyone was seated and holding hands, Daniel closed his eyes and bowed his head. "Dear Heavenly Father, danki for the food You've provided to nourish our bodies and bless these women for their hard work in preparing the meal. Danki for bringing Daisy into this loving family, and please watch over her. Amen."

Anna smiled. "Your prayer was lovely." She passed him the plate of sliced roast beef.

The women nodded in agreement.

"Yes, son, that was a very nice blessing," Mrs. Plank said.

He delighted in being back in the bosom of this gracious family again. They didn't hold back on their sentiment. Their openness was one of the things he held dear about them. "It's a pleasure to be here and praying with you again. Danki." He took two slices of meat and put them on his plate. "Here you go, Leah." He passed the platter to her.

Beth giggled. "Otis and Cotton have been inseparable since you've arrived."

He enjoyed his meal with the Planks. Afterward, he got up and lifted the dish tub. "I'll fetch the water for the dishes." His cheeks dimpled. "I'll dry them if you wash them, Anna."

Mamm pinched the bridge of her nose. "I've got a terrible raging headache."

Leah rushed to the cabinet and took out a packet of aspirin powder. She passed the packet and a glass of water to Mamm. "Swallow the powder and please go to bed. We can take care of what needs to be done before bedtime."

"Yell if you need anything."

Beth went to her side and hugged her.

"Take care, Mrs. Plank." Daniel accepted and dried a glass from Anna.

He waited until Mamm was out of sight and then gave Anna a mischievous grin. He splashed water on her.

She splashed him back and laughed.

Leah and Beth giggled.

"Waa! Waa!"

Beth stood and kicked her chair back. "Daisy's up. I'll warm the milk."

"I'll read her a story and play with her in Anna's room. You can bring the bottle to me and join me until she goes back to sleep." Leah winked. "Let's give Anna and Daniel time without her pesky schweschders around."

"Sounds good to me!" Beth skipped to the icebox.

"Finished!" Anna wiped the counter, wrung out her dishcloth, and hung it over the side of the tub.

"I should go home and gather what I need for my repair jobs tomorrow."

"I'll walk you out."

Otis followed him out, jumped on the bench, and sat.

Anna laughed. "Cotton must've worn Otis out. He's ready to go home." She reached for Daniel's hand. "Daniel, I'm happy you're comfortable with Daisy. In the short time we've had her with us, she's already brought so much joy into our lives. Even before you met her, I had made up my mind to tell you how much I love you and I'm not in love with Noah. I am clear he's a friend and nothing more. Since his return and having spoken with him, I discovered we are not compatible and we desire different lifestyles.

"I fell out of love with him sometime during the year before he left. I was letting the past with him baffle me. You are the one for me, and no one else. I love you, Daniel Bontrager."

His heart thumped hard. With Daisy's arrival, he'd changed his mind about telling her his thoughts until another day. He loved her, but he needed a little time to digest the emotional turmoil he'd been through. He couldn't put it off. He had to tell her. "Anna, I love you and your family. But the time you've taken to contemplate your feelings for Noah has clouded my mind about whether we are right for each other."

Her eyes blinded with tears, she stepped back. "What do you mean?"

"I've been upset our relationship didn't seem solid to you. Your reaction to Noah's return *shocked* me."

"Are you saying you don't want to marry me? Have I ruined what we had together? Please tell me this isn't so."

He couldn't stand for her to cry. His intention wasn't to upset her, but he had to be true to himself and honest with her. "Your declaration is what I've been waiting for, but I'm not ready to set a date for the wedding."

"Do you need time away from me to contemplate what you want?" She wiped her wet face with the corner of her apron, already damp from washing dishes.

He shook his head and gently wiped a tear trailing down her cheek. "I'm sorry I've upset you. I had to share my heart with you openly. I'm not abandoning you or our courtship. I want to continue courting you and see if we can't get back to where we were before Noah returned."

"My head understands, but my heart is breaking. I've been selfish thinking only of my needs, and I've put our relationship in jeopardy."

"I'm thrilled you are clear you want us to marry. I just need to get over the hurt of your indecision at Noah's return. Let's give it time."

She held his arms with a determined expression on her face. "I would marry you tomorrow without any reservation, Daniel."

He wouldn't allow himself to ignore the hurt he needed to overcome before he could commit to marriage with her. "I love you, and in time, I'm hoping to ask you again to marry me. I'm hurting too, and I need to heal." He kissed her lips and hugged her tight. "Good night, sweetheart."

She managed a weak smile and wave. "Will you kumme by the haus Sunday, since we won't have services that day?"

"I will." His head throbbed. The conversation had been a difficult one. If he couldn't get past this, he doubted he'd love another woman for a long time. Had Noah's return and her confusion about the man scarred them beyond repair? He ached at the possibility.

Chapter Twelve

Anna blinked back tears pooling in her eyes. What had she done? Daniel had proven she could count on him from doing the smallest repair to protecting her from harm. He'd promised to provide for her and their future kinner. He was attractive, strong, a devout believer in God, and had everything she'd ever want in a husband. She understood his pain. She'd have felt the same way had their positions been reversed. She wished she could take it all back.

She went inside. Leah and Beth must be in with Daisy. Mamm must've fallen asleep. She poured water from the white porcelain pitcher into a bowl, rinsed, and dried her face with a towel. *Knock. Knock.*

She dried her hands and opened the door. "Noah, it's a little late. Is anything wrong?"

Noah curved his lips in a wide smile. "I was thinking of you and I wanted to stop by for a few minutes. Where is everyone?"

She didn't relish hurting him, but his timing couldn't have been better. She was anxious to show Daniel she'd chosen him. Another way to prove it to him was to tell Noah. She'd explain Daisy's presence first, in case the little one woke up. She told him about finding Daisy on their porch. "She's beautiful, delicate, and no trouble. She's a delight to have around. We love her. Beth and Leah are with her in my bedroom. Would you like to meet her? She might be asleep."

Noah shook his head and wrung his hands. "Anna, I want one child, and I'd like the boppli to be ours. Are you set on keeping Daisy?"

"I appreciate your honesty. It's a lot to consider, but don't worry. What I have to say will ease your mind where Daisy is concerned." She pressed a hand to her throat and swallowed. "Noah, I had doubts about a future with you before you left Berlin. Your return sent my mind back to when we first met, but it didn't take long to figure out I was no longer in love with you. I have given my heart completely to Daniel. I'm sorry. I don't mean to cause you pain, but I must be honest. I care about you as a friend, and I want you to find a fraa who loves your need for change and delights in it."

His shoulders slumped. "I did wish you were more spontaneous like me, and I did try to change you. It was foolish of me, wasn't it?" He frowned, his eyes sad.

"Noah, there's nothing wrong with your choices or mine. We've grown up. Instead of drawing us closer, our differences drew us apart."

He stood and gently pulled her to her feet. "I would marry you in spite of our differences, and my heart tells me to do whatever I can to win you back. My mind agrees with you, because you're right. We are different people, and I was wrong to pressure you to bend to my ways. Daisy is another reason marriage isn't right for us. I'm not comfortable raising another man's boppli, especially since I would prefer to have only one child."

She swallowed the sob rising in her throat.

He rubbed his thumb over her hand. "Daniel's a blessed man to have you in his life. It softens the blow to have gotten acquainted with him and I have no doubt he will take good care of you."

She swiped an escaping tear with her finger. "Will you remain in Berlin?"

"No. I have no ill will toward you or Daniel, but returning to Lancaster would be easier for me. I'll love you for a long time. I wish you and Daniel the best, but running into you in town and church would be too painful. I'm going to approach Mamm about selling her place and leaving with me."

If she were in his shoes, she would want a fresh start too. She hoped Jane would leave with him, so they could be together. She understood his desire to avoid her and Daniel together. "You've touched my life in a special way. I wish you the best, Noah." She fought to control the sob in her throat.

He kissed her cheek. "I wish the same for you, Anna." He gave her a wry smile. "I should go. I'm sure we'll run into each other before I leave. Take care."

She hugged him and noticed his tear-dampened cheeks. She walked him to the door and waited until his wagon was at the end of the lane before closing it. Their discussion had gone much better than she'd anticipated. She wished hers and Daniel's had ended on a better note.

Daniel had taken to Daisy as soon as he'd met her. She sucked in her upper lip. She'd been foolish to think her revelation would end with his proposing to her. She'd concentrated on her feelings and not his. Of course he would've suffered pain with her asking him to give her time to put Noah's return into perspective. Her thoughtless request might have cost her the love of her life. She couldn't bear to think of losing him.

She woke on Sunday morning, changed clothes, and picked up a wide-awake and smiling Daisy. Saturday had kumme and gone fast. She and Mamm had cleaned the haus all day. She was glad for a day of rest. She buried her nose in the boppli's neck. "I love you, little one." She changed her and carried her to the kitchen. Ham and bacon sizzled in the skillet. "Good morning, Mamm. Where are Leah and Beth?"

"They're in the chicken coop gathering eggs. I suspect they're taking their time and playing with the hens and chicks." She leaned forward and kissed Daisy's fat little fingers. "I enjoy the bishop's messages and visiting with our friends after the service, but I'm glad to stay home today."

"I feel the same way, Mamm." Anna balanced Daisy on her hip and lifted milk out of the icebox. She poured some in a pan on the stove and set a clean bottle on the counter. She took a chair and bounced the little maedel on her knee and waited for the milk to warm. She wanted to tell her family once they were all together about her conversations with Noah and Daniel. "When did you get rid of your headache, Mamm?"

"I'd guess about an hour after I went to bed last night. I woke up refreshed. Daniel seemed to enjoy Daisy."

Leah and Beth scampered in the door, interrupting them.

Beth carried a basket of eggs. "I dropped one and the shell broke."

Leah smiled at Anna and kissed Daisy's nose. "I'm to blame. I chased her to the door and caused her to drop the egg."

Mamm grinned. "We've got plenty. I'm glad you have a good time together."

Beth stuck her finger in the warm milk on the stove and poured it in the bottle. She passed it to Anna. "Leah and I heard you talking when we put Daisy to bed. We peeked out and saw Noah. He was here kinda late. Is he upset about something?"

"I'll tell you about his visit when we sit down together."

Mamm scrambled the eggs in the pan, put them on plates, and served them. She sat next to Anna and paused to give the blessing before picking up her fork.

Anna pushed her plate aside and fed Daisy her milk. "First, I'll tell you about my discussion with Daniel. I told him I had already fallen out of love with Noah when I gave my heart to him. When Noah returned to Berlin, I let the past with him cloud my judgment."

Leah got up, grabbed a basket of sliced bread on the counter, and removed canned peaches from the cabinet. She set them on the table. "Was he overjoyed?"

Beth wiggled in her seat and grinned. "I'm excited! I want you to marry Daniel right away!"

Mamm lifted her palm. "Wait and listen to what Anna has to say."

Anna put the bottle beside her plate and shifted Daisy to a burping position on her shoulder. She patted her back. "Daniel's been hurt by my putting him off. I don't blame him, and I'm sad I put a big gray cloud on our relationship. He's disappointed I was so uncertain where I stood with Noah. He's hurt. He's disappointed I didn't have clarity about him and me. He's asked me for time to reconcile this in his mind."

Beth gasped and frowned. "Will he still visit us?"

"We'll spend time together, but Daniel isn't ready to marry me. I'm hoping he can heal."

"Me too." Beth frowned. "He belongs in our family, and so does Otis."

Hours later, Anna rocked Daisy in the chair on the porch and gazed at the wagon kumming down the lane. *Daniel.* She got up and waited by the hitching post for him.

He arrived and tied his horse to the post. "You look lovely." He kissed Daisy's forehead. "She's a cheerful soul."

"I've enjoyed rocking and cuddling her. I'm happy you're here."

"How's your Mamm?"

"Her headache is gone. She's doing well. Let's go to our spot and chat. Noah came by after you left. I'd like to tell you about our conversation." She grabbed a blanket from the back of the chair.

"I'm surprised." He walked beside her to their spot, spread the blanket, and sat next to her. She rocked Daisy to sleep.

"I told Noah what I told you. He admitted he was pushing me to do things his way, and he had noticed, but ignored, my reluctance to do so. Neither of us had a thorough discussion about our differences until last night. He agrees we drifted apart."

"Did he meet Daisy?"

"I told him about her, and he wouldn't have wanted to raise her as his. He is set on having one child and would prefer the boppli be his flesh and blood."

Daniel's eyebrows lifted. "I'm glad you had already told me you wanted us to resume our courtship before he found out about Daisy. It leaves no doubt you didn't choose me because of my acceptance of Daisy."

"Me too. I don't want you to question my decision in any way. I told him I was clear I'd given my heart to you completely before he came back to Berlin, before I told him about Daisy. He is fond of you, and he does wish us well. He is asking his mamm to sell her property and leave with him. He's confident she will agree to go with him. They're so close. He wants to move to Lancaster in a week or so. Mr. Zook will probably look after their place until a buyer kummes along. We ended the evening without animosity."

He blew out a sigh of relief. "I must say, Noah's going to Lancaster does make me feel better. I'm fond of Noah, but his leaving Berlin will make things easier for all of us."

They played with Daisy and enjoyed their time together.

He kissed her good-bye and left. She cradled Daisy and watched him until he turned the corner at the end of the lane. She'd settled her differences with Noah, and she'd declared her love for Daniel. She was ready to move forward and vow before God and all their friends she would stand by his side until her life on earth ended. She wished he matched her immediate desire to marry and was ready to set a date on the bishop's calendar. But she wouldn't push him. She caused this upheaval and she'd have to live with the consequences.

* * *

When Anna and Leah arrived at the shop Monday morning, two gray-haired Englischers were waiting to get in. "Good morning. I'll unlock the door for you. I'm Anna Plank, and meet my schweschder Leah. Are you in search of something special?"

"It's about time you showed up." Hands on hips, the tall woman looked down on them. She pushed past them and barged in the door. "Do you have a remnant box? I'm shopping for scraps of material for my daughter to stitch a patchwork quilt."

Leah gestured her to the back and dragged a box to the woman. "You're wilkom to rifle through these remnants."

The shorter woman followed Anna inside. She smiled and extended her hand. "I'm Irene Tisdale, and the woman who came in ahead of me is Etta Foster, my sister. You have a wonderful display of quilts on the walls. I need swatches for the quilt I'm working on. Do you have another box I can sift through?"

Anna gestured to a box underneath a shelf of aprons against the wall. She pulled the box out for the patron's convenience. "Here you go. Take your time, Mrs. Tisdale."

The kind woman held up a green swatch of cotton. "Do you like this one, Etta?"

Mrs. Foster pinched her lips. "It's not the color I want." She grimaced at Anna. "Do you have another box I can root through?"

Why was this woman being rude? Mrs. Tisdale, her schweschder, was pleasant and jolly. "I have and I'll bring another box out from the back."

"Don't bother. I can walk. Show me where the

swatches are." The woman's demanding, cold eyes stared at her.

Anna pointed to the back room and stepped into the open doorway. The woman brushed past her and bent to sort through the remnants. This woman was quite a challenge to please.

"You can go. I won't steal anything."

"I apologize if I've made you feel uncomfortable, Mrs. Foster. I stood by in case you might like help picking out certain colors or patterns. I'll be out front if you need me." Anna forced a smile and left the woman.

Mrs. Tisdale was humming as she fingered the fabric in the other box.

Leah sidled up next to Anna and leaned close to her ear. "These two couldn't be more opposite."

Mrs. Foster hurried to her sweet schweschder, carrying a fistful of swatches. "I can't find my small coin purse. Do you have it?"

"No! Didn't you put your coin purse in your pocket? Maybe it's in the buggy."

"I wouldn't question you about it if I had it in my pocket! We must head to the livery. I must find it." Throwing the material she carried onto the counter, Mrs. Foster glared at Anna. "I'll be back. Don't let anyone buy these."

Mrs. Tisdale winced. "I'm sorry. My sister can be a bit abrupt. We'll return in a few minutes."

"We'll be happy to hold your choices. I hope you find it." Anna smiled politely at her.

"Thank you, dear." The sweet woman patted her hand.

Mrs. Foster scowled. "Irene, quit dawdling and let's go."

Mrs. Tisdale hurried out liked a scared rabbit.

* * *

Daniel whistled as he weaved his way through the crowd in the hardware store and reached between two Amish men to grab a box of nails off the shelf. "Excuse me."

Both men gave him a half grin and moved aside as they perused the shelf. He scanned the hammers, saws, shovels, and other tools. Should he buy another hammer? *Not today.*

Heading to the counter to pay for his purchase, he tipped his hat to familiar Amish faces and smiled. He paid for the nails and returned to the livery. On his way, he passed a peddler hawking timepieces displayed on a small maple table.

"Beautiful timepieces for sale today! Doesn't cost you to have a look!" The peddler leaned on his weathered cane and tipped his hat as Daniel passed him.

Men and women diverted their eyes from the salesman and rushed by to avoid him. *It must be hard to make a living begging people to buy your products.* Daniel walked fast across the busy street.

"You simpleton! Look both ways before you cross the street!" A man waved his fist and beeped his motorcar's horn. "I almost hit you!"

"Sorry!" Daniel ran the rest of the way across the street to avoid being hit by the other oncoming motorcars, buggies with squeaky wheels, and horses clip-clopping on the street kumming toward him. He went inside the livery and put the nails in his saddlebag. He glanced at Noah and backed away out of the man's sight but kept him in view.

Noah reached in his wagon and lifted a small white bag from under the seat.

I shouldn't be rude. He wanted to say good-bye to Noah. He might not run into him again before he left. Daniel opened his mouth to greet him, but Noah was on his way out.

Two women bumped into Noah on their way into the livery. They frowned, said something Daniel couldn't understand, and glanced back at where they'd bumped into Noah. Daniel squinted, rubbed his chin, and watched them. What had upset them? He inched up a little closer but far enough away not to draw their attention.

The taller woman shouted from the buggy. "My coin purse isn't here." She narrowed her eyes. "The Amish man we bumped into had something in his hand. He looked suspicious, and I'm betting he stole my money. I'm going to the sheriff."

"Etta, you shouldn't jump to conclusions. Let's go back to where we first were when we noticed it missing and look for it again."

Etta shouted, "We're going to the sheriff before he gets away."

Oh no! The women accused Noah of being a thief. He had to tell Noah. Daniel followed the women to the sheriff's office but kept his distance. Etta seemed rude and unreasonable, compared to her companion. Noah would wonder why he didn't greet him earlier. He'd have to confess he was avoiding him. His muscles tensed. Noah's accuser looked like trouble. He had to help him.

The women ran inside. Daniel sat on the bench outside the building and waited. Through the open doorway, he heard the woman raising her voice and accusing Noah of stealing her coin purse. He should check the shops and find Noah to tell him about his accusers. He ran into Noah kumming out of the bakery close by. "Noah, I've got something important to tell you."

Grinning, Noah slapped him gently on the back. "Anna and I came to an understanding about us. It's difficult to accept she and I have no future, but our desires for life no longer match and it's for the best. I hope there are no hard feelings between you and me."

He smiled and nodded. "You're a good man, Noah. I have no ill will toward you. Anna told me you are relocating to Lancaster with your mamm. I wish you safe travel and much happiness in your life." He whispered in Noah's ear. "I came to find you, because I'm afraid you've been accused of wrongdoing."

Taking two steps back, Noah frowned and raised his eyebrows. "Daniel, what are you saying?"

The sheriff approached them. "I'm glad you're here, Noah. I thought I spotted you from the window. Would you come inside, please? Mrs. Foster and her sister, Mrs. Tisdale, have some concerns we need to discuss."

Noah glanced at Daniel and back at the sheriff. "I'm not acquainted with these women, but I'll kumme inside." He shrugged and followed the sheriff and Daniel inside

The sheriff gestured to the women. "Noah Schwartz, meet Mrs. Foster and Mrs. Tisdale."

Mrs. Foster yelled and pointed her accusing finger at Noah. "He's the man who stole my coin purse."

Noah gasped and put a hand to his parted lips. "I haven't stolen anything. Why would you accuse me of such a thing?"

Daniel understood his friend's dumbfounded look. He couldn't believe the woman was so bent on accusing Noah of stealing her property. "Sheriff, I can shed some light on this matter. I was in the livery when Noah came in to retrieve something from his wagon. These women bumped into him on his way out of the livery. He didn't take anything from their buggy."

"Liar! I'm sure you ignorant dullards all stick together." Mrs. Foster waggled her finger at Daniel.

The sheriff turned to the women. "Everyone, please have a seat and let's discuss this in a calm manner. Mrs. Foster and Mrs. Tisdale, this is Daniel Bontrager. I'm acquainted with both these men. They are respectable and honorable gentlemen. In my time as sheriff for the last twenty years, I've never had a single bone of contention with the Amish. They possess a deep belief in God and strive to maintain a peaceful community."

Daniel glanced at the timid Mrs. Tisdale. She had her hands folded in her lap and stared at her feet. She was intimidated by the other woman.

Mrs. Foster leaned forward and splayed her hand on the sheriff's desk. "Tell him to show you what coins are in his possession."

"Madam, are you sure you checked your buggy thoroughly and anyplace in town you've visited?"

She snarled at him. "What kind of sheriff are you? Asking him to show you what he's carrying isn't an unreasonable request."

The sheriff rubbed the back of his neck. "Noah, do you mind?"

"Not at all, Sheriff." Noah unwrapped a plain white handkerchief and emptied the coins on the desk.

"Madam, is Noah holding the exact amount of coins you are missing?"

"I had more. He's had time to hide the rest."

The sheriff leaned toward Mrs. Tisdale. "Did you observe Mr. Schwartz taking anything from your buggy?"

She darted her eyes to Mrs. Foster, bowed her head, and spoke barely above a whisper. "No, but he was leaving the livery in a hurry, and he did have something in his hand."

"What are you going to do about this, Sheriff?" Mrs. Foster crossed her arms against her chest.

The sheriff took off his hat and scratched his head. He put his lawman's hat back on his head with a frustrated expression. "There's nothing I can do. You have no proof Mr. Schwartz has stolen your money. If someone turns in the coin purse, how can I contact you?"

The furious woman huffed. "My sister and I will be staying at the Berlin Inn tonight and leave to go home tomorrow. Please check with me by six in the morning if anyone turns my money in, or if this man confesses to the crime." She sniffed and rolled her eyes. "I doubt he'll tell you anything. I'm already considering my coins gone." She nodded to Mrs. Tisdale. "Let's go. There's nothing more for us to do here."

Mrs. Tisdale ducked her head, glanced at them with regretful eyes and a smile, and followed her haughty schweschder outside.

Daniel met Noah's worried gaze. "I suggest we go tell the bishop what transpired before these women have a chance to tell anyone who listens. Even if they don't, someone may've noticed us in the sheriff's office and ask questions."

Noah shook his head. "Jah, we should tell him. I

don't get why these women are targeting me. Sheriff, danki for your support."

The sheriff pulled out a small can of tobacco and tucked a wad between his gum and left cheek. "I'm sorry to have had to question you, Noah. I believe you, but I can't stop the gossip. I'll bet these women will tell anyone who will listen about how you stole Mrs. Foster's coins. She obviously dropped the purse. I doubt we'll find her belongings. Push Mrs. Foster's accusation out of your mind and go on with your life."

Daniel studied Noah's face. His heart sank for Noah. Being accused of wrongdoing when you're innocent would be painful and frustrating. The Amish worked hard to maintain their honorable reputation and kept to themselves. If the women spread gossip about Noah, would their suspicions tarnish the Amish's good reputation in the Englischers' minds? He hoped not. He rolled his shoulders and tried to relax. No need to jump to conclusions.

He put a hand on Noah's back and guided him to the door. "Danki, Sheriff. We'll be at Bishop Weaver's or Grace's Dry Goods Shop with Anna Plank if you find out anything."

Noah bowed his head, nodded at the sheriff, and left with Daniel. "Bishop Weaver will be upset. Gossip in town about an Amish man accused of stealing will cast doubt in some Englischers' minds. What should I do?"

"Let's hope the women, the sheriff, or someone else finds the coin purse. If not, there's nothing you can do."

"Why me?"

"I don't have an answer for you. I wish I did." He

pulled him between the post office and hardware store, away from the crowds. "Let's bow our heads and say a quick prayer."

Noah closed his eyes.

"Dear Heavenly Father, please intervene and clear Noah's name. We love and trust in You, Heavenly Father. Amen."

Noah opened his eyes. "In spite of what we are going through with Anna, you've stuck by me and did your best to help me today. I won't forget your loyalty."

"You would do the same for me."

Noah nodded. "Absolutely."

They walked a little farther and knocked on Bishop Weaver's front door.

The bishop removed his spectacles. "Daniel and Noah, what a pleasant surprise. Kumme in." He pushed the door open and gestured them inside. "Make yourselves comfortable. Coffee or tea?"

"No, danki. We have bad news." Noah sat and rested his elbows on his knees and folded his hands.

"Has someone been hurt?"

Daniel pressed his back against the feather-filled cushion in the maple chair. His body tensed, and he wished he could do more for Noah.

Noah shook his head. "I returned to my wagon to fetch some coins I'd knotted in a handkerchief and put under the seat in a clean flour sack." He sighed and slapped his legs. "I'd forgotten to take the coins with me when I got to town. Two Englischers, Mrs. Foster and Mrs. Tisdale, ran into me leaving the livery. They had returned to their buggy to search for

Mrs. Foster's coin purse at the same time I was leaving. They are accusing me of taking their money."

"Why are they accusing you of stealing her coins?"

"They noticed something in my hand and assumed what I had in my hand was her coins."

"Did they approach you?"

Noah hung his head dejectedly. "No. They went directly to the sheriff and reported their accusation against me to him."

Daniel cleared his throat. "I was in the livery when Noah returned to retrieve his money. He went only to his wagon. They passed Noah and remembered he had something in his hand, and they assumed his handkerchief was the missing coins. I overheard the women's accusation against Noah. I didn't approach them, but I followed at a safe distance behind them to the sheriff's office. I found Noah and told him about what happened. The sheriff approached us and asked Noah to step inside his office."

Noah groaned and slumped in the chair. "Daniel followed me inside. Mrs. Foster angrily pointed a finger at me and boldly said I stole her money. Mrs. Tisdale bowed her head and darted her nervous eyes to her schweschder. She agreed with my accuser that I had something in my hand and agreed my possession could be her schweschder's coins. I got the impression she was afraid not to."

"Daniel, did you tell the sheriff what you witnessed about Noah in the livery?"

"I did, and he told the women he is acquainted with us and proclaimed we are honorable Amish men. It didn't matter to her what he said or what I witnessed. Mrs. Foster believes Noah is guilty."

"Noah, you're in a terrible bind. I hope these women won't spread the word you're a thief."

Daniel darted his eyes to Noah and the bishop. "They are staying in town tonight and leaving in the morning, I'm hoping her coin purse with the coins is found, and Noah's name is cleared before they depart."

Bishop Weaver took a seat by Noah on the settee. "My heart goes out to you, Noah. Let's bow our heads and ask God to help us." The bishop prayed a prayer to God, and the men raised their heads. "Don't fret. You've done nothing wrong. If the coin purse is not found, the women will leave anyway and gossip will change to something else in no time."

"Your support and encouragement means a lot to me, Bishop Weaver. Danki."

Daniel and Noah bid him farewell and walked to the dry goods shop to speak to Anna.

Daniel had hoped for time alone with Anna and Leah to relay this story without any customers in the shop. Noah was so troubled. The man's shoulders drooped, he barely spoke, and his cheery disposition had disappeared. He suspected Anna and Leah would notice Noah's sad demeanor the moment they laid eyes on him. He walked in the shop with Noah.

Anna and Leah gasped.

Anna approached Noah. "What's wrong? You look troubled."

Noah recounted the story to Anna and Leah and told them the women's names.

Anna's and Leah's mouths dropped open.

Daniel watched Anna. She was stunned and hurt someone would question Noah's integrity.

Anna ran, dragged the remnant box to the front

room, and dumped it over. "Those women came to the shop and riffled through two boxes of fabric. Maybe Mrs. Foster's coin purse is somewhere in the box." She and Leah separated the pieces to search for the coin purse.

Daniel and Noah pushed the pieces aside to search the sea of fabric for the missing coin purse.

Daniel knelt next to Anna. "The purse isn't here."

Leah ran to the back and dragged a box to them. "Mrs. Foster spent more time in the box we checked first. Mrs. Tisdale searched this box." She poured the fabric and watched the pieces scatter on the floor. She and Anna spread the fabric squares.

Anna looked from one piece to another. "Nothing."

Leah dragged the box to the back room, leaving the door open.

She yelled, "I found the coin purse!"

Daniel, Noah, and Anna ran to her.

Daniel approached her. "Where did you find it?"

Leah pointed to the faded cedar chest. "I pushed the box next to the chest, and the coin purse was behind the large piece of furniture. The chest is not far from the wall. You wouldn't notice the purse unless you were looking over the chest. The very reason why we missed the purse before."

Anna pressed a hand to her chest and blew out a breath. "The lantern doesn't provide good light in this room. No wonder we missed the tiny thing."

Noah heaved a big sigh. "What a relief! Here's proof I'm not a thief."

Daniel smiled. "I'm delighted for you, my friend. Let's go and tell the sheriff, your accusers, and the bishop the good news."

Mrs. Foster and Mrs. Tisdale came into the store.

Daniel froze. Noah looked stunned.

Anna's and Leah's faces paled, and they approached them.

Leah waved the coin purse. "We have good news for you. We found your coin purse."

Mrs. Foster snatched the coin purse from her. "Where'd you find it?"

Anna clasped Leah's other hand. "She found the small purse behind a cedar chest in the back room. The purse must've fallen out of your pocket and slid across the floor behind the furniture piece."

Mrs. Tisdale snapped her fingers. "Of course! When my sister changed clothes, I checked the skirt closely and discovered a rip in the pocket seam. The rip was large enough for the tiny thing to slip through it. We were on our way to tell the sheriff how sorry we were to accuse Mr. Schwartz when we caught a glimpse of him through the window in your store. It provided us the perfect opportunity to apologize to you in person, Mr. Schwartz. We are so sorry we accused you of any wrongdoing." She bumped her sister's arm. "Don't you agree, Etta?"

Mrs. Foster lifted her chin and glared at Noah. "What are you doing here? Are these women friends of yours?"

Noah looked perplexed. "They are friends of both Daniel and me."

She glowered and tapped a finger on her cheek. "Did you ask these women to cover up your crime?"

Mrs. Tisdale rolled her eyes. "I'm sorry for my schweschder's ill-mannered behavior. Don't answer her question." She harrumphed and crossed her arms. "Etta, stop being rude. These people have been kind and gracious, in spite of your bad behavior toward them. You have your coin purse, and the explanation is more than reasonable. You owe them an apology."

Mrs. Foster stared at her schweschder with a wide-eyed expression and parted lips. She wrenched her gaze from Mrs. Tisdale and over to Leah. "Thank you for my coin purse." She turned on her heel. "Irene, let's go." She swung her arms and marched to the door.

The kind woman smiled. "We'll tell the sheriff the news."

Mrs. Foster whipped her head around and glared at her schweschder over her shoulder. "He can tell the sheriff. I'm ready to get out of here."

Daniel stepped closer to Noah. "We don't want to trouble you. We'll tell the sheriff. We're pleased you have your coin purse and can leave here assured Noah isn't a thief."

"Again, we are so sorry, Mr. Schwartz. I hope you will forgive us." Mrs. Tisdale gave Noah a shy and apologetic grin.

Mrs. Foster pushed the door open. "Irene, come on. You've done enough apologizing for me to these people. I'm not going to wait much longer."

Noah nodded. "I accept your apology, and I wish you and your schweschder safe travel home."

The women left, and Noah heaved a big sigh. "I'm so relieved this terrible misunderstanding is over. Do you mind if we hold hands and pray?"

They got in a circle, held hands, and bowed their heads. Noah thanked God for Mrs. Tisdale's discovery of the rip in the skirt and the purse being found. Noah pointed to a pitcher of water on a small table. "Do you mind if I have a glass?"

Leah pulled a glass from a small cabinet and poured water from a porcelain pitcher into it. "Here you go." She passed the glass to Noah and chatted with him about the two women and their different attitudes.

Daniel gazed at Anna. Her hand in his during the prayer was small and warm. Her touch sent excitement through him. He thought of her night and day. His mind said wait. His heart said not to.

Chapter Thirteen

Anna met his eyes and pulled him aside. "You were a good friend to Noah to stick by him through all this. You didn't have to go to the bishop's haus or kumme here with him. You are the kindest man, Daniel Bontrager."

"He would have done the same for me."

"I suppose we should join Leah and Noah."

He nodded and followed her.

Leah had given Noah a cup of coffee, and they were chatting.

Anna pressed a hand to her throat. "Noah, you should tell your mamm, the bishop, and the sheriff what happened before they find out from someone else."

"Jah, I should. Again, I'm grateful for everything all of you have done for me."

Daniel opened the door. "I should get back to work. I'll stop by your haus later, Anna. Good-bye, Leah."

Anna told them good-bye and shut the door behind them. Minutes later, the door reopened. "Grace, I'm glad you're here." She recounted her story about the women accusing Noah of stealing.

"That's terrible! How is Noah?"

"He's relieved the ordeal is over."

Leah wrinkled her nose. "Where's Joy?"

"She's with Mamm. I stopped in to chat with Mark, and I wanted to visit with you if you weren't too busy. You and Leah have done a wonderful job displaying the quilts on the walls."

Leah looked up as a customer came into the shop. "I'll help her while you two visit."

Anna motioned to Grace. "Let's go outside for a few minutes."

Grace and Anna sat in the two old wooden chairs out back.

Anna crossed her legs and relaxed. "I'm glad you're pleased with the display." She told Grace more about Noah's accusers, and where they found the coin purse. "I'm sure he'll tell Mark the story." Mark had been a loyal friend to Noah. He'd advised him on life matters and taught him woodworking techniques. He'd paid him to work on his property, and Noah enjoyed his job. Mark hadn't judged Noah for leaving. He'd allowed him to make his own decisions and supported him in his dreams.

Grace and Mark followed Amish law but bent the rules when they supported their friends. She had done the same in her life and was thankful Grace had shown her this through her friendship with Becca Carrington, who had married an Englisch doctor in Massillon, Ohio, but maintained her faith in God and values, getting involved in a church in Massillon.

"Poor Noah. Mark will be shocked. He thinks the world of him."

Anna had been brokenhearted to find him so forlorn. How could Mrs. Foster have been so cruel? She shook her head. No need to dwell on the incident. It was over. "I was proud of him. He kept his wits about him and didn't allow Mrs. Foster to rattle him. Wrong or not, I wanted to lash out at her."

"I don't blame you, but nothing good would have kumme of it. You did the right thing holding your tongue. On another note, are you any closer to a decision between the two men?"

"I told Noah I realized I'd fallen out of love with him before he returned. I got wrapped up in the past, remembering when we first fell in love. I was so shocked when he came back, and those memories confused me. We had a good conversation. He admitted he tried to change me. He thought we could overcome our differences, and he still wanted us to marry. After I pointed out our disagreements and the tenseness between us at times, he agreed I was right."

"He hasn't told Mark yet. I'm certain he will soon. Will he remain in Berlin?"

"No, he's going to ask his mamm to sell her property and relocate with him to Lancaster. Mr. Zook will probably look after the place until someone buys it. Noah's in a hurry to leave. I suspect she will go with him, and I hope she does. They're close, and they'll benefit from being together."

"I agree with you, but Mark will be sad for Noah to quit working for him again. Although, there are plenty of men who've asked Mark for work. He won't have trouble finding someone, and he'll support Noah's decision. He has a soft spot for Noah. Have you had a chance to speak to Daniel?"

"I did. He loves me, but he's not ready to make any wedding plans. He's been hurt by all of this too. I disappointed him by not realizing I had fallen out of love with Noah the minute he returned. I wish I had."

"If God means for you to marry Daniel, He'll heal his heart."

"I hope so, Grace. I love him so much."

Grace covered Anna's hand with hers. "Daniel loves you. Give him the time he needs, and I believe he'll ask you to marry him." She grinned wide. "I heard about Daisy through gossip. I can't wait to meet her."

"I love being a mamm. She's delightful."

"I'm thrilled for you and Daisy. Joy has enriched my life and Mark's more than we could've imagined. I'm certain Daisy will do the same for you. What did Noah and Daniel think of her?"

"Daniel's delighted with her. Noah wasn't interested in her. He didn't want to raise her as his and made his point clear. I'd already planned to tell him I was completely in love with Daniel before he told me his strong opinion about her."

Shrugging, Grace sighed. "It wouldn't be easy for an Amish man to raise an Englischer's boppli as his. I can understand his concern. You're blessed Daniel is accepting of her."

"He's been wonderful with her. He and I want a big family."

"Mark and I are hoping to have more kinner, but no news yet." She squeezed Anna's hand. "Do you still want to work at the shop after you're married?"

She shook her head. "I'm excited to take care of Daisy at home before I'm married. I waited to tell you because I wanted to make the transition smooth for you. Leah's agreed to manage the shop, and Mamm has given her two weeks' notice to the General Store. She'll join Leah here at the shop."

Grace slapped a hand to her chest. "You are a wonderful friend to ask your mamm to work in the shop for me. I love your mamm and Leah, and they already have the experience I need. I'm thrilled. I'm available whenever they need for help or questions."

"I'll help them too."

"You've been through a lot of turmoil lately." She squinted. "I heard about Butch Winter causing trouble with your family before he was finally put in jail. Is it true Daniel intervened on your and Leah's behalf against Butch?"

"Jah, and Leah and I were terrified. He was attracted to Leah, and he wouldn't leave her alone. He came to the shop and bullied her. Another time, he caused Leah and Beth to have an accident while traveling. He shot off a rifle and rode past them fast, spooking our horse. They ended up in a ditch but thankfully weren't hurt. We didn't have proof, but Leah was fairly certain she recognized him. He did a number of things to scare us. Daniel did his best to keep us safe. I'm relieved we don't have to worry about him anymore."

Grace slapped her leg. "How terrible and petrifying! I'm thankful you're unharmed and safe." She picked up a daisy and removed each of the petals. "Tell me more about why you love Daniel."

"He's calm, steady, and enjoys a routine, which is a lot like me. He's happy in Berlin, and he wants to make a life here. It doesn't hurt he's handsome, a devout believer in God, and has all the traits I'm looking for in a husband. He's proven he will protect me, provide whatever I need, and love me unconditionally."

"I'd say you couldn't do any better than him. You're choosing him for all the right reasons. I'm sure everything will work out. Be patient." She stretched her arms. "I need to go home and fetch Joy from Mamm. She's probably worn her grossmudder out."

Grace hugged Anna. "Dear friend, I'm sorry I haven't had a chance to visit you before today, but I'm grateful time doesn't get in the way of our closeness." Anna went back inside, and Grace left.

Anna and Leah worked until five, locked the door to the shop, picked up Mamm, and told her about Noah's trouble with the two women on the drive home. Anna agreed to stay on at the dry goods shop a while until Leah had a chance to train Mamm.

After halting the horse, Anna jumped down from the buggy. Leah and Mamm followed.

Beth, holding Daisy, and Cotton greeted them. "I came outside the minute I heard your squeaky buggy wheels kumming down the lane!"

What a beautiful sight. Anna took Daisy in her arms. "Let's go inside." Anna held Daisy and sat across from Beth at the kitchen table, Cotton at her feet. She explained in general to Beth what happened with Noah and Mrs. Foster's coin purse. She didn't want her to hear the story through idle talk.

"Mrs. Foster sounds like a meanie. Good thing God worked a miracle for Noah."

"You're right, sweetheart."

Leah and Mamm came in and took seats at the kitchen table.

Anna had enjoyed the shop, but Daisy needed her at home to care for her. The boppli had changed her priorities.

She had given Daniel such a hard time about working after their first boppli was born. Daisy's kumming into her life had shown her how ridiculous she had been to suggest such a thing.

She heard a horse's neigh and peeked out the window. *Daniel. What a pleasant surprise!*

He climbed down, tied his horse to the hitching post, and walked to the door where Anna greeted him. "Good to see, everyone!" He put his finger in Daisy's sweet hand. "How's the wee one?"

Daisy cooed and smiled at him.

Beth tugged on his shirtsleeve. "Where's Otis?"

"I left him at home. I'll only be here a short time. I've got a lot of work to catch up on. I'll bring him next time."

Mamm smiled at him. "Stay for supper."

Leah nodded. "Jah, stay."

He shook his head. "I'll join you another night. I have to get home and replace a loose board on my porch and a latch on the corral. I've had so much outside work, I've neglected my place."

Leah took Daisy from Anna. "You two go to your spot and chat awhile. I'll take care of our little angel."

Daniel and Anna walked to the pond, while the rest of her family went inside.

He'd prayed and thanked God for showing him his need to understand Anna's predicament about Noah. He hadn't considered how he would feel if he'd been in her position. He'd gotten clarity through Scripture and prayer, and he was ready to move on with their lives. His heart sprang with joy. He gently pulled her behind the barn. Picking her up, he twirled her around. He lowered her steadily to the ground and held her close.

He raised his head, knelt, and clasped her hand in his. "Anna Plank, I can't imagine my life without you in it. Will you marry me?"

She fell to her knees and cupped his face in her hands. "Of course I will, Daniel Bontrager! I love you so much!"

"Let's set a date with the bishop and ask him to announce our special day to the members. We've waited long enough. I've never been in love with anyone but you. Having had time to study the Scriptures and through prayer, I realize I, too, might have been confused if I were in your same position. I'm ready to get on with our lives."

"Oh, Daniel, I'm so relieved." She hugged herself. "I'm so excited!" She waved her hands in delight. "Let's go tell my family!"

Beth ran out the door and met them halfway. "You're both smiling!"

He grinned wide. "We're getting married!"

"Yippee!" Beth hugged his legs.

He hugged her. "You are a sweetheart. Danki for rooting for me, little one."

"I'm thrilled! I knew she'd choose you!"

The three of them laughed.

Beth grabbed his other hand. "Let's go tell Mamm and Leah!"

Beth grinned as she dragged him inside. "Leah! Mamm! Anna and Daniel are getting married!"

They circled in a warm family hug.

Leah wiped a tear. "Congratulations!"

Mamm dabbed her eyes with the corner of her worn apron. "I'm thrilled for both of you!"

Anna glowed with happiness. "Daniel is asking the bishop to schedule a date and to announce our plans at the next service."

"How wonderful!" Beth clapped her hands.

Cotton barked and jumped as if he understood they were celebrating.

"I can't believe how Daisy can sleep through anything!"

Mamm pointed to the closed bedroom door. "She's a good boppli. She cries when she needs a change, is hungry, or tired. Otherwise, she's content. I don't think a train whistle would wake her."

They chuckled and discussed organizing food with their friends for the wedding meal.

Daniel grinned. "This sounds like women's work. I'll take my leave."

Anna escorted him to his wagon. "I love you, Daniel Bontrager."

He kissed her. "I love you, Anna Plank. Soon your name will be Anna Bontrager and we'll take the necessary steps to legally adopt Daisy."

"The grossmudder left two legal documents along with Daisy the day I found her on our porch. One is from the daed signing over custody of Daisy to her. The other is Mrs. Cooper waiving her rights and giving custody to me. Both are signed by a judge."

"Good. We'll take the documents to the judge in town after we're married and officially change Daisy's name to Bontrager too."

"We have so much to look forward to. I can't wait."

"This would be a good time to visit the bishop. This has taken priority over doing the repairs I'd planned earlier. I'll schedule the date and return."

Anna grinned. "I'll be waiting."

Daniel left and drove to Bishop Weaver's haus. The bishop was on the porch in a rocking chair. He halted his wagon at the old white hitching post in front. "Good evening."

The gray-haired man gestured to him. "Kumme join me." He pointed to the other rocker.

Daniel stepped onto the porch and sat in the comfortable chair. "I've been at the Planks'." He smiled. "Anna has agreed to marry me."

"Congratulations!"

"Danki. Would you consider announcing our wedding date in the service next Sunday?"

"Of course. I'd be happy to." He rose and opened the door. "I'll be right back. I'll get my calendar. We'll schedule a date."

The bishop was being very agreeable. He hoped the kind man would agree to a date early in November. He didn't want to wait long after the harvest.

Bishop Weaver returned and dragged his chair closer to Daniel's. Flipping through his calendar, he scanned the pages. "Do you have a date in mind?"

"Would you agree to November fifth?"

"The harvest will just be over. Are you sure? I have no problem with the date."

"Jah, I'm sure."

Bishop Weaver offered his hand. "We'll tell our friends and neighbors in the service next Sunday. Will Daisy live with you and Anna?"

A thrill of excitement passed through Daniel. He and Anna had a plan. They could forge ahead with their preparations for their wedding day. "Jah, I accept her as my dochder without hesitation." He reached over and shook the bishop's hand. "Danki, Bishop Weaver."

"I hadn't announced Daisy joining the Plank family yet. I planned to tell them Sunday after the service. I'll inform the congregation of both events after I deliver the message." He winced and smacked his arm. "I don't want to rush you, but it's getting dark and the mosquitoes have feasted on me enough tonight."

Daniel stood and grinned. "I should get going too." He tipped his hat and stepped off the porch. The lilt in his step was back. His life would change. No longer alone, he'd soon have a fraa at his side. They'd share meals, work out their concerns and decisions, plan for a family, and enjoy each other. He couldn't wait to tell Anna the date.

He and Noah had had their differences, but he was glad they parted friends. He didn't want him to leave town without a final conversation with him. He'd pay him a visit. Thoughts of getting to his neglected chores went by the wayside.

He returned to the Planks' and knocked on the door.

Anna opened it. "Daniel! What did Bishop Weaver say?"

Stepping inside, he smiled wide. "The bishop scheduled November fifth for our wedding date! He'll announce it and Daisy joining your family next Sunday."

Anna said, "Half the townsfolk have heard from Mrs. Hochstetler by now about Daisy. She's been caring for her, and she's invited friends and neighbors to meet our new addition."

Mamm grinned. "I'm glad the bishop is making a formal announcement to the congregation. His support will mean a lot. I'm certain they'll be happy for us and accept the child."

Mamm, Leah, and Beth gathered around them. They circled Anna in a hug. Beth giggled. "I'm excited for you both!"

"We'll have to get busy planning for your big day!" Mamm grinned.

"Anna, Daniel, I'm thrilled!" Leah bounced on her toes.

Daniel grinned. "Danki, everyone." He turned to Anna. "Would you walk me to my wagon?"

She nodded and went outside. "Oh, Daniel, I'm so happy. November fifth can't kumme soon enough."

"I agree, my lovely Anna." He brushed her fingers with his. "I'm sorry to rush off, but I would like to speak with Noah on my way home. I'm not sure when he plans on leaving for Lancaster, and I'd like to have one more conversation with him before he heads out."

"You're a good man, Daniel Bontrager."

He hugged her and left.

He went to the Schwartzes' haus. Noah was out front on the porch with his mamm.

He climbed out of the wagon and tied it to the post. "Good evening, Noah and Mrs. Schwartz."

Noah waved him onto the porch. "Join us for hot tea."

His mamm stood. "I'll go get another mug. I'm certain it's still warm. I haven't been out here long."

Daniel tipped his hat. "Danki." He sat in the worn maple chair opposite Noah. "I'm here to talk to you about Anna."

Mrs. Schwartz returned and passed Daniel a mug. "I've written down my new address in Lancaster for Anna. I may not have a chance to give it to her. Would you mind seeing she gets it?"

"I'd be happy to give it to her. I'm certain she'll miss you, Mrs. Schwartz."

"I will miss her, too. I'll go inside. Noah will want to share our plans with you. I have a few more things to pack."

"I wish you the best, Mrs. Schwartz."

"Danki for all you did to help my son during his trying time with Mrs. Tisdale and Mrs. Foster."

"I'm glad it's over and he can put it behind him."

"Me too." She smiled and went inside the haus.

Daniel waited until Mrs. Schwartz was out of earshot. "I've got some news I wanted you to hear from me. Anna's agreed to marry me. I've already been to the bishop's to tell him."

"Have you set the date?"

"November fifth. He'll announce the date to everyone next Sunday."

"I'm sad for me but happy for you, my friend. She's a wonderful woman. You're blessed to have her in your life. Take good care of her."

"I will." He pressed his back against the chair. "I didn't want you to avoid us. You're wilkom in our home anytime. If you need help with anything, I don't want you to hesitate to ask me."

"Did Anna tell you about my returning to Lancaster?"

"She mentioned you are leaving Berlin but not a date."

"Mamm and I have said our good-byes. We're leaving Tuesday."

Daniel's eyebrows raised. "Tomorrow?"

"Jah, I figured a Tuesday would be as good as any day to travel. I told Mark I want to return to Lancaster. He understood and, together, we approached another young man to take over my job. He accepted, and I've had time to get ready to leave.

"I asked Mamm to join me. She agreed to sell her property and relocate with me. I asked Mr. Zook to take care of the property until we have a buyer, and he bought the property, plus everything else Mamm didn't want to take with her, for a good price. We are pleased. She'll enjoy reuniting with my aunt and uncle, and we'll benefit from being together. There are plenty of shops in town if she wants to work. She enjoys the bakery here. Leaving our friends is difficult, but we'll write letters and visit." Noah sipped his tea. "I was going to make a life in Berlin for Anna's sake, but I'm anxious to go back to Lancaster."

"Anna and I wish you and Mrs. Schwartz the best, Noah."

"I could tell by Anna's demeanor she'd changed while I was away. Even after she'd put her confusion with my return aside, she was distant. Not in a rude way, but reserved. I hoped she'd get over the hurt I caused her and return to me, but all along I think I knew it was too late. I didn't want to admit we'd grown apart, wanting different things. I worked hard to change her to be more like me. It was selfish and unrealistic."

"Do you regret leaving Berlin?"

"In one way I do because I hurt Anna. In another way I don't, because reuniting with my aunt and uncle was wonderful. My uncle is a talented farmer. He's remarkable with growing crops and maintaining healthy livestock. He experiments with different feed for them and has little tricks he does to grow good crops. He likes to whittle toys and build potato boxes, chests, and tables. We have a lot in common, and we've grown close."

"I'm happy for you. I miss my family."

"Jonathan was brokenhearted after Adele passed until the day he died. They adored each other. Their devotion was written all over their faces anytime I encountered them." He patted the small table next to him. "My daed built this table. I miss him."

"Having the assurance my parents are in Heaven eases my pain, but I mourned them for quite a while. I broke down in tears without warning at the oddest times. When I picked up Mamm's favorite cup or

Daed's favorite blanket. Cleaning out the haus was the worst. I'd healed pretty well until I came here and emptied Jonathan's place."

"I'm sorry, Daniel. Had Jonathan gotten rid of Adele's things? I can't imagine him parting with them."

"He left everything as if she were still living there. I knew her when they lived in Lancaster before they married. She was a sweetheart. It pained me to let go of her things too, but I'm glad I'm getting rid of her things, rather than Jonathan having to have endured the pain to part with them. I can understand why he wanted her belongings around him. She was such a part of him."

"I believe you'll have the same type of relationship with Anna. I hope to have the same loving relationship with the woman I find to marry someday too." Noah cleared his throat. "I'll never forget what you did for me, defending my honor against the women who accused me of thievery."

"You handled the situation well."

"In spite of what happened with Anna, you've been a good friend to me. I don't regret meeting you, and I hold you in high regard."

"I'm glad things are working out for you and your mamm. Is there anything I can do to help?"

"Kumme to the barn with me. I have something to show you."

Daniel followed him to the barn.

Noah uncovered an oak desk and chair.

The craftsmanship was perfect. "Your work is superb."

"I want you and Anna to have this. I didn't build it for her and me. I made the desk and chair before I left to sell in Mark's store. I ran short on time and didn't take the furniture to him. I forgot about the pieces once I moved."

"Noah, are you sure you don't want to sell these fine pieces?"

"No. Take them. I'd be pleased if you'd accept the gift."

"You're being generous. Danki."

"You're wilkom. I wish you and Anna a happy life." Daniel offered his hand.

Noah pulled him into a quick, manly hug. "Stopping by was a good idea. I enjoyed our conversation. Let me help you put your gift in the wagon before you leave."

Daniel and Noah hauled the furniture to his wagon and put them in the back.

Noah smiled. "I wish you and Anna much happiness. I'm glad to have met you, Daniel. Give Anna and her family my best."

"I will. Best wishes to you and your mamm, Noah. Travel safe."

He waved and smiled at Noah as he drove away.

Chapter Fourteen

Daniel headed to his neighbor's haus Tuesday and built new porch steps for him. Noah and his mamm would've left early this morning for Lancaster. He hoped they wouldn't have any problems traveling to their destination. Daniel was glad he and Anna could put this ordeal with Noah behind them. All three of them could begin life anew.

He went home, milked the cows, and fed the rest of the animals. He worked in the garden a little, picked some ripe tomatoes, and made a ham sandwich. Anna would be interested in his conversation with Noah. He'd head over there as soon as he cleaned up.

While he drove to Anna's, his heart fluttered. His parents, Jonathan, and Adele would have adored Anna. They would've enjoyed being a part of the Plank family. He couldn't dwell on what wasn't meant to happen. He had a new family. He was grateful to have them.

He tied his horse to the post. The Planks were outside. They must've just finished their chores after work. They came to greet him.

Anna bounced Daisy on her hip. "Are you hungry? We saved you venison and boiled potatoes for supper."

He kissed Daisy's hand. "You're a sweetheart, Daisy." He gazed at Anna. "No, danki, I'm full. I devoured a ham sandwich earlier. I was really hungry."

"How did your conversation go with Noah?"

"We had a pleasant discussion. He was grateful for my support of him with Mrs. Tisdale and Mrs. Foster. I enjoyed my time with him. I wished him and his mamm the best." He handed her Jane's note. "Here's their address in Lancaster."

"When are they leaving?"

"He and his mamm left for Lancaster this morning. Mr. Zook bought their property, and they were anxious to reunite with their relatives." He smiled.

"I didn't have a chance to talk to Jane before then. I'll send her a note."

Daniel was glad Anna wasn't distressed to discover Noah had left. He didn't think she would be, but he was grateful for her casual demeanor about the matter. "I'm certain she gave me the address so you would stay in touch with her."

Mamm and Leah remained quiet.

Beth grinned. "Everything is working out good for everybody. Isn't that good?"

Anna gave her a loving look. "Jah, it is, little schweschder."

Beth tugged on his sleeve and pointed. "What's in the back of your wagon?"

He'd left the gift of furniture in his wagon to show them. "Noah gave us a present. Kumme to the wagon."

They peeked inside.

Anna gasped and ran her hand over the oak desk and chair. "The table and chair are beautiful! Noah is a talented craftsman." She turned to Daniel. "Are you comfortable with us accepting his gift?"

"Jah. I'm humbled he gave the set to us. He is a gentleman and a kind man. In spite of what we've been through over loving you, we genuinely like each other. I think we'd have been close friends, and we would've spent a lot of time together in the future under other circumstances, but as it is, we parted amicably."

Mamm smiled. "I respect you, Daniel Bontrager. Reaching an understanding with Noah to smooth over things between the two of you before he left was an honorable task. I'm going inside and get some sewing done. You two enjoy this beautiful evening."

Leah took Daisy from Anna, and Beth kissed the boppli's fingers.

"I'm happy things have worked out this way. It's best for all of you." Leah patted Daisy's back. "I'll give this one a bottle and put her to bed."

"Danki, Leah." Anna kissed Daisy's forehead and hugged Leah.

Daniel led her to their spot at the pond. He traced her cheek. "Noah left on a good note, and he's moving on with his life. We have the reassurance we've parted with him without any ill will." His eyes full of affection, he leaned close. "I'm counting the days until I can call you Anna Bontrager." He wanted Anna's mind free of any doubt he and Noah had any bad feelings between them. He suspected her desire was that no one would harbor any bad feelings at the end of this. He would've done anything for her. Talking to Noah was easy. Losing her would've been the hardest thing he'd ever experienced, and he'd suffered a lot of pain in his young life.

* * *

Daniel finished his breakfast the following Sunday morning. This past week he'd been busy catching up on his customers' repairs. He felt guilty for admitting it, but he was happy Noah had left to start a new life in Berlin. His absence from Berlin gave him and Anna a fresh beginning. He was ready for November fifth to arrive. He couldn't wait to call Anna his fraa. Reaching over, he scratched Otis's ear. "Anna will be living here soon. You and Cotton will be family. You'll visit the Planks often."

His family would've been so happy for him today. He'd never forget when he'd been told his parents had been killed. The pain had eased over time, but the longing to hug them once again lingered. Adele's and Jonathan's deaths were no less tragic or painful. The verses in the Bible explaining about Heaven had brought him comfort. His family was happy and healthy and he'd be with them again someday. This truth got him through these sad moments.

Daniel whistled while he dressed into a clean white shirt and black pants and snapped his already attached suspenders over his shoulders. He harnessed his horse to the wagon and drove to the church barn.

Anna couldn't wait for Bishop Weaver to announce their news to their friends either before or after the message in this morning's Sunday church service. After their wedding date was announced, it would be exciting to discuss plans for the wedding meal.

She didn't regret not seeing Noah again before he left. There was nothing more to say. She had made her peace with Noah the day she told him she wasn't in love with him. They'd had a good conversation and wished each other well. It had been almost a week since Noah had left. His departure under good circumstances allowed her a free conscience and to enjoy her upcoming life with Daniel with no regrets or guilt. She'd gotten up early and written a danki note to Noah for his gift and a separate note to Jane telling her she'd miss her. She'd drop them at the post office in the morning before work. She'd meant to do it earlier, but this week had been busy.

She spotted Daniel and waited for him. "Good morning, my soon-to-be husband. I finally got around to writing a danki note to Noah from us, and one from me to Jane. I'll drop them by the post office tomorrow morning."

"I'm not sure when they'll arrive, but they'll enjoy your notes. I'm going to like hearing you call me 'husband' after we're married. I'm excited the bishop will let our friends and neighbors know you and I will be married right here on November fifth." He shrugged and grinned. "I wish I didn't have to wait until then!"

She chuckled. "Me either, but we'll make the best of it. There's a lot to do!"

They went inside.

Daniel sat with the men on one side of the barn.

Anna joined her family already seated on the other side with the women. She nodded to Grace and Sarah before sitting on the worn wooden bench. A sea of black dresses and white kapps filled one half of the church, and on the men's side, an ocean of men's black hats decorated the other.

Bishop Weaver stepped to the front, led them in song, and opened his Bible. "Please turn with me to John, Chapter One, Verse Nine. *'If we confess our sins,*

*He is faithful and just to forgive us our sins, and to cleanse
us from all unrighteousness.'"*

Bishop Weaver delivered the message. "Please bow
your heads for prayer." He prayed and opened his
eyes. "Please remain seated. I have two announce-
ments. First, Anna Plank met a woman with child and
her grossmudder in her shop a short time ago. The
woman's husband left her when he found out she was
with child. The woman has since died in childbirth,
and the grossmudder is not in good health and is
unable to care for the boppli. She left Daisy with a
note to Anna telling her this information. She included a document signed by the boppli's daed giving
up all rights to the child. The Plank family graciously
took the child in to raise. Please meet Daisy today
before you leave."

Friends turned and smiled and nodded at Anna
and her family, who nodded and grinned in return.
Most of their friends and neighbors had heard
through the gossip chain about Daisy.

The bishop removed his spectacles and pulled a
handkerchief out of his pocket. He wiped the sweat
from the bridge of his nose. "Second, Daniel Bontrager
and Anna Plank have set a date for their wedding.
Daisy will live with them after they are married."

Excited gasps riveted through the crowd. Grace
and Sarah smiled wide at Anna.

"The date will be November fifth. The harvest will
be finished, and it will be a good time for the wedding." He offered another prayer of thanks to God for
the after-service food and dismissed them.

Grace hugged Anna. "Congratulations! I'm so happy
for you. Now we can make your wedding plans out in
the open."

Sarah patted her arm. "I'm thrilled for you too. I'll bring boiled potatoes, carrots, and green beans."

Anna beamed. "You can bring whatever you desire, but perhaps we should start a list to keep track of food donations."

Anna sat with her friends, and they discussed what food to cook for the after-wedding meal. The men had Daniel cornered, and he looked happy. They were having a wonderful day.

Anna rose from her bed and peeked out the window. The bright sun warmed her face, and the birds chirping was a wilkom noise. September and October had passed quickly leading up to her wedding day. She had stayed home with Daisy and Beth. Mamm and Leah had taken over managing Grace's Dry Goods Shop. Grace, Sarah, and her other friends had visited and oohed and aahed over Daisy. They wished her the best and had committed to bringing a number of meats, vegetables, potatoes, and desserts to the wedding meal. The boppli was such a pleasant and content little maedel. She and Beth had more alone time when Daisy napped. She loved her family, but she was ready to become Mrs. Bontrager and start a future with Daniel. Today was her wedding day. She could hardly believe it. November fifth would forever be a very important date to her.

She touched her white kapp. Leah had done an excellent job. She'd treasure the delicate bonnet for years to kumme.

Beth had stitched her two kitchen towels, and the stitches were a little crooked but she'd done a good job. She ran her hand over them. Her little schweschder was growing up fast. She had worked hard on the precious gifts, and the gesture warmed her heart.

Mamm had stitched her dark blue dress. She held it and swayed. Her handiwork was perfect. She couldn't ask for a better mamm to have prepared and taught her how to be a good fraa. She'd written on paper Anna's favorite recipes and given them to her in a little wooden box she'd purchased from the store of Grace's husband, Mark King. She would make good use of them.

Her mamm had taught her to sew, to bake, and to cook. She'd also taught her patience and discernment in settling disputes with her schweschders through the years. The most important thing she'd learned from her was to seek God's will in her life when making decisions. Her mamm had shared notations in her Bible she'd made to refer to Scriptures special to her. Anna had jotted the same reference notes in her Bible. She needed all the help she could get when she encountered life's bumps in the road.

Leah and Beth pushed her bedroom door open.

Leah grinned. "Today's your big day! Are you nervous?"

She shook her head. "No, excited!"

Beth bounced on her toes. "Me too!"

Mamm joined them. "I'm a little sad. I'll miss having you around here, Anna."

Stepping inside, her family gathered around her. She would miss living among them. Walking to her mamm's or schweschders' rooms to share something with them or ask a question, doing chores together.

Beth traced Anna's arm with her finger. "You won't be here when I kumme home from school. I'll have to go to Mrs. Hochstetler's. She's wonderful, but I will miss our time together."

"I'll schedule time to kumme over. We can still have meals and time together. You can kumme over anytime."

Mamm said, "I stitched an apron for you to wear in the kitchen. I wanted something you could use along with the recipes I wrote out for you."

"Mamm, the apron is beautiful, and I'll tie it around my waist and neck often with you in mind. Danki." She hugged her.

Beth laughed and pointed to Daisy's cradle. "Our little schweschder can sleep through anything. She hasn't moved a bit."

Anna yawned. "She was up last night each time the thunder clapped."

Knock. Knock.

Cotton barked.

They went to greet the person at the door.

Anna pushed the door open. "Grace! Mark! Joy! Kumme in."

They exchanged a wilkom greeting.

Grace had a wrapped package tucked under her free arm. "We won't stay but a short time. I'm certain you have a lot to do, but I didn't want to wait to give you my present." She handed Anna a wrapped gift.

"Danki!" Anna unwrapped the gift and unfolded the quilt. She spotted the pocket and plucked out the letter inside. *"Dear Anna, The day you walked into my shop and asked for a job, I knew you were special. Your smile radiated on your face. You stepped into my life, and we've become close friends. You've listened to my woes, shared my joys, and loved me unconditionally. I don't have to hold back on what I tell you. I wish you and Daniel the best. Love, Grace."* Anna swiped tears staining her cheeks. "Grace, your gift is perfect. I love what your letter says, and I'll treasure your written words always."

Her eyes pooling with tears, Grace hugged her. "I mean every word. I'll leave you to get ready for your big day. We're off to help with organizing the dishes before the service. I'll meet up with you in a little bit."

Grace, Mark, and Joy bid them farewell, went outside, climbed in their buggy, and headed toward the church.

Mamm, Leah, and Beth admired the quilt.

Leah grinned. "Grace's gift couldn't have been more perfect. She shared her heart with you in the letter. You are very special to her."

"I love her too. I hope I've helped fill a void with her friend Becca living so far away."

Mamm patted her shoulder. "In my opinion, you've accomplished your wish. Do you need help getting ready?"

"I can manage, but danki."

"We'll be planning for Leah's wedding day before long."

Smiling, Mamm shook her head. "Oh, I hope she waits for a while. I'll have a difficult time adjusting to your not living here. I enjoy our tight-knit family."

Beth picked up a wrapped package tied with twine. "I'll hold Daniel's surprise!"

Smiling, Anna squeezed her little schweschder's arm. "Danki, sweetheart." She couldn't wait to watch Daniel's eyes light up when she handed him her handiwork. She put a lot of love into each stitch.

Mamm said, "The time is getting away from us. We should be on our way. I'll harness the horse to the buggy."

Leah changed Daisy, and Beth finished getting ready.

Anna stared at her bedroom and sighed. Her life was about to change, and it was exciting! She joined her family in the buggy and smiled, picturing Daniel standing before her and saying "I do."

Daniel met them halfway. "You look lovely, Anna." He couldn't believe their wedding day had finally arrived. She was a kind and loving woman. She was everything he wanted in a fraa. Their meetings these past weeks had brought out they were in agreement on the importance of communication, raising a family, and finances. She brought joy into his life with her sweet demeanor and cheerful attitude. From the time he'd met her in the shop, she'd left an indelible impression on him. He'd been smitten with her from that day to this. From now on she would be at his side. He was a very happy man. She'd stolen his heart, and so had little Daisy.

"You look handsome yourself, Mr. Bontrager. You look like you're getting married today." She laughed.

"As a matter of fact, I am, and she's the prettiest woman in Berlin." He winked and grinned.

Leah balanced Daisy on her hip, and Mamm and Beth joined them.

Daniel clasped Daisy's hand. "Are you ready to move into a different haus, little one? We'll take the documents to the judge in town after we're married and officially change Daisy's name to Bontrager too."

She held out her arms to him and grinned.

Leah stepped away from him. "You can't hold her. She could dribble on you and leave a wet spot on your handsome black jacket."

Anna smiled. "My schweschder is taking care of us. She's making sure we'll be presentable for our big day."

He nodded. "Danki, Leah. I can use all the help I can get."

Beth tugged on his arm. "Will you bring Otis over to visit us a lot?"

"Absolutely, and you can bring Cotton over to our haus anytime."

She grinned big. "And maybe you can throw ball with me again."

"I'd be disappointed if we didn't."

Mamm exchanged a thankful look with Daniel. "You're good with kinner."

"Daisy and Beth make it easy."

They walked into the church, together, as a family.

The bishop beckoned them. "Anna and Daniel, please join me outside."

He led them to a shady spot under a cluster of big oak trees. "Do either of you have any reservations about the commitment you're going to make to each other? In our meetings these past weeks, you've not shown any."

Anna and Daniel shook their heads.

"Daisy's addition to your family won't allow much time for the two of you to adjust to married life alone, as a couple. Remember what we talked about. You'll both need added patience and understanding with her in mind. Any questions for me?"

Daniel and Anna shook their heads again.

Bishop Weaver read I Corinthians, Chapter Thirteen, Verses Four through Seven. *"'Charity suffereth long, is kind; charity envieth not; charity vaunteth not itself, is not puffed up, Doth not behave itself unseemly, seeketh not her own, is not easily provoked, thinketh no evil; Rejoiceth not in iniquity, but rejoiceth in the truth; Beareth all things, believeth all things, hopeth all things, endureth all things.'"*

He closed his Bible. "Read these verses together when you have a disagreement or become discouraged. You'll find comfort in them." He bowed his head and prayed with them. "Let's go back in. Congratulations on your special day."

Daniel and Anna followed Bishop Weaver and took their seats on opposite sides of the church.

Daniel stole glances at her through the songs and during the bishop's message. She was beautiful. He would take good care of her and Daisy. He'd worked long hours bringing in the harvest the past weeks. The crops had been healthy and plentiful. After they enjoyed a bountiful and superb meal after the service, he'd present her with his gift. Woodworking wasn't something he had much time for, but he'd stayed up late and risen early to work on his gift for her.

He couldn't wait to have her to himself. He would love and cherish her for the rest of his life. To have a partner to listen to and share life's ups and downs with would be a wilkom change. He'd shouldered problems alone since his family's passing. Now he would have Anna.

Daisy had the sweetest personality. She was such a pleasant boppli. He accepted her as his dochder and couldn't imagine her not being a part of their new beginning together. Anna's family had been supportive, warm, and wilkoming from the time he'd met them. Marriage would bind him to them until he parted this earth. He had a family again. What a good feeling.

The bishop asked him and Anna to step to the front with him. His heart raced. He grinned and faced her before the bishop. Her eyes sparkled and glistened. Her smile told him they were tears of joy. He had to restrain himself from reaching for her, holding her close, and telling her how much he loved her.

Bishop Weaver read I Corinthians, Chapter Thirteen. He talked about fraas submitting to their husbands, and husbands respecting and loving their fraas. "Daniel Bontrager, do you commit to love, cherish, protect, and provide for Anna and accept her as your fraa until you pass from this earth?"

"I do." He exchanged a loving smile with Anna. He wanted to shout from the highest hill in Berlin how much this day meant to him. Committing to Anna was the easiest thing he'd ever done.

Bishop Weaver gestured to Anna. "Anna Plank, do you commit to love, cherish, obey, submit to, and accept Daniel as your husband until you pass from this earth?"

"I do." Blushing, she lowered her eyes and smiled at Daniel.

The bishop prayed and lifted his head. "Daniel and Anna, I pronounce you husband and fraa."

He'd wait to kiss her lips, pick her up, and twirl her around but, in his mind, he was doing it already.

Her mouth spread in a wide grin, and she threw him an endearing gaze.

Pressing his arms against his sides, he heaved a jubilant sigh. They would never forget their special day.

Bishop Weaver prayed again for the feast. "You're dismissed. Let's enjoy food and fellowship together."

Friends surrounded them and wished them the best. The crowd soon gathered outside and the women had the tables full of succulent dishes and an array of desserts.

Daniel pulled her under their usual after-church-services spot by the big oak tree. "I love you, Mrs. Bontrager! I wish I could hug you tight. I'm the happiest man in the world."

Anna beamed and her happiness was all he needed to feel like the most blessed man anywhere. She chose him to wed and share her life. He'd won her heart, and she'd won his.

Anna blushed. "Our wedding day finally arrived! I'm thrilled to be your fraa, Daniel!"

Grace and Sarah approached them. Sarah had one child on her hip and another holding her hand. "The food is getting cold. You two get something to eat before your favorite dishes are gone."

Daniel laughed and stood. "You don't have to tell me again."

He and Anna followed her friends to the table. They filled their plates and joined Grace, Mark, Sarah, and Levi.

Anna glanced at Daniel as he spoke with Mark and Levi. They were laughing and having a good time together. The two couples were good examples of loving marriages. She valued Grace's and Sarah's advice. She wanted to get better acquainted with Sarah. She hadn't had much of a chance, since Sarah kept busy caring for her home, husband, and kinner.

Grace hugged her. "You and Daniel looked like you might burst with love as you agreed to commit to each other. You made the best choice. I love Noah, but he will fall in love with another woman one day. You two had grown apart and sought different things. There's nothing wrong with either path, but it wasn't meant for the two of you to be together forever. Having mutual desires in life will make marriage a lot smoother." Her eyes damp, she wiped her cheeks. "Mark is probably telling Daniel this as we speak. He built you a maple bed and two dressers. He thought you might like to have your own instead of using Jonathan and Adele's in Daniel's haus. We'll drop the furniture off to you sometime later this week. The large pieces were cumbersome to move, so he didn't bring your gift today. He wanted to leave the wagon empty to help deliver the gifts you receive today."

"What a wonderful and generous gift! Danki, Grace! We will cherish your present." She kissed her cheek. "In regard to your statement earlier, I couldn't have said it better, Grace. I'm at peace with how Noah and I left things. We parted on good terms. I sincerely wish Noah the best in his life and in finding a woman to share his dreams." She smiled and glanced over at Daniel. "I have found the perfect man to share my dreams." She hugged Grace and joined her husband.

Daniel eavesdropped on Anna's conversation. His heart soared. She was certain he was the one for her. Her conversation with Grace thrilled him. "Are you having a good time, sweetheart?"

"This is the best day."

Beth glanced at him and bounced Daisy on her hip. "Do you feel married?"

Daniel grinned. "I do, and it feels good. What do you say, Anna?"

"I do, but I'll have to get used to answering to my new last name. I've been signing Plank for a long time." She chuckled.

Daisy reached for Daniel. He took her and held her up. "I'm your new daed, Daisy."

She reached out to grab his nose.

They laughed.

Mark approached them and rubbed Daisy's back. "Daniel, are you ready for an instant family?"

"I've spent time with Daisy and accepted she came with Anna if we married. I'm looking forward to raising her. I've always loved kinner." He'd wanted bopplin soon. Daisy had made his dream kumme true sooner than expected. He was delighted to be the daed to this child. Sarah Helmuth came alongside her. "Levi and I want to invite you to our haus soon. These kinner of mine keep me busy, and I haven't been getting out socially much. I apologize."

Anna waved a dismissive hand. "Daisy is a handful, and she's only one child. I can't imagine the work involved with more kinner. Although, I'm looking forward to having a hausful if we're blessed to have them."

Daniel and Anna enjoyed their food and conversation with their friends for the next hour.

Grace tugged at Anna's arm. "Everyone is gathered to present you and Daniel with gifts. Kumme and open them!"

Daniel and Anna got up and followed Grace to two chairs set aside for them. They sat next to each other. Grace sat next to her and passed the guests' gifts of sheets, towels, kitchen utensils, wooden boxes with several recipes in them, cloth nappies for Daisy, bottles, potato and bread boxes, aprons, white kapps, and flour and sugar.

Mark nudged Daniel's arm. "I built you a new bed and two dressers. I'll bring them to you when it's convenient for you to receive them. I left the wagon empty to help load and deliver the gifts you'll receive today."

"Mark, danki. I'm grateful to you."

"Here, let me help you with the men's gifts." He passed each one to him.

For the next two hours, Anna and Daniel chatted and held up one gift after another to admire and show to the wedding guests.

Daniel stood. "Anna and I danki every one of you. We'll put each of your gifts to good use. Danki for the food, gifts, and what we treasure most—your friendship."

Daniel scanned the grounds. The crowd had dwindled, and the tables had few dishes left on them. Women cleared, and the men stowed the maple tables and benches in the barn and locked the door.

Mark patted Daniel on the back. "Levi and I will follow you home with our wagons and unload your gifts."

"Danki." He would enjoy getting better acquainted with these men in the future.

Mamm pulled Anna aside. "I had Leah put your present for Daniel under the seat in his buggy." She smiled. "We'll take Daisy home with us for a day or two, so you and Daniel can have time alone. It will give you a chance to adjust and get settled." She circled an arm around her waist. "This day couldn't have been more perfect. Witnessing you and Daniel marrying has brought me such joy. I love you."

"I love you, too, Mamm." Anna swiped a tear of happiness.

Daniel and Anna bid her family farewell, and she climbed in next to him. "Your mamm was kind to take Daisy for a couple of days."

"She's always been a thoughtful mamm."

Mark and Levi followed with their gifts piled high and secure in their wagons.

Daniel gently squeezed her hand. "The sunshine, clear blue sky, and slight breeze added to our perfect wedding day. Even if rain poured and the sky grayed, the weather couldn't dampen my enthusiasm in wedding you today, Mrs. Bontrager."

She chuckled. "I didn't notice the weather. I was so caught up in becoming your fraa!"

He exaggerated a wince. "You got me! Here I thought I was the mushier one."

They laughed. Butch and all he'd put them through, Daisy being abandoned on Anna's porch, and Noah's return had been a lot for them to contend with, but their love had survived each obstacle and brought them closer. If they could get through all those things, he had no doubt they could conquer any problem in their future.

They arrived home and he, Levi, and Mark unloaded the gifts and brought them inside the haus. Anna carried the smaller things.

Daniel bid his friends farewell. He went inside, picked Anna up, and twirled her around. Something he'd wanted to do all day. "I love you! I love you! I love you!"

Anna giggled and held tight to his neck. "I'm getting dizzy!"

He sat on the settee and pulled her onto his lap, planting a firm kiss on her lips.

She'd returned his kiss, lifted her head, and grinned. "I've got something for you. I'll be right back." She ran out to his buggy.

He grinned and waited. What did she have for him?

She carried a big package wrapped in brown paper and tied with twine. Placing the present on his lap, she grinned. "Open it!"

He untied the bow and ripped the paper from the gift. His eyes wide, he lifted out the beautiful white-and-blue wedding quilt. He spotted the pocket and tugged out the letter tucked inside. *"Dear Daniel, Our*

*road to love has been a rough one at times with the trials
we've faced, but we've conquered each one and our love remained strong for each other. I love you with all my heart,
and I always will. I believe God picked you for me and for
Daisy. I'm looking forward to everything the future has in
store for us. I love you, Anna.'"*

His throat dry and his eyes damp, he pulled her
into his arms and hugged her. He choked back the
tears threatening to stain his cheeks. Blinking them
away, he composed himself. "Danki, Anna. I love your
gift. It's perfect. I'll read your letter often through our
years together to remind me of this day." He stood
and offered his hand. "Kumme with me. I have something for you."

Anna clasped his hand, and he led her to the barn.
He uncovered a beautiful cedar hope chest. She
gasped and knelt to run her hand over the top. She
lifted the lid, took a deep breath, and grabbed and
pressed the quilt to her cheek. "I remember you
bought this the first time we met in the shop."

"I wrote you a letter."

She searched for the pocket on the quilt and
pulled out the note. *"'Dearest Anna, The day I met you,
my heart raced. Leaving the shop, I couldn't get you off my
mind. You'd made a lasting impression on me. The more we
talked, the more I fell in love with you. Even though we've
had some harrowing things to deal with, I'd do it all again
to have you in my life. Marrying you makes me the happiest
man in all of Berlin. I promise to honor and cherish you
until the day I die. I love you with all my heart. Daniel.'"*

She clutched the note and hugged his neck. "It's
perfect!" She let go of him and took a deep breath.
"Daniel! It's beautiful and I love the cedar scent. I
can put many of our wedding gifts inside, and I can sit

on the top of the chest to put on my shoes. How thoughtful of you!"

"Jah, my idea was for you to use the furniture piece to sit on or stack things on. Your choice."

The sparkle in her eyes and the radiant smile on her face told him all the late night hours he'd spent working on it with the help of a few lanterns were worth it.

"You handcraft things? I'm shocked you never mentioned it before. You did an excellent job. It's exquisite."

"I haven't had much time to handcraft things, since I met you. Jonathan and Adele's haus required clean-out and work, and the problems you and I have had to contend with, and managing the farm and repairs for others, I had to put my woodworking interest aside. Then when you agreed to marry me, I bought the wood from Mr. Zook and worked on your gift whenever I got a chance."

"I'm pleasantly surprised, and you couldn't have given me a more suitable and amazing present."

Daniel gently took her in his arms. "Everything I have is yours, Anna Bontrager. You can do anything you want to the haus to make you happy here."

"You're all I need."

Pennsylvania Dutch/German
Glossary

boppli baby

bruder brother

daed dad, father

dochder daughter

Englischer non-Amish male or female

fraa wife

grossmudder grandmother

haus house

jah yes

kapp covering for Amish woman's hair

kinner children

kumme come

mamm mother, mom

schweschder sister

wilkom welcome